KRONO

Charles L. Harness

Franklin Watts

New York   Toronto   1988

C.3
SF

Library of Congress Cataloging-in-Publication Data

Harness, Charles L.
    Krono.

    I. Title.
PS3558.A62476K7   1988   813'.54   88-26087
ISBN 0-531-15087-9

1

In a post-holocaust future, a time-travelling field agent travels into the distant past to save an endangered Earth colony.

Demmie

The flight steward (young enough to be his son?) nods respectfully, hands him his ten-kilo bag, and Konteau trudges off down the landing ramp. Already the dubious gravity on Deimos, the smaller of the two Martian moons, is making him queasy. But he has been here before, and he knows he'll get used to it. He finds a U-Drive miniskit and after a few jerks, sets off down the hollow echoing corridor to his rooms in the East Wing of the great satellite resort. He passes an old porter leaning on an auto broom and gazing with profound melancholy at the clutter and detritus spread out along the hallway: plastic plates, cups, a mask that was once gilded but is now smeared and broken, silly hats, beer cans and wine bottles, paper streamers, syntho-rice, some sort of cast-off lingerie. Konteau sympathizes with the porter but passes on. We all have our problems, he thinks, mentally addressing the old man. But look on the bright side. Because the fun-lovers ignore the waste chutes, you have a job.

The trip out from Terra on the Xanadu Express was only four hours, but he is weary. He'll clean up, take a nap, then look for some action. One week's vacation. He's got to make the most of it. A two-month backlog of surveys is waiting for him on his return to Terra. The Field Chief made that very clear.

He is gloomy. His heart is not really in this.

His rooms (as he anticipated) are furnished in frenzied opulence. The decor is so ridiculous it almost cheers him up. The walls are papered with synthovelvet, mercifully hidden for the most part under tapestries showing someone's ideas of Martian landscapes. The carpets are deep red and are deeply padded. He tosses his valise onto the fur-trimmed coverlet of one of the two beds. Here and there are foldout desks, tables, and chairs of genuine plastic teak and mahogany.

An hour later he is strolling down the crowded Concourse. All the vacationers seem to have turned out to mark the death of the old Overlord, the Vyr of Vyrs. Konteau has been looking at the faces. Nobody seems to be particularly grief-stricken, but why should they be? The great religious leader was rarely seen. In fact, he probably hadn't left his palace during the past ten years.

No, nothing sorrowful or solemn here. Quite the contrary. A raucous festive air grips the Mall. Rather like Carnival, muses Konteau, as he watches the chains of masked dancers.

He seeks the semi-safety of a doorway as a brass band in motley strides by, totally out of step, and totally off-key, banging out an ancient bawdy marching tune. A girl crowds beside Konteau to escape the troops, but a grinning youth wearing an eye mask breaks ranks long enough to spray her bare legs with very cheap, very pungent perfume. She screams happily and runs off down the Concourse ahead of the band. Konteau assumes she is hoping for a repeat.

Too violent for me, he thinks. And the noise is getting to him. Maybe he should have asked the girl to stay awhile. They could talk. But she obviously had other things on her mind. Also, he had the impression she was not entirely sane. At least not just now. And just now he could do with a spot of sanity.

Find a bar. Let's see. Somewhere down this alley, Twin Moons. There should be some less excitable ladies sitting around, waiting for a middle-aged krono on the prowl.

An insistent voice snags at him. "Aphrodisiacs! Love potions! Potency pills from tyrannosaurus testicles! Fresh, time-traveled ground triceratops horn! Genuine dried archaeopteryx gut! *You* sir!"

Konteau locks cold eyes (one real, one false) with the person behind the stall. (Male? Female? No way to tell for sure.) Me, impotent? He ponders the question—the implied accusation—briefly. Ask me again in the morning. No, don't ask. His mind-set shifts. From an inner jacket pocket he pulls out his leather-cased membership card in the Gamma 300 Chess Club and flashes it for a split second before the barker's startled eyes. "Grayjacket plainclothes," he says icily. "Ten thousand kroner fine, a year in Delta prison, if that stuff is controlled prehistoric material."

The miscreant's face contorts and is suddenly bloodless. "Oh, Kronos, sir . . . of course not . . . just ground chicken bones. . . ."

Konteau sighs. He improvises further. "And also there's Section Nine-Eleven—common cheat. You think just because there's no jail on Xanadu there's no law here?"

"Oh, sir. Perhaps if you could come back into my . . . sitting room, you could explain. . . ." The head turns slightly, and the lacquered eyes leer at him from their corners.

Yuk! (And he still can't make out the sex of this creature.) "Watch it, honcho," he growls, and passes on.

A hundred meters down the Concourse he stops again. He listens to a metallic voice.

"The Overlord is dead! Long live the Overlord! But, who shall he be? Whom shall the Conclave select? Discover for yourselves the name of our next Overlord!"

The speaker is invisible. The sound is from a bank of loudspeakers. Konteau looks up at the hastily contrived holo-placards blazoning the stall-front. These are brief clips of a bare-chested man with a turban and loose red breeches holding a snake with one hand and gleaming scimitar in the other. In subsequent clips the blade flashes, the reptile is beheaded, and bloody hands rip out the long convoluted entrails.

Konteau's mouth wrinkles in revulsion.

The grating voice continues. "I hold the Striped Bands from the College of Augurs, maintained personally by the Vyr of Delta. I have sat at the feet of the great Tages himself. I have prophesied before the noblest houses of the Four Continents, and I am known world-wide for my accuracy. I use only the freshest entrails. Next divination in ten minutes. Fee, two silver jeffersons. Group rates, see the management. Children under six, free when accompanied by an adult."

The kron-man grimaces, then his attention is drawn to a couple talking behind him. "Biggest scam in the Mall. Snakes—like hell! He uses rabbit guts, garbage from the restaurants. Not even time-traveled."

"The king cobra is supposed to be good for divination, but my cousin says nothing beats human entrails."

"I've heard that, too. A time-traveled woman is the best of all."

Konteau's stomach suddenly convulses. This place, he thinks, is sick. These people are sick. Why am I here? Why did I come? For oblivion, for girls, for noise, for everything, for nothing . . . so I wouldn't have to think of *her*. But I *do* think. I do remember. I can't think of anything else. Helen . . . Helen . . . Helen. . . .

Hunching his head down between his shoulders, he turns away and jostles through Xanadu's variegated guests.

A heavy but subtle perfume draws him down-corridor to the next booth. Mimosa? he wonders.

The spieler's hypnotic chant has brought a cluster of the curious around the stall. "Ladies and gentlemen, you are privileged to observe a classic exhibition of *papillon-choix,* or butterfly's choice, a form of prophecy honored since classic days. No crowding, please. Room for all. And at the ridiculously low price of one small jeff. Thank you sir, madam. Thank you, thank you." He pulls in the coins almost faster than they touch the hard plastic tabletop.

To one side of the stone table stands a small beaker full of a clear amber liquid, apparently kept molten by an auto-heater.

Konteau frowns. It's another Overlord divination. He has

figured out the technique, but he can't quite fathom the hot amber liquid. Interesting. He decides to linger and see the thing through. He listens, and the litany continues. "As we all know, there are but three benevolent, rational souls suitable as choices to be the new Overlord. First, Willem the Wistful, Vyr of Nieuw Amsterdam. Second, in distant Cathay, Li the Lowly, Vyr of Biching. And finally, in Maryland Ancienne, Paul the Pious, Vyr of Delta. As you see here, each is represented by a flower, in these three vases: Willem by his native tulip, Li by his native rose, and Paul by blossoms of his favorite mimosa."

Konteau's nose wrinkles. He suspects right away that the tulip and rose will turn out to be scentless. In a moment he'll check it with Mimir, his prosthetic eye.

The barker's beady eyes glint as they search his audience. "Wagers, anyone? Even money. Bet your guess against the butterfly?"

"Ooo, I love prophecies," coos the dowager to Konteau's right. "Two jeffs on Li."

The booth-master takes the coins.

"One goldie on Willem," says the youth in front of Konteau. There is the clank of metal.

"What kind of butterfly?" demands a third voice. "How do we know this is on the up-and-up?"

The spieler heaves a great traumatic sigh. "Sir, your question cuts me to the quick. *This* is the butterfly." He holds up a tiny wire cage, not as big as his fist. "Here you will recognize a 'red', the smallest known of the diurnal *Lepidoptera*. She is indeed barely the size of the nail of my little finger. She was freshly hatched from her tiny chrysalis this very morning, and her only goal in life is to make an honest selection of the next Overlord for you, sir."

A *philomimosa*, muses Konteau. The female lays her eggs exclusively on the twigs of the mimosa, and the caterpillar eats only mimosa leaves.

He senses his oculus mentally. "Mimi, prepare for an olfactory assay." He senses, rather than hears, tiny air ducts opening in his false eye, the tiny fan drawing ambient air in and through the diminutive turbinate chamber where it is searched for specific esters and certain long-chain alcohols. He murmurs mentally, "Start with the tulip."

Mimir's response forms soundlessly on his cerebral cortex. "No scent. The tulip is a scentless variety."

"The rose?"

"Also scentless."

"But plenty from the mimosa?"

"Plenty."

Some choice! Oh well, as the froyds say, it's healthy to have your intelligence insulted occasionally. Keeps you humble.

A dozen more bets. "Table closed," calls the keeper. "Here we go." He holds up the cage with one hand, drops the clasp with the other. The tiny door drops with a barely audible squeak of its hinge, and there is a sudden flash of iridescent crimson.

Philomimosa sits on the furry mimosa sprig, wings pumping slowly, her coiled sucker searching amid the ball of pink bloomlets.

Konteau listens to collective groans of disappointment. Only two people—probably shills—had bet on Paul the Pious.

The group begins to break up.

The stall-man holds up his hand. "Wait . . . that's not all." In one sweeping motion he pulls a small glass vial from beneath the table, sweeps the little butterfly into it, and holds up the container. "A simple killing jar, friends." He grins. "She has done her work, and now she goes to her immortal reward."

Konteau frowns. He conjectures that the inner walls of the vial must be cyanide-soaked. Stupid and cruel. Why couldn't she have been left on the mimosa? Or at worst, just let her go? So what now?

He doesn't like any of this, but he is fascinated, and he watches with the others. He cannot help himself. And now he breathes in sharply. He is beginning to understand.

With tweezers, the showman pulls the lifeless winged one

from the capsule and plunges her into the little cup of hot amber. The wings tremble, then fold out slightly. Quickly, he pulls her out again. The liquid is apparently aerobic-catalyzed, for it hardens instantly into a small pear-shaped drop barely encompassing the sparkling red wings. Konteau notices then that the stall-man attaches the amber drop to a very elegant silver chain, with clasps. *Philomimosa* has become the scintillating pendant of an elegant silver necklace.

The executioner looks triumphantly about the expectant faces. They all know what is next. "Bidding," he says, "starts at three goldies."

"Three," says the youth in front of Konteau. A young blond woman stands next to the bidder. Her arm is interlocked with his. Konteau thinks he recognizes the newlywed couple that sat in front of him on the ship coming out. They are still dressed in their white marriage robes, as though determined to advertise their new status in life, and he notes there's still a sprinkling of syntho-rice in her hair. He assumes this is their honeymoon trip. Probably both have saved and scrimped for this one big splurge of a lifetime. But a goldie was probably a month's salary for this man, and he had bid three. Where did he get that kind of money? Oh well, none of Konteau's business.

"A priceless memento," intones the stall-man. "When Paul is Overlord, you'll have it to remind you that you were first to know."

"Five," says a girl in Konteau's rear.

A brief silence. "Twenty-five!" declares the dowager harshly.

Even the stall-master is astonished. "Twenty-five. Thirty, anyone?" But they all know the bidding is over.

No, thinks the krono, perhaps it is not over. He has yet to place *his* bid. He sends a message along the nerves contacting his false eye. "Mimi, can we do it?" The dowager is shoving past him even as he is communing with certain very sophisticated microchips in his artificial eye. Yes, we can do it, barely. The problem is to encase little redwings in her time frame of five minutes ago, then warn her to get the hell out.

He listens to the clank of coins on the table. The exhibitor hands the woman the necklace. She holds it up for all to admire, and her rouged cheeks contort happily. The tiny scarlet wings sparkle like gem-flakes.

There is a sudden faint flash of light—so faint that only Konteau sees it.

The woman jerks back as the miniscule wings flutter in her face. She stares at the amber drop, uncomprehending. It no longer contains the butterfly. Her mouth drops, revealing bad teeth. Someone points—what is it? Something tiny, flying in flashes past the ceiling lights. And gone.

She turns an enraged face toward the stall-master, who looks back at her, more astonished even than she, and not really understanding anything.

A voice whispers in Konteau's ear. "James, that was very naughty of you." He looks down. It is Zeke Ditmars, of Corps Bio-tech. The old researcher pulls him away. "She's going to wreck the joint. This is no place for honest men."

Konteau agrees. "There's a bar just around the corner."

"The Twin Moons. By all means."

Konteau looks back. The only faces clearly visible are those of the newlywed couple. Their eyes search him like laser beams, then suddenly turn away. He notes spectral light flashes at the man's sleeves. Diamond cufflinks? Interesting. He thinks of a pair he used to have. Now long gone, but no regrets.

Behind them the screeches, general demolition, and howling laughter gradually fade. Konteau is feeling better and better. Day one is getting off to a fair start.

Ten minutes later he is following with vague disinterest the fluid movements of the dancers over the grav-table in the Twin Moons. Their graceful airborne arcs and loops synchronize perfectly with the pre-programmed on-off gravity circuits under the table. Colored lights flick over their enameled bodies. And over all, like an eternal sky or sea, the soft subdued songs drift in from hidden speakers. The voices are winding up *Ratell's Roundelay.*

Oh, sing with me the song of Time,
   Tiempo, Temps, Zeit.
Got no reason, got no rhyme,
   Vremya, Tempus, Tijd.
Oh, nine equations that they wrote us,
Delivered by Ratell and Kronos. . . .
Oh, sing with me the song of Time,
   Tiempo, Temps, Zeit.

There's barely a pause, and now they are off into some sugary sentimental ballad. "Though you flee beyond the Moon someday I'll find you now, now, now, let it be now. . . ."

Konteau watches the dancers and finds himself wondering about the programmer. "Some very fancy footwork there," he mused.

"Eh? Oh, the programming? Quite right, James. Glad you asked. All spare-time work, done by a very talented amateur."

Konteau frowned faintly. He couldn't recall asking anything. "Really?" he said politely.

"You want to meet her?"

"Her?" He blinks. Is there actually a woman of intellect and poetic accomplishment out here?

"You got a hearing problem? Her. A girl. A woman. Isn't that why you're here? To meet some interesting women?"

Konteau shrugs.

Ditmars's mouth wrinkles into a parched grin. "You wait here, I'll put in a call for her."

"She's here on holiday?"

"No. Actually, she's working. You wait. Give me a few minutes."

The old man disappears.

Konteau doesn't mind the wait. Here the noise is soft, muted. He likes the sheltering anonymity of strange tongues, secret syllables blending into dull invariant white sound, such as one might hear from an ancient seashell held to the ear.

Like snowflakes the soft numbing lyrics continue to float

down. "I roam the stars . . . looking for her . . . where is my love tonight. . . ." Dull, pleasant noise, thinks Konteau. Neither good nor bad. Just nothing. Pointless even to think about it.

Helen, where are you tonight? When you left you took nothing—except my brain (both hemispheres), heart, lungs, guts, muscles, bones. For days I walked around as a hollowed-out corpse.

He looks up. The old scientist is back with a woman in tow. After the brief introduction ("Demmie, this is James Konteau.") she sits at the bar, next to him.

During the opening small talk he studies her covertly. There is something at once nondescript yet impressive about this woman. Age? Young enough to be his daughter. Under thirty, certainly. Her clothes have a severe tailored look, as though she is traveling incognito and they are part of her disguise. As long as she is still, and silent, and looking away, the camouflage works fairly well. She blends in, unnoticed, with the ladies of the night, the johns, the furniture, the glassware on and behind the bar. But when she swivels on that stool, in that fluid, graceful motion, and looks at him with those cool brown eyes (questing, yet authoritative), she loses all claim to anonymity. By the Four Horsemen, woman (he thinks, squinting and blinking, and embarrassed by her fine figure), you don't belong on a bar stool. Who are you?

They dispose of programmed gravitational dancing in about two minutes, then move on to mutually agreeable banalities. Isn't it nice how Deimos was reconstructed to be a great interplanetary resort? With that disposed of, they proceed to a discussion of the inner moon, Phobos, that actually spins around the planet faster than the planet rotates. And then to Mars itself. And then all of a sudden the irrelevancies cease, and they are into a hot argument about the possibility of life on prehistoric Mars.

Konteau needs moral support, and he looks around for Ditmars, but the ancient researcher is gone.

He is on his own. He tries to explain that there had once been life down there, life of sorts.

"Impossible," Demmie protests. "No air, no water down there. Just a frozen desert."

"That's true today, but there used to be air and water."

"No! You're teasing me."

"Oh, it's so." He lays it all out, item by item, as though he is checking off a shopping list. "There used to be rivers, lakes, even oceans. Volcanoes, mostly in Tharsis, were spewing out water vapor, carbon dioxide, carbon monoxide, nitrogen, by the cubic mile. To this day you can see flood-marks down the whole length of Valles Marineris. And there was truly primitive multicellular life on the planet then, quite similar to our algae back home. They lived by photosynthesis. They took in carbon dioxide and water and excreted oxygen. Two billion years ago the oxygen content of the Martian atmosphere was really quite respectable. You could breathe the air."

"How do you know all that?"

He lapses into momentary reverie. How did he know? He knew because he had been there. He had stood on the scarp of the great Valles, and he had watched the awesome torrent of a river four miles deep and so wide he could not make out the opposite shore. That great river roared through a canyon three thousand miles long, down to a shallow sea.

He could still hear her question. Ah, how did he know? How could he explain to her what it was like, standing on the edge of that gorge, work boots dug into the rubble, flailed by the mud-flecked spray. He had shouted and screamed and yelled his exultation.

A few kilometers east of the Valles was this relatively quiet tributary, where the water flowed in hyacinth curls, as though in obedience to poetic command. He had stared, fascinated. (Hyacinths. Helen of the hyacinths. Always, *hyacinths.*) And all the while, it had rained, rained, rained. And when the rain finally stopped, the skies were actually blue. The solar spectrum was scattered here the same as on Terra, and it had surprised and delighted him.

But what could he tell her of this? He didn't know how to explain it. In fact, he wanted *not* to explain it. It belonged to *him,* and he refused to share it.

Today, of course, the terrain was all different. So in a way, she was right. The only water was underground, hidden as permafrost.

She is saying something to him, and her voice is mocking, skeptical. "So what happened to all that air and water?"

"It mostly escaped. The problem was a mix of molecular speed and escape velocity. You see, in the upper atmosphere nitrogen ions combine with electrons to produce high speed atoms traveling about six point three kilometers per second. That's less than Earth's escape velocity, but greater than Mars'. So Earth keeps its nitrogen, but Mars loses it. It's much the same story for oxygen and hydrogen."

"How about water?"

"UV light converts it into oxygen and hydrogen, and off they go into space. It's not quite the same on Earth. Again, Earth gravity is sufficient to keep oxygen, but not enough to keep the lighter gases, such as hydrogen and helium. Back home, we're losing the lighter ones almost as fast as they are generated by volcanic outgassing. It's even worse here, of course. Once, though, there was plenty of air and water. Air pressure was once as high as 800 millibars. Men could live."

"You're being very silly."

"No. Two billion years ago, back in our Proterozoic, men could live on Mars."

She gives him a look that says; not only silly, crazy.

He takes her by the hand. It is cool, pliant. His eyes take her eyes. "Listen to me. It's a question of simple math. Hydrogen escapes at the rate of two times ten to the eighth atoms per second per square centimeter of Martian surface. Nearly all the hydrogen came from water, by UV-dissociation. If this has been going on since the formation of the planet, that's enough water to cover the entire planet to a depth of a couple of hundred meters."

"So what? It's all gone now, except for a little permafrost."

"Once, though, long ago, it was *there.* It was all different a couple of billion years ago. You could have planted a whole colony back then—a full five million people."

She peers at him with a sudden strange intensity. "Five million people? A full colony? Ridiculous!"

"No," he replies mildly. "It could be done."

"Prove it!"

"I could, if I wanted to."

This amuses her. "Big talk, James."

He growls, "I'd need a lot of stuff out of the library."

"You're serious?"

He shrugs.

"Well, then, I know the librarian. I can help."

He thought about that, then signaled the bartender for a repeat. "Nyah. I'm here on R and R, not to write some idiotic report."

They sip at their drinks, and they look at each other.

Something about her reminds him of his wife. He can't bring himself to say ex-wife. And who are you sleeping with tonight, Helen of the hyacinth curls?

Demmie breaks into his thoughts. "You'll need an assistant, somebody to keep things in order. I can make your kaf, massage your neck, get the data you'll need."

He hesitates. He can't decide. A Martian colony. A dream. Yes, but. . . .

Her mouth lifts in a mocking grin. "You don't really mean it, do you, James Kontcau? You're just bragging? You can't *really* put five million people on a frozen, dry, airless desert?!"

"Sure you can. It's just that it's a bit more complicated than you think. To start, you'd have to prepare time-pilots for several different areas. Remember, we're talking a couple of billion years back—during Earth's Proterozoic. On Mars the epoch doesn't even have a name. The pilot crews won't have a picnic. Space outfall is unpredictable. Of course, you can look at the map, and you can pick clear areas, with no meteors, back to about one billion years. Beyond that, though, the dust storms have pretty well leveled the craters to flat regolithic plains. So after you've worked out the time-pilots, and after you've tagged the craters and set out warning buoys, *then* you send in your survey crews, and they lay out the sites for the colony and the individual boros. And finally, if you haven't killed too many people by then, you send in the construction crews with concrete and prefabs and hammers and nails." (Oh Kronos, he wants to command this project! He presses his tongue against his teeth. He can actually taste his craving. Kraw of Kronos, he's salivating! In sudden embarrassment he brushes his mouth with the back of his hand. Does this woman know what she is doing to him? She knows. Damn her!)

And what is she doing during his very patient and lucid explanation? She is laughing at him.

No more talk. He takes her by the wrist and they go off together to his cramped suite.

And so it starts.

In cleaning the stationery and directories out of his desk they find the Book of Kronos, put there (and, he supposes, in all rooms) by the ubiquitous Malthusians. He can tell the black leatheroid covers have never been opened. He creases the front cover back and reads the red-and-gilt inscription:

> "The realization of a happy society will always be hindered by the miseries consequent on the tendency of population to increase faster than the means of subsistence."
>
> *Thomas Robert Malthus (1766–1834)*

There is something chilling in the statement. He tosses the book in the wastebasket without even a glance at Demmie.

They get organized.

She has contacts. She has Maintenance install a printer in a corner of his little studio, and she compiles a list of service reports, with all kinds of accessions from Earth libraries. The abstracts pour in, and he begins to scribble, painfully at first, and without method. She has to show him how to make an outline, and what should go in certain sections.

Demmie . . . the necessary ingredient. The essential catalyst.

The hours pass, and the sheets of manuscript fall to the floor, and she picks them up, numbers them and reads them but reserves her comments and questions, waiting until he takes the next break. She gets his meals, cleans his room, makes their beds.

Once in a while he thinks of her as a woman. In her free, undemanding way, she is very pretty. Undemanding? What is he thinking! She demands—*commands*—this damned report. That's all she wants . . . all she ever wanted of him. No sex. Desire is irrelevant. He sighs. What day is it?

2

Hyacinths

Drifting out on the day's twilight tide. In his mind, it is all in quotes. There is no real day here. The day on Xanadu is arbitrarily and artificially taken to be identical to that of Grinch, the underground colony in ice-bound Anglia. The Martian day is actually thirty-seven minutes longer, and this occasionally introduces oddities. But nobody cares. The light inside the great resort dims at 'night', lightens up a little at 'dawn', is blazing relentlessly by 'noon', and begins to soften again at seven in the 'evening'.

And though there is no visible water down there, and no tide, nevertheless he drifts.

They sit in the inner observation lounge and watch the planetary desolation sweep by in slow vistas on the mosaic of giant screens. As always, Konteau is hypnotized by the stark austere beauty of that landscape, and he wonders whether Demmie sees the beauty too. He will probably never know. Her mind is a mystery. *She* is a mystery. No matter.

He ponders this project.

The last thing he had wanted to do here was something useful. And yet, despite his lackadaisical resolutions, he had got involved, and now this weird undertaking had completely consumed him.

He tries to think back, tries to pinpoint the exact moment that this spider-woman captured him, entangled him, and began the torture that had produced this damned report. There was a certain time there, back in the bar. Was that it? It had been fast, yet orderly, almost gradual. Rather like going under in surgical anesthesia. That report was all she had wanted, from the very beginning. Had Zeke Ditmars known? Very likely. I ought to be mad at both of them, he thought. But I'm not. That study is a remarkable thing, a real tour de force. Actually (he acknowledges grudgingly) I'm proud of it.

He had got a sense of accomplishment from the simple sensual act of writing and composition. He liked the ready response of his pen (the same one he used in the field). He liked the contact of pen nib and paper (those pages from surveyor's notebooks that he had had Demmie bring in from a Mall stationery shop). Never in his life had he written so much in such a short time. Once he had got started, there had been very few corrections. He knew exactly what he wanted to say and how to say it. He took pride in the precision of his ideas, the clarity of his explanations. Toward the end, the report became a part of him, like a third hand, or (bad comparison!) a second eye. It developed a life of its own.

As he wrote, sometimes he had looked up, frowned, and tried to remember how and why Demmie was there. Once, after he had stopped writing and had stared at the wall in front of his desk for a full ten minutes, she had stood behind him, and she took him by the shoulders, and shook him, and commanded him to get up. "What time is it?" he had asked in a slurred voice. She said, "Nine in the morning. Why don't you go down to Bio and visit Ditmars?"

And so two hundred pages lie in a neat stack back on his studio desk. Neat apple-pie order. *She* did *that,* of course. After all these hours, days, nights, it is done, finished. He can quit. But his mind and body are still racing. He has got to slow down.

Strange, strange. . . . *Whose* report, he thinks. Hers? Mine? She pushed me into it. Without her . . . almost as though she had given him an official field assignment. Except he'd never before written a Comprehensive, a prospectus for a full col-

ony—five million people—not even on Terra. And his Field
Chief would never pick him, a mere field krono, to draft a
Comp. And the hell with it. But there it is. It now exists, even
though it has no reason for existence.

Just now he and Demmie are having their kaf in the observation lounge. The auto-contour chair has adjusted so pleasantly to his spinal column that he barely feels the support.
Ah, perhaps he can begin to relax. . . .

They take a long last look at the Martian desert. One by
one the screens are switching over to the newscast in general
and to the ex-Overlord's funeral in particular.

It's a good time to be away from home base, thinks Konteau. Because of the death of the old Overlord, schools and
shops were closed. Bells in the Terran Kron-temples tolled.
Many thought it a holiday, just as here in Xanadu, and
parades and carnivals sprang up spontaneously in the Terran
colonies.

And now he and she sit here in this great resort carved out
of the outer Martian moon, and they watch the funeral of the
old Overlord. They are shown the serene ashen face as the
casket lid is closed. The brain-dead corpse is still breathing
with its macabre life support system. Four black horses draw
the hearse over millions of rose petals (to muffle the clomp
of hooves and the scraping of wheels on the pavement) down
the boulevard to the launch-pad.

Konteau is curious. He asks the woman, "Ever seen a
horse before?"

"They had one in the farm-museum, back in firstschool."

He nods, and thinks back, and decides on silence. He saw
dinos before he saw horses.

Back to the funeral.

The procession has reached the tarmac. The gantry takes
the casket from the hearse and lifts it with smooth mechanical grace into the waiting jet-capsule. The capsule doors
close. The cameras shift to the podium, and the master-of-
procession steps up to the lectern and begins his eulogy.

Demmie twists uneasily in her chair.

Konteau turns to look at her. "Odd-looking chap, isn't
he?"

"Look at his eyes."

Konteau has already noticed. The speaker, Paul Corleigh, Ninth Vyr of Delta, has eyes with elliptical pupils. A mutation, probably, thinks the krono. And hardly unique. He has seen elliptical pupils before. On certain reptiles; the rattlesnake, for example. Ah, Paul the Pious, can those great slack jaws uncouple to swallow your prey whole?

The woman asks, "Ever met him?"

"No. My crew once surveyed a boro in Delta, in the upper Triassic. But it was all done through the Corps. We had no contact with the chancellory."

"He's a dangerous man. Stay away from him."

He shrugs. It's moot.

She insists on making her point. "He's on a collision course with the Council and the Corps."

At least (he thinks) she knows the amenities. In talking to a kron-man she calls it the Corps. Quite proper. When kron-men talk to each other, they call it the Black Widow, or simply the Widow. All a question of idiomatic courtesy.

Demmie continues. "And if the Conclave elects him the next Overlord. . . ."

He yawns. "I'm not involved, you're not involved. It's all a lot of political hot-air. Forget it."

She does not reply.

He ponders politics a moment. How does she know—or seem to know—all this stuff? You could hear all sorts of stories. Myths, actually. In one of the myths, the new Overlord slays the old one with a ritual axe. Or a dagger. Or by strangulation. Did anything like that really ever happen? Probably not. Anyhow, today they wait for the old Overlord to die a natural death: old age, accident, whatever. And then the god Kronos appoints the new Overlord. Actually, of course, the so-called appointment by the god is simply symbolic terminology for the selection process at the great Conclave of Vyrs. And the Vyrs are coming now from all over the world to Delta, for the Conclave.

He asks politely, not really caring, "Do you know how they make the selection at the Conclave? The mechanics, I mean?"

He thinks she looks at him queerly. But she replies simply, "I've heard certain things."

"Such as?"

"It's rather a blend of animistic savagery and the best computer science. They use . . . mammalian tissue . . . with a sort of laser readout." Her mouth twists grimly. "It's all very horrid and very secret. Don't get involved." She laughs shortly. "I keep saying that, don't I?" But her voice is hard.

What's going on? He doesn't like this. He doesn't pretend to understand politics beyond the broad outlines. The Vyrs, along with their inquisitors and grayjackets, ran the colonies. As the colony-populations overflowed, the Council, through the Kron-Corps, was supposed to have new boro sites ready and waiting. That was government, briefly stated. Of course, the Vyrs and the Council were always fighting, with each trying to absorb the other. The power play had been going on as long as he could remember, and he found it all very boring, totally unrelated to his daily work in surveying sites for new boros and new colonies.

He nods toward the screens. Back to the ceremony.

The speech of Paul the Pious is done. He steps down from the podium, the mob melts away with him, the capsule engines ignite, and the molecules defining the residue of the former Overlord are on their way into solar orbit. The men who had known the late Vyr of Vyrs will be dead long before the batteries that power his space coffin.

Konteau feels a momentary gratitude for his functional detachment from the political scene. He realizes very well that Paul, or any other Vyr for that matter, could squash him like a brontosaurus stepping on a Mesozoic insect. But he has no intention of attracting attention. In his line of work he has no direct contact with these seats of power. Even if he wanted to (Kronos forbid!) he has no opportunity to antagonize the Vyr-structure. And he is determined to keep it that way.

Demmie nudges him. The cameras are now switching to downtown Delta Central.

Like vultures, the Vyrs are gathering there from all over the world for the Conclave. They would soon elect one of their number as the new theocrat. Which Vyr has rendered the greatest service to the god? Who has done what? The delegation from Rho, in central Gallia, proclaim their lord's expedition to Centaurus. Not that the Rho-Vyr had gone to the star personally, but certainly he had financed the project. The adherents of Sigma Vyr, in Espania, sneer; their master has sponsored research that developed synthobeef, cultured from algae. Willem the Wistful, on the other hand, has built a fantastic cathedral dedicated to Kronos. Li points to his forty-hectare Botanical Gardens, where new radiation-resistant vegetation has been invented that might provide good ground cover for the deserts . . . and on and on.

The cameras show strangers walking up to other strangers in the street and starting arguments as to which Vyr has served Kronos best . . . how the politics go (or ought to go) . . . who owes what to whom . . . too bad such and such Vyr has no chance. . . .

R and R (thinks Konteau) certainly came at the right time. Here in the great resort the Conclave excitement is bad enough. Back in Delta it would be impossible.

Except for the two of them, this outer deck is deserted. Demmie brings the tray and puts it on the stand in front of their chairs. She hesitates, then makes a motion as though she might leave. But he says, "Please stay. Please." She smiles and sits down in the chair on his left, on the side of his good eye. He leans over and pours two cups. He takes his kaf black. She adds cream and sweetener to hers.

It is good to relax. What was the word? *Drift.* After all, that's why he's here.

Demmie is trying to get his attention. She is asking something. He frowns. He doesn't want to talk. He just wants to sit here, an empty shell on a distant timeless seashore.

She repeats her question. "How long have you been in the Corps?"

How long? He closes his eye, as though to shut her out. "Too long," he mumbles.

"Where are your Hourglasses?" she asks, half accusingly.

A kaleidoscope of expressions flashes across his face. He doesn't know what to say. In any case, none of her business. The Black Widow gave you the Hourglasses for twenty-five years field duty. Generally, nobody cared—or noticed—whether you wore them or not. They were de rigueur on only one occasion: when you were a pall-bearer at a funeral of a fellow krono. For thirty years they added diamond clusters. You could choose a lapel insigne or cuff-links. He chose the links. Either way, the black-enameled hourglass looked like the underbelly of a black widow spider. Once you had the Hourglass, you were entitled to call the Corps 'the Widow'. Personnel didn't like it; they sent out annual memos warning against the practice. The Glassers paid no attention. For the award, there was an exclusive little banquet and a nice ceremony. Only Hourglassers attended. Another little banquet when he got the diamond clusters. There had been black jokes. Diamonds is a death sentence.

But there was one very nice thing about those diamonds. They were worth money. So, Ms. Demmie (who knocks on forbidden doors), I can answer you truthfully, I don't know where my Hourglasses are. Because I sold them, and with the money, I. . . . He lifts a hand to touch a faint bulge in his inner jacket pocket. Does courtesy require that he give her some sort of reply? Well, all right. He nods in her general direction and growls something unintelligible.

She responds with a forgiving smile and a shrug so elaborate that it might even be taken as an apology for her question. She switches to safer ground. "Do you come here often?"

"Once a year. Just a short vacation."

"I'm here off and on. I never noticed you before."

"I come, and I hide."

"Do you like it here?"

"Sometimes. It was something to try."

"When was your first vacation? . . . here, I mean."

"Oh, four years ago, I guess."

"Why did you pick Xanadu?"

How could he answer that? The Widow had paid for the first one. It was a medical prescription, actually, a thing the meds and froyds insisted on after Helen left. That or indefinite suspension from the Corps. He pulled farther into his

shell. He didn't want to get into *why*. That would just raise
still other questions. "I think I'll take a nap," he mutters. He
closes his eyes firmly.

He thinks back. How had he got involved with those meds
and froyds in the first place? It had been Helen, of course,
but it had developed in a rather curious and roundabout way.
About four years ago, shortly after Helen had left, he had
had a minor auditory problem, and he had mentioned it
rather casually to the meds. A low hum, barely audible,
comes and goes. Nothing serious, he insisted. It didn't really
bother him. Just an intermittent nuisance, that's all. So the
regular meds at the Widow clinic had given him all the
routine hearing tests. They poked him with otoscopes. They
had checked the functions of his inner ear, the malleus, the
incus, the stapes, the cochlea, all those things with the funny
little names. They rotated him, standing and prone, then
checked the movement of his one good eyeball. "Nystagmics
normal," they grumbled. (He could have told them that.)
They had rayed his auditory nerves and checked the range
of his auditory response. They added it all up and shook their
collective heads. One of them muttered, "Not tinnitus. No
ringing in the ears. Or roaring . . . or clicking . . . or hissing.
. . . No otosclerosis, no detectable organic damage." Where-
upon his case took a dramatically different turn. "Do you
hear voices? Does Kronos talk to you?" He was ready to
drop the whole thing, but they wouldn't let him. "How about
other sounds? Continuous musical notes?" He read up on
audio hallucinations. There were historical cases. Centuries
ago a composer, Robert Schumann, had continually heard
the note of A, and he had jumped off a bridge in ancient
Vienna. Konteau did not protest vigorously when they
turned him over to the froyds, who, he suspected, were delighted to get him.

For the initial consultation there was this older man, with
a pince-nez and flabby forgetful eyes, and with him a
younger assistant, very respectful, yet very knowledgeable.
Both wore white coats. They told him their names, but he
forgot them instantly. They took a moment to read the clinic

results while Konteau sat on a stool in his skivvies and wished he was somewhere else.

The two froyds were talking.

"A psychomnem?" the assistant asked the chief.

"Maybe."

Konteau had scowled. Psycho? . . . hell. He knew these quacks. Give it a name nobody ever heard of, you think you've got it under control. Right in front of him, they were talking about him. That wasn't courteous. Worse, they didn't know what they were talking about. "What's a psycho—whatever it is," he grunted.

"Psychomnem. Just a little teaser from your subconscious," said the older froyd. "Something reminding you of something you'd like to remember, but which is going to hurt if you do."

"So it's all very indecisive and ambiguous," added the assistant helpfully.

"I don't have anything like that," declared Konteau. "I'm in full control of my memories and my subconscious."

They didn't reply. They didn't even look at each other. He suddenly realized they probably heard this from every lost soul that wandered through the examination rooms.

Watch it, Konteau, he warned himself. If he bucked these cookies too hard, they could give him a bad medical. They could even force his retirement. He couldn't handle that. His job was all he had. With Helen gone, it was the only thing that held him together. His voice was lifeless. "Let's get on with it. Tell me why I hear a hum."

They put him in the sound room, and they began a reconstruction of his hum. Actually, he took a grudging liking to the analytic process. It was mostly fun. Very scientific.

"The average human ear can sense sound over a frequency range of about sixteen to 20,000 vibrations per second," said the assistant. "Human speech uses a range of about 300 to 4000 cycles per second. The lowest bass note of a pipe organ is about sixteen cycles per second. A hum would of course be in the lower part of the sound spectrum. So first of all, let's try for the general range. Listen to this. Is your hum lower or higher?"

"Lower."

After another couple of tries, they agreed it was eighteen, plus or minus two. "But it's not that simple," he insisted. "My hum is actually a composite. I think it's actually two hums—sort of blending together."

That really fascinated them. "Out of sync?" asked the chief white coat.

"No, I don't think so. If they were out of sync, say two different frequencies, I think I would have heard a beat."

"Do you think the two hums come from the same source?" hazarded the assistant.

"Why . . . yes, I think so."

"A motor?" They were both firing questions at him now.

"No. . . ."

"Two humming transformers?"

"No."

"What are some natural hummers?" the assistant asked himself. "Hummingbirds?" he said brightly.

"No. Wingbeat too fast." Konteau sat up suddenly. "But wait. Something flying. It's overhead."

They looked at him. "Go on," said the chief evenly. "It's flying overhead. One thing, but it makes a composite hum. Not a bird. How many wings?"

Konteau put his hands over his ears and closed his eyes. But he was hearing and seeing snatches of things . . . sounds . . . scenes. . . .

"What is it?" persisted the chief. "What is making the hum?"

"I think . . . a dragonfly."

The assistant objected. "A dragonfly? Impossible! The wing beat would produce a frequency far too high."

The chief held up his hand. "You said four wings?" he asked Konteau quietly.

"Four. The front pair goes up while the back pair is coming down. Then they reverse. It can hover."

"*Was* it hovering?" asked the assistant.

He didn't answer at first. It was coming back, in the beginning slowly, then in spurts and gushes, then finally the full torrent of memories, cruel, beautiful. He and Helen were lying alone on the moss under the great scale tree, dozing after lunch, back in the Upper Carboniferous, three hundred and ten million years ago, in that great green forest of giant fern-like trees that would eventually make coal. It was hot and steamy. They were in shorts and casuals; it was the hour when the sea breeze had stopped but the land breeze hadn't started yet. The forest was absolutely dead. Not a flicker in the fronds. The rest of the survey crew had gone off on a side trip, down the shore of ancient Appalachia, collecting air samples and making temperature and air pressure readings. Suddenly the girl had shrieked and grabbed at him. And simultaneously he had looked up and heard the hum and had seen the creature: a gorgeous *Meganeura,* a giant dragonfly, with a one-meter wingspread. It was there for just an instant, then gone, frightened away by her cry and the movements of their bodies. Ah, but he had seen it. He remembered that great beautiful insect with almost painful explicitness. He remembered the body length, the long slender abdomen, twig-size legs, the gigantic bulbous eyes. The eighteen-per-second beat converted the wings into a vague blur. He remembered thinking at the time that this creature, this primitive *Odonata,* was a biological impossibility.

And then. . . .

When Helen opened her eyes his face was over hers, and he was looking down at her nose and lips. He eased the weight of his body away a little so she could breathe. He noticed for the first time that her hair was a cluster of individual curls, like the petals of the hyacinth. Her eyes closed again as he kissed her. She put both arms around his neck and shoulders.

Their life together had begun with a hum.

He listened to the two froyds talking back and forth in low voices. "I think he's got it."

Yes, he had it, but he wasn't sure he wanted it.

That encounter with the froyds was the first, but not the last. That one had happened a few months after Helen left him. Had it helped at all? Actually, yes. The hum vanished.

He was never troubled with it again. And he could now pass the florist shop (displaying hyacinths in pots) without palpitations or shortness of breath. He had found the "misplaced" volume of Edgar Allan Poe in the disorder of his bachelor apartment. *("Helen, thy beauty is to me. . . .")* He found it on his night table, where it had been all along. Maybe he was actually getting over the shock of her departure.

But solving the hum wasn't the end of it. They assigned a special trio of froyds to him, three females who worked as a group, and he checked in with them quarterly. Actually, he had started coming here to Xanadu at the insistence of those three—whom he had never actually seen, and knew only by their voices. He would lie on that soft couch, under soft pink lights, in the talk-room, and the voices would float in dreamily. Before the first session had been well underway, he had been able to distinguish each of the three voices. He was somehow reminded of the Three Norns:

First voice (Norna, rough, firm): You have lost ten kilos since your last physical. You need rest. You must get away. It will take your mind off Helen.

Second voice (Verdandi, contralto, beautifully modulated, concerned): Try Xanadu, on Deimos.

Third voice (Skuld, soprano, a bit squeaky, exuberant): You always liked Mars.

First voice (Norna): You could write a Comprehensive. You have long wanted to write a Comprehensive for a Martian colony.

Second voice (Verdandi): In any case, you could meet some girls.

Third voice (Skuld): Find a girl who can help you with your report.

Odd how it had worked out. Almost as if the Widow had forewarned Ditmars, and Ditmars had lined up Demmie. But what was Demmie's stake in this?

He shook his head. Forget the report. Forget Demmie . . . Ditmars . . . even the Widow. There was only one truly important thing, and that was Helen. All mental paths turned back finally to Helen, like passages in an artful maze, or roads to ancient Rome. Even the Norns led to Helen. Especially the Norns.

Funny about those invisible three.

Once he had complained. "Is this normal? Why can't we do this face to face?"

"It might interfere with our usefulness," said Norna.

"Are you ladies some kind of monsters? You think the sight of you might frighten me?"

"For the moment, James, we won't pursue the question of what we look like." (This from Verdandi.) "If you have a sudden life and death emergency, this could change."

"Now that's reassuring. If I see you ladies, it's because I'm about to die." He intended that as a mixed statement and question.

It was Skuld's turn to respond, but there was no answer.

He takes a covert peek toward Demmie. She is breathing softly, regularly. Maybe she's the one that needed a nap.

He sighs, and his thoughts turn once again to Helen. She needs nothing, no one. Not their son Philip. Not her work. Certainly not me. How did she ever achieve such detachment? *Is* it an achievement? Whatever it is, it's awesome.

In past sojourns on Xanadu he would sit here, alone on the observation lounge, thinking of Helen, and of his son, and wondering whether he would be killed on his next assignment, or the next, and whether anyone would care.

So, Madame Demmie, or whatever your true name is, you want to know what happened to my diamond-clustered Hourglasses? You want to know the fate of the sole tangible testimony of thirty-two neck-risking years with the Widow? I sold them, my persistent little friend, and with the money I bought something of value: three filmy soft-focus oil portraits, by the great Ingrim. Ingrim, no less. The originals were in a vault back at Sigma, but before storage he had had miniature vocal holos made, which he kept hidden in an inner wallet. In past carousals here, he would put the triptych on the bed, or on the credenza, or even on the floor, set the sequence going, and his lips would shape the words along with the vocals:

One:

> If thou of fortune be bereft
> And in thy store there be but left
> Two loaves—sell one, and with the dole
> Buy hyacinths to feast thy soul.

(He had sold both loaves; both diamond-clustered Hourglass cufflinks, that is, and no regrets.)

Two:

> I sometimes think that never blows so red the rose
> As where some buried caesar bled,
> That every hyacinth the garden wears
> Dropped in her lap from some once-lovely head.

(He thinks: if I can just understand about hyacinths, the knowledge will make me invulnerable. I can survive. I can make a life without her.)

Three: *(This one was a nude.)*

> I touched her sleeping breasts
> And they opened to me suddenly
> Like spikes of hyacinth.

In his mind's eye he considered this elegant flower. The hyacinth was a bulb perenially flowering from a central stalk into a dense growth of six-petalled florets, with tips that curled back toward the stalk. The visual and olfactory impact could be dramatic, especially with the darker hues. Some women—Helen was one—had hair that coiffed naturally into hyacinth curls.

He had watched Ingrim at work. "Hyacinths!" breathed the great painter. "Oh, marvelous!" And from one photograph he had painted one canvas a day for three days, while Konteau had basked in the artist's enthusiasm.

The profoundest image of all, the Poe vision, he had not entrusted to Ingrim. It was his own private property, not to be shared even for the purposes of rendering it immortal. For it was already deathless.

> *Thy hyacinth hair, thy naiad airs*
> *Thy classic face have brought me home . . . .*

The naiad under the great Lepidodendron tree, on that probe into the distant Pennsylvanian Period. Oh, he would remember her forever. The great humming dragonfly had left, and the silence had come again. And the only sounds were the gasps from our sweating bodies. And so you, Helen of the Hyacinths, became the mother of our son. Twenty-two years ago. Or was it 310 million?

So now, Xanadu. And thank Kronos for Xanadu. During past vacation days here, everything sort of got mixed up, blended together, and nothing was real. He would sit here (in this very chair?) and close his eyes, and float in an amniotic sea. Xanadu was a sheltering womb.

In the "evenings" of holidays past he had liked to wander through the shop-lined Mall. The walkways were generally crowded with wanderers like himself: men on the prowl for women, and vice-versa. In the beginning he had been astonished at the number of very rich females that showed up here. He had met several from the noblest houses of Terra.

Dress-marts, beauty salons, boutiques, and fast-food bars seemed to alternate with each other, like braids. He liked to stroll by the beauty parlors and look in the windows at the hair styles. Last year there had been a big holo of a woman's hair done up in hyacinth curls. He had stared at it for several minutes, fascinated. He imagined he could sense the pungent, attar-like scent of Helen's hair. Next evening the holo was gone.

But this year it was different. Very little time to wander around. Demmie had kept him at the damned report. She nagged, she pressured. Odd thing, he could never decide whether he resented it. Even when it was finally completed, he didn't know.

At least on this trip it was almost as though he had a purpose; even though (as he now suspected) it was actually the purpose of this mysterious female. Demmie had shoved it down his throat. He hadn't known what was happening until it was all over.

He was trying to think back, trying to put it all together. When had it started? If old Zeke Ditmars was in any way involved, it might even have started as early as a year ago. Last year, the day he arrived he visited the Council's Experimental Laboratories to say hello to his old friend, the retired theoretician who had designed Mimir, his prosthetic eye. The conversation had somehow ambled off into a discussion of how to cope with Earth's population overflow. The kronman had recommended the Martian Proterozoic. "You could put a whole colony there, Zeke, five million people. Start with one boro—five thousand. Then another and another. You can siphon off the Terran overflow, say a hundred thousand a year at first."

The old scientist eyed his friend thoughtfully. "You'd need a lot of preliminary work."

"I've been down there. I *know.*"

"Sure you do. But *they* don't. The Council would need a full report, a Comprehensive, before they would think of sending in even a preliminary survey team."

"I know. So forget it. I think I'll hop around to the Stately Pleasure Dome and check out the girls." He added politely. "Join me?"

Ditmars was thoughtful. "Not this time, James. Next year, perhaps. You'll be back next year?"

"Yes, I guess so."

"Next year, then. Next year for sure."

Konteau realizes now that the ancient scientist had planned this rendezvous with Demmie as early as one year ago. He laughs mournfully.

He has been set up.

3

"A Quake is Coming"

So they sit here on the observation lounge, and Konteau broods, and Demmie asks an occasional question.

Demmie: "Are you in the field a lot?"

Konteau: (Groans.)

Demmie: "Is that how you lost your eye?"

Konteau: (No answer.)

Demmie: "It's a marvelous report."

Konteau: (His thoughts are morose, unutterable.) "What the hell do you know?"

But she is not offended. He nags at her. "And who cares, anyway?"

"I care."

He thinks, and maybe you really do. And maybe someday, somehow, that might turn out to be important. Demmie—a woman with ideals, and a mission. No time for men. Last year the idea of Demmie would have made him feel fragile, adolescent, uncertain. But now, it just doesn't matter. He realizes, though, *that* wasn't necessarily good. What *does* matter? There are still a few things left. Work. Helen. Phil. Funny about the order. When had Helen dropped down to second place? And did *that* mean some sort of progress? He wishes to Kronos he knew.

She is asking him something. He has to think back a little.

What did she say? Ah, he has it now. How long has he been a kron-man.

His reply is weary, flat. "Thirty-two years."

Too long, yet not long enough. The question opens the gates to memories: some trivial, some awesome, some horrible. Helen of the curls had been a kron-surveyor. That was how he had met her. He and she and Devlin and Quincy, on that assignment in the late Mesozoic. Devlin was group leader. They had all warned Quincy: Don't take chances. But the light-hearted Quincy had been very confident and very careless. Quincy had got himself killed. They couldn't even bring the body back. Scavenger insects, ants and beetles as big as your foot, had eaten Quincy within minutes. Even the bones. Even the titanium dog-tag. Devlin had never got over it. The group leader had barely escaped court-martial. Poor Devlin.

So now he and this girl sit together in the observation lounge, linked in near-silence, like old people. He notes vaguely that she watches him from the corner of her eye. He clears his throat. His voice is somber, thoughtful. "I have a son, approximately your contemporary."

"Is Philip a krono too?"

He jerks. He has missed something? The conversation is weirdly out of sync. But what? How? He can't bring it into focus. She has asked a question about his son. Just making conversation? . . .

He replies, "No, he's not a krono. He's finishing up his doctoral in low tensors. I told him I'd kill him if he joined the Service." The intonations are modulated, matter-of-fact, rather like a weather summary over the Marineris. He smiles his lop-sided smile. "Not to worry. He's perfectly safe. He gets his degree this summer, out of Prime Teknikon. That's in Lambda 421."

"I know. I was born in Lambda, in Illinois."

"You weren't born in 421?"

"No, 618. But I've *been* to 421. I've seen the Teknikon. Your son is very fortunate."

Now he has it. She had known his son's name, Philip. He

hadn't told her. He files the bit of data away mentally. "I have a snap of him." He pulls the picto from his wallet. "That was last year, when he got his second level in math."

She looks at the little rectangle. The face is simultaneously arrogant, sneering, pleading. The moving lips seem to cry out, "Father, love me!" She steals a look at the man. He sees the look, and he says, as if in combined refutation and explanation: "But I *do* love him. I just don't know how to say it. I don't know what he wants of me."

She hands it back without a word. He replaces it carefully. She says, "You tried to call him last night?"

"Yeah. He left word on his recordak he was in studylock—out for twelve hours."

It is almost casual, the kind of trivia two near-strangers might exchange idling away an hour in the club room of an express. He wants to tell her about his wife, but he knows it wouldn't work. How could he explain something he didn't understand himself? Helen had announced that she was leaving him as soon as Philip was settled into the collegia. That was three years ago, and he had not believed her. Yet that was exactly what she had done. For a time he had walked around in a sort of mechanical stupor. How had he offended her? He couldn't imagine. There were no other women in his life. His vices were without distinction. What did she want? Just her freedom? Was that all? But she had always been free. As the months rolled on, he finally realized that he had never really known her, that all these years she had lived in a Helen-world from which he was excluded. After the physical fact of separation there followed the dull legal details. He would pay her something, but she would still have to work. What would she do now? She'd take some refreshers and go back into kron-surveying. And why not? After all, that's how they had met. (He smiles, thinking back.) Philip had been conceived under the cathedral branches of that giant fern tree. Philip, an insouciant citizen of the Carboniferous. That tree was long gone, bladed out by the construction crews that followed Devlin's survey team. He happened to know that a skitter-wash now occupied the sacred spot. Progress.

And so she had left, and he had buried his wounded ego under field-work and reports. But nothing really helped. It was like trying to run with broken legs.

Helen was free. He was in chains.

He starts. Demmie is tugging at his sleeve. "Is your son as handsome as you?"

That makes him laugh. It is a spontaneous explosion, almost happy, and it is contagious. She laughs with him. He calms down. "He *is* a good-looking kid, isn't he? He gets his looks from his mother."

She smiles. It is a knowing smile, and it irritates him. He switches the subject.

He muses aloud. "Odd how things are named. Two billion years ago, during our Proterozoic, Mars was warm and wet and green with algae. Not red at all. It was warm because of the greenhouse effect of the carbon dioxide in the atmosphere: it let sunlight in, but retarded radiation back into space. But all the time, water was dissolving surface rocks, and carbon dioxide was reacting with the dissolved minerals to form carbonates, limestones, dolomites. And so the carbon dioxide disappeared, then the planet cooled, the algae died, the water evaporated, the oxygen reacted with iron, and the planet turned rust-red. But I'm digressing. The point is, the great number one river, the Alpha, that flowed in a massive torrent through the Valles Marineris. Alpha in the surveys, but Alph for short. And where is the Alph?"

"In Xanadu, . . ." she murmurs. *"Where Alph, the sacred river, ran/Through caverns measureless to man/Down to a sunless sea.* Except that Xanadu is up here on little Deimos, not down there on the planet."

His face contorts into something very like a grin.

"So you were really there," she says quietly. "You breathed the air, and you really saw the great river."

He grunts something unintelligible.

She asks, almost diffidently, "What does it feel like . . . when you go back in time?"

And now he looks at her, very grave, very serious. "Little friend, don't ever do it. If some fool offers you the chance, don't take it. Not even as a one-time observer. Not for fun, not for kicks, not for the experience, not for any reason. Do you understand me?"

"Yes."

She is not really offended, just impressed. Fair enough.

He mutters, almost apologetically, "Who knows? Maybe one day the report will actually reach the Council's Planning Commission. Maybe somebody there will actually read it. But will it really persuade anybody to start a colony down on the planet? No. Never."

She is silent.

He continues. "If they don't do something soon on Terra, they'll have to start killing people."

"Gracious! Are we that crowded?"

He does not reply. He stares at the Valles Marineris on the screen and he is lost in faraway thoughts. In silence she pours them both more kaf.

He says, "A quake is coming." He is not talking to her, perhaps not even to himself.

She shows more concern than he does. She whispers, "Here, on Deimos?"

No reply. A shadow passes over his face.

"Where?" she says. "When?"

He closes his eyes. "Not a geo-quake. It will be a quake in the flow of time. Kronos sneezing, as they say in the Service. When?" He is silent again. He thinks, I have to get a psychic fix. It would have to affect a boro his team had surveyed. He had laid out a great many. Over sixty. But of these only three were vulnerable. One in Epsilon, one in Omicron, one in Delta. And for each and every one of these, he had recommended triple stabilizers. So why was he worried? Even if his son were perchance in one of these three, he would be safe. The triples would absorb anything.

"Forget it," he says. "No danger. Anyhow, maybe I'm wrong."

But he is uneasy, restless. He can't relax anymore. He has to be up, moving around. He gets to his feet. "I think I'll go down to the East Wing for a little while."

"The Experimental Lab? Ditmars?"

"Yeah."

Obviously he doesn't want her company.

"Tell Zeke hello for me."

This season the old scientist is working with primates. "In this cage," he explains, "we have a young rhesus monkey— we call him Beta—perfectly normal in all physical respects. He's well-fed, well-treated, with not a care in the world. You can even stick your finger through the mesh, and he won't bite you. Whoa! Don't try it! Heh heh. Now, overhead here,"—he points to a holo screen—"we have another rhesus: Alpha, Beta's father. At the moment, the real Alpha is several million kilometers distant, down on the planet, in our research facility in Marsdome. He, too, is at peace with the world. He has just dined on syntho-bananas and is contemplating a nap." He looks at the wall clock. "Our little experiment begins in thirty seconds. Ready?"

"Ready."

The scientist presses a button on the bench. A holo of something sinuous and scaly begins to form in horrid coils around Beta's cage, and Beta begins to scream in terror.

Konteau frowns and starts to protest, but Ditmars holds up a hand. "Holo of a South American anaconda. Monkeys are deathly afraid of them. Beta's reaction is old stuff. Not the point of the experiment. *Look at Alpha.*"

The holo of the parent simian is also in hysterics, flailing about in his holo cage.

"Enough." Ditmars flips off the snake holo and the two monkeys gradually subside.

"Telepathy?" hazards Konteau. "The father sensed his offspring was in danger?"

"Something like that. And of course telepathy is not unknown. But that isn't really the thrust of the work."

"Oh?"

"We can induce the characteristic, James. The technique is really quite simple. The rhesus ovum is fertilized during time travel. The resulting scion is able to convey certain feelings telepathically to one or both parents, generally the father. The ability is functional over great distances of space and time. In this particular instance, Beta's parent ovum was artificially fertilized during a passage forward from the Silurian. Passage through the lines of time appears to develop a latent hereditary faculty in the genes. Like imprinting migration routes on the cortices of certain birds, or homing traits in salmon. We've even done it with plants. Damage to a daughter mimosa makes the leaves of the parent fold up. If we kill the daughter plant, the leaves on the parent actually drop off. We've even worked out time-rate parameters for a number of species."

"I'm not sure I understand."

"Well, take the rhesus ovum. To develop the property, the ovum at the instant of fertilization has to be moving through time at the rate of about seven hundred thousand to a million years per second. For example, coming up from the Silurian of four hundred and five million years ago, the crew would have to reach the present in about forty minutes, their elapsed time. That's about the usual transit time, anyhow, isn't it?"

"Roughly," agrees Konteau. "Did you actually time-travel the female monkey?"

"Oh no. We did the rhesus work in vitro."

"You have pictures?"

"Of course. We timed everything to the microsecond, with microviewers. Are you really interested?" He looks at the krono doubtfully.

Konteau thinks of Helen, and long ago, and love under the lepidodendron. "I'd like very much to see your work."

The old man putters about through the piles of cassettes, mumbling to himself. "Maybe . . . yes." He blows dust off the cover, pulls out the little rectangle. "Really ought to . . . some day. . . ." He dims the lights and turns on the holo screen. "Magnification, five thousand. There you go."

Konteau peers into the 3-D cube.

"The little wriggler is the spermatozoon," explains the sage. "The big ball is the ovum. Step one, the sperm buries his head in the ovum. Bang! That's the instant of conception. Look at the excitement in the ovum! She knows she's been fertilized. And one sperm's enough. Step 2, she forms a protective shell all around herself. It stops other wrigglers from getting in. Step 3, the ovum nucleus begins slowly to whirl, like a micro-carousel. This draws the sperm head inside. He leaves his tail outside. It wiggles a bit, then stops. It has done its job, and it dies. Step 4, the sperm head begins to swell up. Hah! See there? It's a nucleus, loaded with its own packet of chromosomes, a unique donation from the male. It now joins the ovum nucleus. They fuse together, to make one nucleus. Our gametes are now one zygote. Two haploids equal one diploid. After this, we simply transfer the diploid cell to the host mother, for normal gestation."

"How much of this has to be going on during time-transit?"

"We think just Step One, the instant of fertilization."

Konteau is thoughtful. "Fascinating. Beautiful work. Have you tried it on human ova?"

"Not yet, though we've applied for permits. Of course the technique with humans would present even greater difficulties than those we encountered with rhesus."

"How's that?"

"Well, with rhesus we fertilized and time-traveled in vitro. We had a measure of control. With *sapiens,* we'd probably have to use a real live woman. The ovum would have a journey of several inches along her oviduct, on the way to the uterus. The spermatazoon—one of some quarter billion— seeks out the ovum, fertilizes it in the oviduct. At that instant, that absolutely unpredictable instant, the woman has to be moving in time. Conception in transit, as it were. Her effective time gate is only half an hour or so. Nah." He shakes his head. "Far too complicated. If it ever gets done with humans, it'll be by accident."

As he returns to chambers, Konteau thinks back. It always seems to go back to Helen, one way or another, starting with their first passionate lovemaking under the great fern tree, with its bark scales spiraling upward. The curling scales always reminded him of hyacinth petals, and of Helen.

An interesting point to ponder: at which exact point in time had son Philip been conceived? No way now to know for sure. Several hours needed for some two hundred million sperm to ascend into the oviduct. Was an ovum waiting there? A microscopic haploid cell, waiting for that even smaller wriggler? Quite possible. And then the miniscule male gamete burying its head into the massive female ovum, which instantly wraps itself in a defensive membrane to prevent entry by other spermatozoa. That is the instant of conception. The rest is inevitable: the twenty-four chromosomes of the sperm mixing with the twenty-four of the ovum to form a new diploid nucleus. The question is, at the instant of Philip's conception, were they returning from the late Paleozoic at the correct rate, over a hundred thousand years per second? Intuitively, he knows it is so. But so what? The odds were astronomical that the distant Philip, nose deep in his research texts, would ever find himself in deadly danger and cry out to him. He thinks of his son and he smiles. Philip, to Kronos born; already over three hundred million years old. Conceived in transit. A true child of time.

Returning, he passes by the entrance of the game room. He pauses and looks in.

Once Demmie had said, after he had been writing all day, and then into the small hours, "Let's take a little walk, then you have to go to bed." She had taken his hand. She guided his silent somnabulistic steps down labyrinthine, disorienting corridors. They paused at the entrance to the dim-lit game room. In the center was that post painted to look like a lepidodendron tree trunk fresh out of the Carboniferous. Mocking him? And there, near the doorway, the chess table. Odd, he had thought there might be a cowled figure there, waiting for him. But no one was there. The pieces should have been set up, in that problem position. But the board was empty. In fact, the whole room was empty. Generally there at least would be a few people bent over the transportation exhibit, punching buttons to make the models move: the oxcart, the Roman chariot, the automobile, the ancient moon-lander, a modern spacer, even a funny little thing called a steam locomotive. He liked to flip the switch and watch it clickety-clack around the rails. You could make it go almost as fast as you liked. Going around the curves, magnetism held the wheels to the rails. The micro-pistons exhausted their dead steam up the little smokestack with a staccato puff-puff-puff. You could switch it into the little station, and it automatically slowed down and whistled as it entered the station side-track.

But he isn't interested in the game room just now. He turns away, finds the route back to the observation lounge. Demmie is still there. He sinks into his chair, and in a moment he is dozing.

Finally his head jerks. He must have fallen asleep. How long have they been out here? Other guests are coming out now. The revelry in the Mall is apparently finally subsiding, and people are coming out here to collapse. What time is it? He glances at his watch. Mid-morning, Deimos-time. He groans and stretches a hand out to his kaf-cup. The stuff is cold. He puts it back, comes to a decision. "I have to go to Message Center. I'll be back in the suite in, say, half-an-hour. Meanwhile, would you mind dropping around to the library and see if you can get a couple of cassettes?"

"Of course. Which ones?"

"Poems. Goethe's . . . and Poe's."

"Goethe, Poe. Fine. And how about some of the modern poets? Or even some from Renaissance Two? Barsel, the great lyricist. And Mahmud, for hypnotic chants? And I'm sure they have Thergan. I've always loved his images. I listen to him, and I can actually hear the sea."

"Not for me. For yourself, if you like."

She smiles, and nods. She doesn't demand an explanation. Thank Kronos for that. He doesn't have an explanation.

He stride-floats off to Message. There he fills out the text and feeds it into the receptor:

INFO GENERAL: 1. ANYTHING UNUSUAL REPORTED FOR EPSILON 005 OMICRON 772 OR DELTA 585? 2. IS HELEN MARTIN 951-135-642 STILL AT DELTA CEN-TRAL? 3. IS PHILIP KONTEAU 612-951-304 STILL AT LAMBDA 421? REPLY Y/N. WAITING. CHARGE JAMES KONTEAU KRON 612-001-763.

He waits patiently, and he thinks. He has never been in a timequake. His surveys always stress triple stabilizers where there's the slightest danger. So there is absolutely no reason for concern. So why is he worried? Perhaps because he is just a little insane. If you stay in this business long enough your mind turns to mush. You get off by yourself, and you think. And what do you think? You think you have solved one (or all!) of Ratell's Paradoxes.

Just look at them.

Paradox Number One. That slab in Harvard Museum with the dinosaur tracks, dug up forty years ago. And next to it, a holo of the identical tracks, made fresh in that same Mesozoic mud, and next to those tracks, a couple of Ratell's own footprints. Prints of the actual naked feet. He put his feet there within minutes of the passage of the dino. In the holo you could even make out the friction ridges on the bottom of the right big toe. So why hadn't Ratell's footprints been carried over on the solid Harvard exhibit? What had Kronos done to make the time-master's footprints disappear, some time during the last ninety million years?

Paradox Number Two. The Mediterranean Sea existed today because Ratell and a crew of twenty-fifth century engineers had broken open the Gibraltar bridge and let in the Atlantic thirteen million years ago. But how could the Mediterranean be formed by forces that would not come into existence for another thirteen million years, and which indeed the formation of the Mediterranean would be required to produce? It didn't make any sense at all. If you thought about it too deeply, you could go crazy. No matter. The fact that it had been done was the important thing. If it had *not* been done, if the great mid-sea had *not* been formed, where would history be? Where would *he* be? Or Ratell, for that matter?

He had read Ratell's report on the grand opening. The time-scientist had visited the great sunken basin three times. He had checked the land bridge at Gibraltar, and he had decided it would hold back the Atlantic forever unless artificially breached. In North Africa the Nile would continue to cut through deep gorges down into a dead shallow lake. There would be no annual flooding, and Egypt would never be born. There would be no daring Phoenicians sailing out through the Gates of Hercules to barter at the Tin Islands. There would be no wine-dark seas on which the Greek marines could challenge the Persian hosts. Xenophon would not have his thousand-mile Up-March, and his mercenaries would not finally rush down to the shores with their wild exultant cries: *"Ho Thalassa!* The sea! The sea!"* Octavian would not destroy Antony at Actium, nor would Christianity halt Islam at Lepanto. Civilization would never be born.

At the middle of the Miocene Ratell returned for the last time. He brought his engineers and his earth-moving equipment, and he opened the great sluice for the Atlantic to enter and flood the sunken desert. For more than a hundred years the waters roared in, and the basin was finally filled. And so were born Egypt, the isles of Greece, the Italian peninsula, and the scene was set for *Homo sapiens* and for history. And the whole proposition (thinks Konteau) is preposterous, absolutely outrageous.

And finally, Number Three, the ultimate Ratellian Paradox. It was alleged that the Time-Master stood on the shore of that limitless Archeozoic Sea, the great Proto-Oceania, lifeless, yet rife with organic soup: adenine, thymine, guanine, cytosine, uracil—the whole DNA/RNA orchestra tuned up and waiting for the conductor. And then Ratell (so they said) emptied the R-cell culture into the waiting waters.

That fantastic toss was not merely symbolic, as when centuries ago, Governor Clinton had poured a quart of Atlantic water into the Erie Canal, as a sign that the Great Lakes were now joined to the Seven Seas. No indeed. It was totally functional, as when (in the olden days) the brewer added his special yeast culture to the waiting wort. Or as in that tale by the Prophet Jules Verne, where the little girl throws a shard of ice into the supercooled lake, and it instantly freezes over, and off they go on ice-sledges.

Konteau had collected the scattered reports, and he tried to reconstruct several that seemed to have disappeared, perhaps destroyed as too fantastic for indexing and storage. From what he could piece together, Ratell had stood on the shores of Tethys, the Proto-sea of three billion years ago. He had analyzed samples of the seawater, and found in it all the organics necessary to start life. Ratell had stood there in that strange eternal rain—it rained for three million years—and through his helmet he had looked out over the thrashing water at the gray-green sky, continually laced by U.V.-produced fluorescent flashes. There was no oxygen; the atmosphere consisted almost wholly of nitrogen, methane, and carbon oxides. Conditions were ideal for formation of life in the sea; but there was no life. Ratell checked lagoons, mudflats. Nothing. Maybe not warm enough? He investigated warm pools around volcanoes, where heat dehydrates amino acids. He found polyamides, but no life.

Evidently he was too early; so Ratell waited two hundred and fifty million years and checked again. He sampled seawater all over the world. Nothing. Not even one elementary strand of viral DNA. This alarmed Ratell. He checked one more time, two and a half billion years B.P., in the Archeozoic; still nothing.

That did it.

He had the Bio Lab brew a special culture—a colony of cells, absolutely primitive, yet unique in their predictability to mutate when exposed to the proper mutagens, such as terrestrial radioactivity and cosmic rays. These R-cells ("R" for Ratell) would initiate life in its simplest, most elementary forms. Yet they would readily mutate with changing environments. They would be capable of evolving into the gene of the simple virus, one two-thousandth of an inch long and containing 170,000 genetic steps. Then into a bacterium, one four-hundredth of an inch long and containing seven million steps. And then eventually into the three-foot long DNA with six billion steps in the chromosomes of *H. sapiens* as well as eight-foot strands for frogs, which need additional genetic directions for metamorphosis from tadpoles into frogs. Each R-cell carried within its simple walls everything needed to respond to mutative selection and evolution over the next several billion years. Stromatolites were first, then algae, protozoa, jellyfishes, mosses, worms, things with shells, fishes—in and out of the water, land creatures, reptiles (great and small) . . . finally, mammals, primates, *Homo sapiens,* and Ratell. Full circle. (For rumor held it that those original R-cells were based on clones from his own flesh.) Devlin had sworn he had seen the culture flask, as recovered from metamorphosed magnesia-limestone way up in the Dolomites. Like hell, Devlin. That flask must have been a plant, a hoax. Konteau was reminded of Professor Beringer of eighteenth century Wurzburg, whose prankish students planted synthetic fossils for him to find. The good doctor even found a silicified bone inscribed with Hebrew characters, spelling out his name. No, you had to draw the line somewhere.

He had heard reports of kronos who had grasped the Harvard Paradox and the Mediterranean Paradox, but he had never heard of anyone who truly understood the R-Culture Paradox.

Whether Ratell had actually opened the Med, or had actually started life on Earth, he didn't have to decide. Fortunately, it couldn't happen again. Nowadays of course there were very strict rules. If you were going to transfer something from Present to Past (or vice-versa) you had to get an HIS, an Historical Impact Statement, proving the thing wouldn't affect history in the slightest. On the other hand, suppose the Historical Office was wrong, and it *did* affect history? How would anyone ever know? Maybe every piece of junk that ever got shifted into the past has already changed history—and our memories to match—so that it doesn't matter at all. We don't know a thing about it. It's all part of the normal past. Maybe (he thought) my putative ancestor, Gork the Caveboy, forty millenia removed, got killed by a bear I should have killed during one of my surveys, and maybe I'm not really me.

His reverie breaks. The Message bell is beckoning. Ah, the report has finally come in. He stops pacing and strides over to the screen.

FOR JAMES KONTEAU I N 2 & 3 Y CHG 26.00

So. No quake reported. And neither Helen nor Philip in one of the possible time-fracture zones anyway.

He takes a deep breath. Absolutely no reason for this sudden insane anxiety.

4

The Nightmare

On his way back to his apartment he passes the game room. From the corner of his eye he notes that the chess table is still empty, but that someone is pushing buttons over at the transportation exhibit. He hears a rhythmic click-click. It is the little steam train. Who cares? He shrugs and walks on up the corridor.

As he opens his door, he sniffs and notes that Demmie has lit a piece of somno-incense in the burner, a bit of black ceramic shaped in the traditional open maw of the god Kronos. Very good! What was the legend? Kronos ate his children, but Zeus finally escaped, slit the majestic belly of time, and freed his brother and sister godlings. Maybe that's what we should do with our excess population: toss the hapless wretches down the time-gullet.

But wait. He sniffs. It's the odor of hyacinths. He doesn't need a confirmation from his oculus. The scent is sharp and clear. The incense is the insidious Malaysian variety, the kind that sends questing tendrils into quivering memories and awakens patinaed irrealities. If he let this go on, Helen would soon be standing there in the middle of the room and he wouldn't know for sure which of them was real.

He blinks the forming images away. Where is Demmie? He turns

The girl is waiting by the audio unit. She is smiling, and

he supposes this means the library had the cassettes. "Goethe first," he says.

"It's in German."

"Of course. Index for *Mignon.*"

"Mignon? *Darling?* Who was she?"

"A young girl, twelve or thirteen, kidnapped in Italy by a wandering troupe of actors and brought over the Alps into Germany, where she was eventually rescued by an aristocrat, Wilhelm Meister. One morning she awakens him with that famous song. She asks him if he knows her homeland, the land of flowering lemon trees, soft winds, blue skies, the land of laurel and myrtle." Konteau stops and says lamely, "I'm boring you. . . ."

She shakes her head. "The key is *home.*"

Home? Was there really such a place? Was that where he and Helen and Philip had once lived? Genuine artificial turf, a tree, a dog, a cat, a dozen kids on the street for Phil to play with. At night, the floating bed. He could fling an arm over her. . . .

Demmie pushes the button. The holo forms. It is a young actress, black-haired, with great limpid eyes. She is dressed in a simple white frock, tied high at the bosom with a pale blue sash. Small satin slippers are visible at the dress hem. She looks at her audience, and begins in a charming, questing soprano:

> *Kennst du das Land wo die Citronen blühn?*
> *Im dunkeln Laub die Gold-Orangen glühn, . . .*

Demmie is pensive. "A poem for me, for you, for the psychologically homeless. Did Mignon ever get back home?"

Did she? He couldn't remember.

Home.

He awakes at morning in a foreign land, and he thinks of home. He cannot rest, his heart is wild with pain and loneliness. . . .

So wrote the pre-No great, Thomas Wolfe. True, Thomas (he thinks), but not what *I* am searching for.

The key was Helen, Poe's *Helen*. The key was a face enhaloed by hyacinthine curls, the iridescent body, radiant with fairy-grace; the classic profile. His wife, his woman, the mother of his son.

Helen. You named her rightly, Edgar Poe.

If he ever had a secret ambition, it was this: to confront the great Poe and persuade him to reveal the identity of the real Helen. Undoubtedly some marvelous southern lady, probably well-known in history for her glorious beauty, her lovely hyacinth hair, her aura of fresh entry from elfland. Edgar Poe would tell him about the real, the true Helen. The two Helens, his and Poe's, would become one, and he could relax for the rest of his life.

Except, of course, it could never happen, for the nine-teenth century was tightly clamped in. No time travel permitted in post-Columbian America. Too close to the present. One little mishap, and the entire fabric of the Present might change. Extant citizens might vanish before your very eyes. (He doubted that.)

"What's in the Poe?" he asks.

"The standard stuff. *The Raven, Annabel Lee, The Bells, Ulalume* . . . but no matter. You want to get to sleep. I'll turn it off."

"No, put it on."

"Any preference?"

"Anything." He wasn't going to mention *Helen*. It was just too private.

Silently, she makes the selection. And there's the poet. So young? Looks barely twenty-one. About five feet, eight inches tall. No raven locks? No mustache? Cool gray eyes. So deep, so sad, under the broad brow. Good make-up on the actor. Fine voice, clear, resonant.

> *Helen, thy beauty is to me*
> *Like those Nicean barks of yore,*
> *That gently, o'er a perfumed sea,*
> *The weary way-worn wanderer bore*
> *To his own native shore. . . .*

He takes a deep breath. That incense (he thinks) is getting to me. And how did Demmie know to select *To Helen?* This woman is damned perceptive. Or else she knows a lot about me that she has no right to know.

> *On desperate seas long wont to roam,*
> *Thy hyacinth hair, thy classic face,*
> *Thy naiad airs have brought me home. . . .*

Home. Home. His mind wanders. Home is where you are, my Helen, my once-girl, gone away. Hyacinthine Helen with the faerie aura and the profile of a classic Greek goddess. Gone.

Gone.

All I have left is a two-hundred-page report. Not even mine. A treatise created in perfumed opulence, of, by, and for a woman of memorable face, figure, and intellect. Demmie, you witch, you planned it this way from the beginning. All you wanted was my report. The rest was playful nonsense. And there was that other thing. Philip. Demmie had known Philip's name before he told her. Demmie, who are you?

He drifts away into a vague, troubled dreamland, barely taking note that she pulls a light coverlet over him, dims the lights, and that finally she relaxes into the nearby chair.

He is asleep, and dreaming of Samuel Taylor Coleridge, of Alph the sacred river, flowing through the Valles Marineris, then pounding through measureless caverns, down to a sunless sea. This is what he is dreaming when he falls—along with five thousand churning bodies—into the dark torrent, and he begins to scream.

He awakens to find Demmie standing over him, gasping and alarmed. Her hands are on his shoulders, as though to steady him.

She calls for the lights, and they come up. This helps him burst the bonds of his nightmare.

He sits up, sweat-drenched, panting, staring. The flesh of his reconstructed right cheek is hurting and throbbing. He has pain sensations in his non-existent right eye—"phantom-limb" feelings. He fumbles around on the night table, finds

Mimi, and claps her into the empty orbit. Mimi gets to work instantly, searching out and canceling the pain harmonics in his cortical neurals. But it's not over yet. His guts are still tingling, tingling, tingling. His body had talked to him, is still talking to him: "Danger . . . danger . . . danger. . . ."

Demmie takes it very well. She mops at his face and chest with a warm towel. She says quietly, "You had a bad dream. I'll get you a capsule."

"No. No dream. A whole boro—five thousand people— gone. I'm pretty sure it was Delta Five Eighty-five."

She stands back and looks at him. "That's one you surveyed?"

"Yes. Help me up. The Message Center. I've got to call Delta Central."

Her fingers are meshing and unmeshing as he leaves. She calls after him: "Your clothes are sticking to your body."

Finally, after passing a gauntlet of deputies and in-betweens, he gets the Vyr's First Secretary. Eleven minutes to Earth, a delay, then eleven back. It could have been worse.

KONTEAU YOU DRUNKEN IDIOT DON'T CALL FROM A
MARTIAN CATHOUSE TO TELL US A WHOLE BORO HAS
VANISHED. THIS GOES ON YOUR RECORD

As he reads, shivering, the woman brings in a robe and drapes it over his shoulders. He clutches it absently. He still shivers.

She walks him back to the rooms. He sits on the bed, staring at her but not seeing her.

"Whatever's wrong, no matter what," she tells him matter-of-factly, "you've got to get out of those wet clothes."

He moves in slow dream-like pauses. She helps him change. He mutters disconnected nonsense. "Helen works at Delta Central . . . no reason for her to be . . . Philip . . . he was at Lambda . . . anyhow, already checked on both of them . . . they're all right . . . they say I'm crazy . . . I hope they're right. . . ."

He comes out of it long enough to note that she has walked

over to the intercom and is talking to somebody. Did the thing ring? Was somebody calling *him?* They were talking about him. She hangs up and turns to face him. She says, "Did you get that? Tex from Delta Vyr, First Secretary. The express left Deimos a few minutes ago, but is returning to pick you up."

It is so. There *has* been a time-quake, and Delta Five Eighty-five is gone. Five thousand people. (But how can he be so sure?)

He temporizes with a murmur. "The First Secretary?"

"The First Secretary."

This is serious. This isn't through channels. This is straight from the chancellory, and not through the Widow. Should he notify his Field Chief? Or should he assume that the First Secretary has already done that? And there are other problems.

The Chief will be sure to ask him why he went over his head in the first place, direct to the Vyr. And there isn't any perfect answer to that. His sole defense will have to be, it was an emergency, and there was no time. And thinking about it, he can see that won't be good enough.

He is in trouble now, no matter what he does.

Through his confusion he notes that Demmie is at the intercom again. Had it rung? Yes, he remembers. And she is talking to him again. "Zeke Ditmars wants to see you before you go."

"I can't do that. No time. Tell him goodbye for me, would you please."

She looks at the wall clock. "You still have ten minutes. He said it was important."

His eyes narrow in suspicion and bewilderment. "How did he know I was called back?"

Her reply is cool, measured. "Word gets around."

Obviously she had told Ditmars. Probably had got him out of bed. But there is no apology in her returning stare.

"What does he want?"

"He wants to explain . . . something. Go on, talk to him. I'll take your bag down to the exit."

He nods vaguely. Things are going too fast.

She tugs at his sleeve to get his full attention. "One more thing. What about your report?"

The report? What difference does it make? No, it is important. If he gets killed looking for Five Eighty-five, that report will be the only thing he will be remembered for. He has to think. Ah, an idea. The Council is rumored to be in session in the West Wing right here in Xanadu. Behind locked doors and intensive security. Less than one kilometer away. But he doesn't know anybody on the Council. He doesn't know how to get the document in to them. So near, yet so far. They might as well be on Pluto. Sad. "Forget it. It doesn't matter anymore."

"I know the Directrix for New Colonies."

It's almost as though she has been reading his mind. He stares at her in disbelief. "The Directrix? . . . On the Council? Meeting here?" He realizes he sounds very stupid.

She continues. "I can get your report to her."

There is something surreal about this. He thinks a moment. "All right. You can try." He looks over at the manuscript, stacked carefully on the middle of the desk. Mentally, he pats the edges. So that's that.

And now he has another thought—a series of thoughts, actually, a fantasy. Helen has her own little office in Delta Central, in the same enormous labyrinthine complex crowned by the chancellory. Somewhere on his way to his encounter with the Vyr he would meet her. They would have a brief, very pleasant exchange of greetings. A word about Philip. They'd make a date for dinner. Candlelight, soft music. Ah, Helen, thy beauty. . . . He tightens his jaw and grimaces. It is absolutely ridiculous. He orders Demmie, almost angrily, "Help me pack."

"Of course." She starts folding his clothing neatly into the little ten-kilo bag. She separates out the things he has worn. "Do you think you will be back?"

"No. They will need a scapegoat. I'm headed for jail. Maybe worse."

They walk down the corridor together and stop at the

turn. She says, very seriously, "In that case, can I have your son?"

That makes him laugh. "If you can find him."

He leaves her and hurries down the hall toward Ditmars's lab. The tousled-haired scientist is waiting for him in bathrobe and slippers. Konteau glares accusingly at the antique cherubic face. "I understand you want to see me."

"Why yes. First, dear boy, relax. You have plenty of time. And they'll announce the ship in here as soon as it docks."

"So what's so important?"

"Manners! Manners!" Ditmars rubs his hands together. The sound is like the wrinkling of ancient parchment. "Just a little going-away demonstration. Come over here." He pulls the krono over to a bench by the side wall.

"And what's all *this?*" Konteau asks curiously. He points to the long transparent plastic pipe at the back of the bench, with a little platform at the upper end and a small metal dish at the lower end. A centimeter-size ball bearing rests at the upper end, held by a cup release.

"Part of a very interesting experiment," explains the old man. "It goes with *this.*" He picks up a small metal instrument from the bench and peers up at his friend. "Looks like a pistol, doesn't it?"

"Sort of."

The scientist snickers as though greatly enjoying the kronman's perplexity. "Actually, it *is* a pistol. A shooter. Only it can't hurt anything."

"A toy? A fake?"

"Oh dear me no. It shoots live ammo. Very live ammo. It shoots *time.*"

"Like bullets?"

"Of course, James. Time has mass, you know."

Konteau's face shows that, quite the contrary, he *didn't* know.

Ditmars frowns at him, as though showing disappointment in a backward student. "Oh come now, James. It goes back to Einstein. $E = MC^2$. C is simply the velocity of light and is distance divided by time, or d over t. Solve for t, and you get t equals d times the square root of m over E. So time has the dimensions of distance, mass, and energy, and is directly proportional to the square root of mass. *Now* do you see?"

Konteau shrugs.

The savant sighs. "Well, anyhow I suppose you are still a first-class marksman?"

"Fair."

"Take the gun." He hands it over to his visitor. "When you're ready, tell me. I'll hit the switch and the steel ball will start rolling down the tube. When it reaches the clear area, shoot it. Can you do that?"

"I think so." He sights along the pistol barrel. "Ready."

And here comes the little ball. Slowly at first, then faster. But Konteau is always able to keep a bead on it. When the ball glints out into the open part of the tube, he squeezes the trigger.

Ping.

The ball vanishes.

Konteau gives the beaming Dr. Ditmars a quizzical look. "So where is the ball?"

"Why *there* it is, dear fellow." He points to the ball, rolling once again down the incline. "You understand now, don't you?"

"The gun bangs it into the past?"

"Exactly. Not into the *distant* past. Not the Ordovician or the Precambrian, or any of *those* silly old epochs. Actually, in this particular case it moves back only two and a half seconds; that's why it materializes back at the top of the incline. Because that's where it was two-and-a-half seconds ago. And don't look so surprised. You did a very similar job on that little red butterfly a couple of days ago, using your oculus. Remember?"

"That was completely different," demurs the krono. "I simply had Mimi set up a field. I didn't shoot the butterfly."

"The very point, dear boy. You won't always be close enough to form a field—which would necessarily be of very limited geometric compass in any case, a few cubic centimeters at most. Occasions may arise where you might want to shoot something or someone coming at you from a distance of several dozen meters. Not to kill, mind you. Just to transpose the thing very briefly back in time. To do that, you'll need a time-pistol."

"Very, very interesting." Konteau turns the gun over and over in his hands, then gives it back to the little scientist. "How do I get one of these?"

"You have one already, James."

"But. . . ."

"It's one of the more esoteric features of your oculus. There's a simple adjustment. I simply forgot to mention it, until now. Take it out."

Konteau removes his artificial eye and gives it to Ditmars.

"Here's what you do," says the old man. "See? The eyeball is the handle. Press here, the barrel rolls out, the trigger folds down. It's permanently set for thirty seconds, one hundred kilos, and one hundred meters. It carries only one charge. Takes about twenty-four hours to recharge, so aim straight. Understand?"

Konteau nods and replaces the oculus in his eye-socket.

Ditmars accelerates his explanations. "Now, there's one more thing you can do with your oculus. I haven't mentioned it before because we don't have all the bugs worked out yet. So don't try it unless it's a life-and-death situation. That's the transmission of polarized time. You can spray matter, and polarize it, and then *if* you're in good sync, you can pass through. I've imprinted the instructions in your oculus. Ask her for 'Polar-X'. Got it?"

Konteau nods. Actually, he hasn't the faintest idea what the old scientist is talking about. "I have to run." They both pause and listen. It's the warning horn for the Terran Express.

Just before he enters the airlock he turns back to wave at Demmie and Ditmars. Quite a pair. Especially you, Demmie the Mysterious. *You* did this to me. You have hidden depths. You know Philip and Ditmars and the Directrix for New

Colonies. Who else do you know? He decides not to think about it.

The lock whistles shut behind him, and he is gone, and thinking either not at all, or perhaps of other things, such as five thousand people missing.

On the Terran Express

As he shaved in the tiny washroom of the Terran-Ex, Konteau made a glum appraisal of his face. Long ago, as a boy, his mother had told him (perhaps in a burst of exasperation) that as soon as she had seen his new-born face she had filed an application with the Sperm Bank. Evidently she hadn't meant it. As it turned out, he was their only child.

Certainly he wasn't handsome, nor in any way memorable, save perhaps for a certain amount of patchwork on the right side of his head and body. He had lost his right eye in that Kappa-5 fiasco. The artificial replacement had certain remarkable features, thanks to Ditmars and the Bio Lab on Xanadu. Bio had engraved M I M I R on the outer surface. MIMIR was an acronym for something very polysyllabic and complicated. He immediately settled on Mimi. Despite Mimi's accomplishments (of which there were many, and some of them quite astonishing), he would nevertheless prefer his lost natural eye. But he never told Mimi this.

As he wiped the lather from his face, he decided his mother had a point. He was far from handsome. The merciless rivulets of time had eroded his face down to its essential melancholy features. And since the accident, half of his face always looked dissipated, the other half staid and solemn.

(How can you have a bag under only one eye? His face perpetually demonstrated how.)

And so what? Looks didn't matter too much in his line of work. How had he begun? He thought back. By the time he was eighteen he had rejected two personality implants and the evaluators had told him (sadly) that his personality index was several magnitudes outside the Permissible Deviation. He was socially unacceptable, a loner. A loner and a wanderer. Is *that* why Helen left him? But it wasn't supposed to be that way. Not in the lines that drifted through his mind whenever he thought of his ex-wife.

> *. . . gently, o'er a perfumed sea*
> *The weary way-worn wanderer bore*
> *To his own native shore.*

He was that wanderer, weary and way-worn, and he was entitled to be borne across a perfumed sea to his lost love. But he knew it would never happen. She would never return. He luxuriated for a moment in a satisfying surge of self-pity.

So, where were we? Oh, trying once again to trace back how he had gotten into this crazy business. Well, that was easy. With his uncorrectable Deviation, he couldn't become a normal, routine working member of a boro. That left the fringe professions: the Grayjackets, Government, or the Kron-Corps.

Despite his father's bitter protests, he had chosen the krons.

As far as the work went, he had no complaints. His father had warned him, and he had entered the profession with no illusions. Surveying in past geologic epochs was dangerous. Even if he stayed sane, he could be badly hurt, even killed. No matter. He would never have met Helen if they had not both been on that survey team, years ago. (*Oh, thou art fairer than the evening air/clad in the beauty of a thousand stars.* Marlowe knew you, Helen my once wife!) No, he couldn't complain.

And so now, homeward

Home: the grand illusion of the homeless, the rootless, the

wanderers. *Home is the sailor, home from the sea.* The great poets understood this. He thought of the holos, back there with Demmie. *Thy classic face, thy naiad airs have brought me home. . . .*

Well, at least his own son had a home. The Widow would never get Philip!

Of course the medics had done a lot in recent years to treat the time sickness. At his last exam they had told him he had a good chance of staying fairly sane. On the other hand they were now calling him in for check-ups every four months. And last time the psycho-physical had taken a disconcerting turn. He never actually met his psychs—froyds, as the kronos called them. The Three Norns were in a separate room, and they talked to him by audio, as he lay on an airbed.

    Norna: Do you dream?

    Konteau: I guess so, doesn't everybody?

    Verdandi: Yes, of course.

    Skuld: Do you have a recurrent dream?

    Konteau: Funny you should ask. Yes, I think I do.

    Norna: Tell us about it.

    Konteau: I've never been able to put the whole thing together—just snatches.

    Verdandi: That's all right. Tell us the snatches.

    Konteau: We're playing chess, this cowled figure and I. His name is D. D means something, but I don't know what. Perhaps I don't want to know. There may be a couple of other people, too. Sometimes in daydreams . . . introspections . . . I see D, and he and I talk.

    Skuld: Perhaps we can help. While you sleep, we can record your alpha, beta, gamma cortical waves. We can decode them and synthesize them into a moving holo. Sometimes it's clear, sometimes it isn't. Even when we get a good technical product, it might defy psychoanalysis.

    Konteau: (What did he have to lose? Maybe he could find some answers.) Go ahead.

They showed him a holo of his dream. He noted with surprise that there was a door behind the chess table. Just a door. Not a door in a wall, or a door into a building. Just a door. The chess game ends. He and the other player rise from the table, open the door, and pass through. And, strangest of all, a woman accompanies them. *He knows her!* And the two men . . . he can't see their faces, but he knows *them,* too!

"Who are they?" asked Norna.

Sudden block. The recognition faded. . . .

"What does the door mean?" asked Verdandi.

Why couldn't he answer? It was on the tip of his tongue. *"Door. . . ."* he stammered. "In an ancient alphabet. Greek? Hebrew? Phoenician, maybe?"

But they weren't getting anywhere. End of session. The froyds heaved a collective sigh. "Think about it. 'Door.' Something you've encountered in a kron project?"

Yes, think about it. Door. What he needed was a door into his own brain. A futile irony.

He couldn't remember when or how it started. Probably in the beginning there was just himself, just introspecting, an inward musing. As time went on, he visualized someone to talk to, this faceless figure in the cowled uniform of a Corps apprentice. The figure sat facing him across a chess table. Who are you? he wondered.

You don't know? asked the other.

Not yet. Are you Death?

Am I?

Perhaps. I'll call you D for Death. How do you like that?

D: Fine with me. Do you think of me often?

K: Yes. The Norns say if you don't mind dying, you're sick. With them, that's a given, an axiom. Do you agree?

D: Debatable, isn't it? Just another axiom. How many of Euclid's axioms survive?

K: Hardly any. Einstein started killing them off centuries ago. Ratell finished the job when he worked out the equations of time.

D: They shouldn't have done that. You've got to *care.* It's the guts of the game, don't you think?

K: I don't know. What game? This chess game?

D: Suppose everybody felt like you? Suppose everybody knew it was just a game? The whole thing would collapse, wouldn't it?

K: Now look who's asking questions?

D: So what about your son.

K: That's not fair. Of course I care about Philip. And Helen. I care about lots of things.

D: Including your job. Isn't the Black Widow real?

K: Yeah. And you're being impertinent. You're an outsider. You're supposed to call it the Corps, or the Service.

D: Outsider, am I? Well, well. But let it pass. Back to you. Your teams have surveyed sub-zones for sixty-three boros. That's over three million souls. Doesn't that count for something?

K: There's no pleasing you. You know I'm a loner. Actually, I can't stand the thought of all those people. They nauseate me.

D: But if a boro disappeared—five thousand people— what would you do?

K: I don't know. Maybe nothing. Probably I'd wait for instructions. Do it by the book.

D: It happened once before, you know?

K: Not one of my surveys.

Last year he began to see the chessboard quite clearly. In fact, he realized then that he and D had been playing this one game all along. A few months ago they came down to a rook-and-pawns ending, evenly balanced, and probably headed for a draw. Konteau wasn't really fighting; just playing casually, as he might play skittles with a friend at the Club, or in a gameroom somewhere. But D was dead serious. D studied the board intently, made his move carefully. What was D afraid of? It was just a game.

The conversations shifted.

K: Do you have a face?

D: Of course.

K: Why do you never let me see it?

D: Because you haven't yet decided what I look like.

K: A grinning skull?

D: Oh, come now!

K: Is it the same face for everyone?

D: Only in that I am always what he or she expects.

K: So you could have a billion different faces.

D: If that's the current terrestrial population, which I doubt.

K: Oh hell. You don't make a lot of sense.

D: It could be worse. Suppose everything started making sense—everything finally falls into place. Is that what you want?

K: I don't know. Well, sometimes. . . .

D: (Something unintelligible.)

K: I know your big secret.

D: Do you?

K: Form no attachments. That way you're safe. Nobody can get to you.

D: You don't believe that. There's Helen, Philip, the Widow . . . or should I say, the Corps? The Corps, then. You can never leave the Corps. Once seized by the great god Kronos, you cannot escape. It's a deadly addiction.

K: (Silence.)

During the last few sessions the chess position had somehow shifted significantly. How had it happened? It was no longer a probable draw. It was now a sure win for D, who had the black pieces. The computers had worked out this exact position before Konteau was born. It was in all the end-game books. And yet D still played slowly, carefully, with life-and-death deliberation.

Well, if that was the way it was, that was the way it was. Let it be so. From here on in, it was just a question of time. Kronos, what a pun!

No matter.

He accepted it all. On his first field trip, with Devlin in the Upper Permian, the old master had told him how to survive. You have to rearrange your mind. You have to devalue the idea of being alive. You have to not require the things that other men need—including the great essential need to exist. To be or not to be becomes irrelevant. It can never be a consideration in the field. It's rather like the conquest of fear, but simpler, really. Just a matter of forbidding your mind to react to certain unpleasant possibilities. Don't try to stay sane. Don't keep asking yourself, am I still sane. You'll start to hurt if you do. Aim at acceptance. Aim at indifference. Take it as it comes. Mental rearrangement, that's the secret.

So spake Devlin—zonked out of his skull twenty years later. How are the mighty fallen. And am I next?

He worked his way back into the passenger compartment, eased into his seat, and closed his eyes. It was a four-hour trip, and they had an hour before planetfall. He was tired. Perhaps he could just drift off for a few minutes. . . .

He was jarred from his reverie by a whisper in his ear. "Incoming message for you, sir." The attendant was leaning over him. He could smell the aromatic oils in the youth's long hair.

"Oh? Who? . . ."

"It's a crystal, sir, priority red." He handed Konteau the small message box. "Do you have a player?" he asked the kron-man.

"Yes, thanks."

The steward looked "overhead" in the luggage compartment. "In your bag, sir? Shall I hand it down?"

"No. I keep it with me. I can manage from here."

"Of course." The other backed away discreetly.

From the corner of his good eye he noted that four or five of the passengers in adjoining seats were turned part way toward him and were carefully seeming not to watch him. He suspected that very few of them had ever received a crystal message, and probably none on a planetary express. He sighed. Lacking a personal compartment, there was only one place where he could read this thing in privacy.

Interesting. On the trip out to Xanadu the passengers were laughing, singing, boisterous. On their way to a carefree holiday. Returning to Terra they were dour, dull, silent, hungover. But they would do it again next year. As would he. This ship, he thought, defines the human condition.

The faces followed him like tracking radar as he got up and worked his way back to the restroom. He closed a cubicle door behind him, sat down, and opened the little wooden case, no bigger than a child's hand. The lid hinged back, and he saw that the crystal—gray piezoelectric quartz—was quietly resting in its padded cushions. He extracted his oculus, slid back the crystal door, lifted the special tweezers from the box lid, clipped the crystal into its pocket in the little brass sphere, then reinserted Mimi into her accustomed socket. And now, he thought, let's find out what this priority red is all about, and who from, and why it had to come in scrambled. He closed his good eye and waited for the descrambler to synchronize with his alpha, beta, and gamma cortical waves.

The myriad electric impulses were coming through, now, and were strongly at work on his occipital vision lobe and his audio cortices. From Corps Psych! It hit him so hard that he blinked and lost the signal briefly. Back again.

As he watched the visual, he was struck by another revelation. He was finally actually seeing his assigned froyd trio, the three Norns. There they were, sitting cross-legged in a row on a bare wooden floor. This was alarming. He recalled their earlier warning, "You will never see us except in a life-and-death emergency." He moaned faintly.

The central figure nodded. "Greetings, James." (He recognized the voice of Norna.) "We have been working on your recent dreams. Analysis is not complete, but in view of the findings so far, and other circumstances, we thought it best to give you our conclusions to date."

The shadowy central figure in his mind paused a moment: her eyes came into momentary focus and seemed to reach out and seize Konteau's one good eye. The eidolon continued. "Dreams are the work-product of the subconscious mind, James, messages to the conscious mind, as it were. When the subject matter is extremely unpleasant, dreams will substitute symbols for the real things. The problem then is to discover what the symbols mean. Generally this can be accomplished only with the help of the dreamer. We can say now, James, you have been most cooperative."

Kronos! thought Konteau. Get to the point!

The figure on the right now took up the narrative. The tones, modulation, and phrasing identified Verdandi. It was the only way he could tell them apart. The facial features of each of the three appeared to be practically identical.

"James, your dreams always seem to start with a chess game. You are one player, and you have the white pieces. Your opponent is a figure in the cowl of a Corps apprentice, whom you call 'D'. You cannot see his face. You seem to be always losing the game, yet it never ends. Lately, you have added two people to the scene. They are watching the game. One is a man, the other a woman. Behind the cowled figure is a door, a big metal thing, bronze perhaps. And now the game adjourns without decision. 'D' remains seated, while you arise. You, the woman, and the third man open the door and pass through. The door is not in a wall. It is simply a door, standing there, alone in space. When the three of you are beyond the door, you look at the man who has passed through the door with you, and you see that he is dead."

There was something preposterous, and chilling, about this. Konteau's mind was reaching for explanations, but there was no way to ask questions.

The figure on the left took up the statement. "In our sessions," said Skuld, "you have mentioned that the letter 'D' brings to mind ancient tongues, as well as death. In this you are quite right. Your subconscious mind has chosen the cryptic symbols in a most elegant and sophisticated fashion. I'm sure you are aware that our alphabet comes from the Phoenicians, who passed it on to the Greeks, who gave it to the Romans, and so finally to us. In the original Phoenician the letters were named for various things, for example 'A' was called 'aleph', which meant ox. The Greeks altered it just a little, to alpha. 'B' meant 'beth', or house, and the Greeks called it beta. 'D' was from 'daleth', which meant door. The Greeks called it Delta."

Tiny beads of sweat began to collect on Konteau's forehead, and he was breathing very fast.

Skuld's voice continued relentlessly. "And where do you see Death, James? I speak now phonetically, of course. Look at the word 'Daleth'. Extract 'Al'. 'Deth' remains. You know someone named 'Al', don't you, James?"

Konteau nodded dumbly. No, that wasn't quite so. Just a rumor. He hadn't tried to confirm it.

And now Norna was summing up. Her voice had become

tense, as though it was growing difficult for her to speak. "You are warning yourself, James. There is grave danger in Delta Colony. Someone is going to die. You think, probably yourself. You believe that you and a woman and 'Al' will pass through that bronze door, and that Death waits for you on the other side. You are warning yourself. I join your subconscious in this warning, James. *Stay away from Delta!*"

As he watched, fascinated, the figure on the right moved to center, and merged with the central figure. Then the one on the left followed; and his froyd was one entity. This astonished and confused him. The three Norns had coalesced into one woman.

And it wasn't over. As if to emphasize her warning, the seated figure threw her head back, and from her mouth flowed a shattering animal cry that chilled Konteau's blood. Then she collapsed forward on her face.

The time-man was paralyzed. He wanted to rush over (to where?) and help her up, hold her, reassure her (how?) . . . but even in the depths of his horror he realized this was impossible.

As he sat there, panting, sweating, the single image blurred, waffled, faded. Then a dead blank. But in his own mind he could still see her, and that terrible final shriek would echo in the corridors of his brain forever. He thought about her for a moment. Those three were indeed actually one woman. She was a triple-schizo. Of course, the schizo's made the best, most sensitive froyds. They had been there, shivering in the darkness, and then sometimes they came out, and tried to help people like him, often at considerable risk to their own mental well-being. She had tried to save his life at the risk of her own sanity. She had now returned into the shadows. He knew he would never see her again. There was no way to thank her. She had left his life.

He gritted his teeth.

From the moment he stepped off this express, he was in considerable personal danger.

And *Al* . . . damn. Did that mean the woman was Helen? But how could *she* be involved? No way. After all, it was only a dream. Hardly surprising he would be thinking lethal

thoughts about her current boyfriend. What was his name?
Al Artoy, something like that.

"Mr. Konteau." It was the intercom, just over the mirror.
A woman's voice.

"Yeah."

"Landing in fifteen minutes. And the Vyr reminds you
that a car will be waiting." The voice was veneered with
cautious respect.

"Gotcha." His mouth twisted in a sardonic grin. The crew
knew damn well who he was, but they didn't know whether
he was being brought in for execution or to be given a new,
highly heroic assignment. Or maybe both. They couldn't
adjust to the ambiguities. He said, "Switch me to Communi-
cations."

"Yes, sir."

There was a click and a hiss. A lazy voice said, "Com."

"I want to send a line to Delta."

"Number and charge?"

"Government 407. Charge Kron-7630."

The voice seemed to snap to attention. (He wondered if the
snap would wither a bit if the signalman knew that Government 407 was the Gatehouse at Ratell Park, and that the
message would be received by an occasionally near-lucid old
man.) "Yes sir! Your message, sir?"

"Assemble."

"Assemble?"

"You got it."

"Yes sir, *assemble.* Signature, sir?"

"No sig."

"Very good, *sir.* On the way."

One last thought. Back to Demmie. He had never caught
her last name. She knew him, he didn't know her. That was
the way it had worked out. Remarkable woman. Oh, how she
had manipulated him! He had gone to Xanadu for his usual
week of careless carousing and forgetful dalliances (one or
more). And what had happened? He hadn't laid a finger on
her. Or on any other woman, for that matter. Instead, he had
written a report. For her. He had been had. He was a prime
moron. On the other hand, his two-hundred-page report was

a fact. It existed. *If* by some strange happy accident it fell into the right hands . . . *if* it actually reached the Directrix for New Colonies, Earth's population overflow might well find a home in the Martian Proterozoic.

All conjectures rebound to you, Demmie. How did you know about Helen, and Philip? What did Ditmars tell you, and what did you tell him? And most important of all, *who are you?*

The intercom interrupted his thoughts. "Landing in five minutes. Delta Interport. Fasten belts. Ship now adjusting to vertical."

A few minutes later he followed the steward to the exit door. He paused briefly on the landing stage, blinking in the harsh sunlight, then started down the metal rollaway stairs.

Interport. He had used ships in and out of this place many times. And today, as always, he sensed the hundreds of thousands of arrivals and departures that had accumulated here over the years, like the monomolecular layers of a dark brooding pearl.

As he descended the stairs, he let his eye rove over the port complex. Half a kilometer distant from the landing pad stood the gray walls of Delta Prison. A grim irony, he thought: the tightest bonds adjacent to the greatest freedom. Did those hapless souls ever dream of breaking through their walls and dashing up the landing stairs of these waiting express ships? Why this strange juxtaposition of spaceport and prison? He could guess. For one thing, lack of space. And for another, in case of launch or landing mishaps, the ships might as well crash into structures housing the most worthless occupants. It all made some sort of cruel sense.

6

Ratell on Time

An aide dressed in the livery of the Delta Vyr met Konteau at Passengers Incoming, took his bag, led him through the terminal to the check room, and checked his bag.

"Now wait a minute," protested the kron-man. "I'm going to need that."

The aide gave him a cold look. "We'll have it sent over to wherever you spend the night. You can't take it into the chancellory. Not permitted."

Konteau wondered if he'd ever see it again. Helen had given it to him years ago.

On their way to the main exit they had to wait twice to let patrols pass.

"What's going on?" asked the krono, stopping to watch the striding grayjackets.

His guide, if he heard, chose not to answer.

In a moment they were outside, and the aide opened the door of the waiting skitter and slammed the door behind Konteau. There was a secondary clink. He was locked in.

"Hey!" He stared out the window as the aide melted back into the crowd.

"It's for your own safety, chum." The voice of the driver rattled back to him as the vehicle moved out into traffic. "Vyr's orders." In the oncoming lane, gray vehicles with the triangular Delta insigne alternated with marching patrols of grayjackets.

He was suddenly very uneasy. Should he try to break out? And then what? He would be a hunted man, and he might never find out about 585. No, he needed that meeting with the Vyr. If he lived through that, he could still break away. Maybe.

Play along. Find out all he could.

"Why all the troops?" he asked curiously.

"Where you been, chum?"

"Away," said the passenger curtly. "What's going on?"

"You knew the old Overlord died?"

"Yes. I saw the funeral clips."

"Then you know the Vyrs are coming in from all over the world to elect the new Overlord. Must be fifty here in Delta already. Just yesterday I picked up the Anglo Vyr and the Russ Vyr. The militia is out simply to keep the peace, preserve order."

"I see. In this election, the Vyr who proves the greatest devotion to Kronos is supposed to win?"

"That's the general idea."

"So who's going to win?"

"You want the straight scut?"

"Yeah."

"You're on your way to meet him right now."

"Corleigh? Delta Vyr?"

"X."

"He did something . . . big?"

"So they say."

"Like what?"

"Nobody seems to know for sure. Just rumors."

"Name one."

"I just drive a government skit, chum. I ain't paid to talk."

Konteau fished a clunker from his purse and tossed it over into the front seat. A gray glove flashed out and the coin vanished in mid-air.

The driver said, "The big talk is, the Vyr gave the god a gift nobody can come close to."

Konteau frowned. "Gift? What gift?"

Silence.

He tossed another clunker over. "What do the rumors say about it?"

"All I know is, it's supposed to solve the problem of over-population."

Well, now, that was interesting. He had no idea Paul the Pious took a serious interest in demographics. Perhaps the Vyr would be interested in the Martian colony. He should have brought a copy of his report to present to the Delta ruler. Things were definitely looking up! "Tell me more," he said. "Just exactly how is the Vyr going to deal with over-population?"

"Now, as to *that,* chum, I ain't got the faintest idea."

Konteau fished in his pockets once more.

"Nah, chum. Save your money. It's Kronos' truth, I just don't know."

"Who does know?"

"The Vyr, I guess. You're gonna see him. Ask *him!*"

The kron-man didn't know whether the driver was being sarcastic or constructive. His conjectures were interrupted when he noted the skitter had drawn up at a booth at the roadside. A grayjacket sergeant came out, checked the driver's papers, then waved him on.

"What was that for?" asked Konteau.

"Routine check."

"Who are they looking for?"

"Who knows? The Conclave votes tomorrow night on the new Overlord. They don't want any trouble."

Konteau nodded. That was certainly reasonable. On the other hand . . . he had a sudden flash of insight. Perhaps the Delta Vyr's gift to Kronos might not receive universal approval. Perhaps major potential dissenters were now being rounded up. Was *he* affected? He doubted it. The Widow was completely outside politics. But the Council was another matter. The Council and the Vyrs were sworn enemies.

He shook his head. More conjectures, more speculations.

They would get him nowhere. He had to prepare for his confrontation with the Vyr. The central issue at the moment was, had Delta 585 been hit by a time-quake? What did he know about time-quakes? Not much.

"How much longer to Central?" he asked the driver.

"Another twenty minutes. Thirty if the traffic gets worse."

He had time. "Does your CRT access Delta library?"

"Sure thing. Just enter 9."

He punched in. A computer voice came on. "Library."

"Ratell," said Konteau. "What have you got on Ratell?"

"*The* Ratell?"

"Yes. The Ratell. Raymond Ratell."

"Your clearance, sir?"

Clearance? Of course. He had forgotten. The great Ratell was proscribed. As a Corps student, Konteau had read the explanation in one of his texts. The wizard of time was quoted for his own proscription: "What's here for the likes of me, or you, kron-man? What do you really want to do, or be? If you don't find it here, go back in time. Explorer? Go back! Riverboat gambler? Go back! Composer? Gun-totin' western sheriff? Go back, go back, go back!" Some irreverent apprentice krono had put it all together:

> Want to broaden out your mind?
> Go in for a life of crime?
> *(Chorus:)* Go back in time, young man, go back!

Small wonder that the time-king's writings were forbidden to lay readers, thought Konteau. The Council, of course, justified the censorship by fears that someone might actually go back and change the Past in a way that would alter the Present. Later on, they mentioned that the quoted exhortation was also immoral and tended to corrupt youth. And just to be on the safe side, they set up those time barriers at the gates of the year 1492 to preserve local history, including themselves. So far as he knew, those barriers had been penetrated only once, by the time quake of 2332.

"Clearance?" repeated the metal voice impatiently.

"Yes. Of course." He put his card in the I.D. slot.

"Confirmed. Are you looking for something in particular?"

"Somewhere, Ratell mentioned time-quakes."

"Time-quakes. Searching, sir. Nothing by that name. Synonyms?"

"Not sure. Breaks. Slides. Fractures."

"Searching. Breaks. Slides. Fractures. No such titles."

"List all Ratell titles."

"Coming."

He watched the entries scroll up on the screen. "Hold. Give me that one." He read, line by line:

Time

Learned men say our society has an extraordinary number of expressions using 'time', starting perhaps with *Ahead of time,* through *Mark time,* to *Time without end.* And we have numerous nouns and synonyms for Time, as the Esquimaux have words for different kinds of snow, and the Bedouins have words for various kinds and conditions of sand.

We are totally immersed in Time; yet we don't know what it is. (Saint Augustine: I know what it is, unless you ask me.) If we can understand Time (whether theoretically, or intuitively, or in any way whatever), we understand All.

I have had small experience with Time and I have made certain equipment for taking my fellow humans and their artifacts back in Time. I have seen the sun rise on Archeozoic seas, and I have provided means for establishing our excess populations in stacks on a very young Earth. All this is done by Time-control.

So let us talk of Time.

What is Time most like? Light, perhaps, as considered in its broader aspect of electromagnetic radiation (not that we understand EMR!).

Like light, Time can be *reflected.* That's how the walls of cities in, for example, the Cambrian stay in place (when properly stabilized): they reflect those Cambrian days outside, and so hold back that particular sea of Time.

Like light, Time can be refracted. It flows more slowly in denser media. And so it can be focussed. And so, with the proper instruments we are able to penetrate distant epochs.

Time fluoresces: this was the mechanism of my first movement backward. One can absorb Time at one frequency and re-radiate it at another. So one takes in Today and sends it out as Yesterday. The effect is analogous to exciting Hg vapor to give off U.V., which impinges on phosphors that re-radiate visible light. And it's like the Compton effect, where x-rays strike matter and bounce back with increased wave lengths. (Thus we radiate the instruments with Today, and they show us Yesterday.) And travel in Time is like the Raman effect, where light floods a liquid, which then re-radiates the original frequency and a higher and a lower spectral spread.

Like light, Time can be polarized. We are very close to achieving a practical use for this phenomenon.

(Konteau paused. Mimi's new Polar-X? Is *this* where it originated? But time pressed; he read on.)

Like light, Times from two different sources set up interference patterns when the two Times meet. Proving Time moves in waves? Not necessarily. Indeed, in one aspect (again like light!) Time is particulate. Consider Einstein's Relativity equation: $E = mc^2$. But what is c? Distance/time. So $E = m(d^2/t^2)$, and t is proportional to the square root of mass. Thus Time has dimensions of *mass* (and distance, and energy), and thus consists of particles. Call them wavicles!

(And *that,* thought the kron-man, is where Zeke Ditmars got the idea of a time-gun. Keep going!)

These similarities are cold comfort, for basic differences in Time and light remain. Unlike light, Time has discontinuities, almost as though intermittent earthquakes open chasms under us.

(Aha! thought Konteau. Here it comes! He read on.)

We were surveying a site in the Permian, and suddenly, without rhyme, reason, or warning, we are in the Pennsylvanian. We lost twelve million years and we fell ten meters. A crew member was killed. That was before tumble-suits. It took us six weeks to repair the equipment and get out again. Explanation? Some tried to hold to the EMR analogies, and they said that Time "skipped", just as radio waves skip over long distances, and then are reflected back to Earth by the ionized Kennelly-Heaviside layers. I say otherwise. I say Time has warps and ripples that have to be accounted for in our charts, the way a mariner makes compass adjustments. And these changes themselves change with distant Time.

What causes these discontinuities? I offer three possibilities: (1) The universe is expanding, and it does this by stretching Time until it fractures. (2) When continents break up, local Time is momentarily shattered. (3) When a sizeable comet or asteroid strikes, it smashes local Time.

Survey crews must be alert to detect these Time faults, existing and latent. City walls must be given extra protection in danger areas, else whole villages may be lost. If a stabilizer is jarred out of place by a Time-quake, the whole village will totally disappear as far as current Time is concerned. If this happens, the only remedy is to go back in and try to find the stabilizer. Replace it and hold it in place until Time gels around the village walls.

(Hold it in place for how long? thought Konteau.)

The skitter drove into an underground garage and the driver turned back to Konteau. "Hey, chum, you awake?"

The krono looked out the side window. Two grayjackets stood by the skitter door, which now opened automatically.

"They gotcha from here on," said the driver.

"Have a nice day," muttered Konteau. He got out. The skitter zoomed away.

"This way to the elevators, sir," said the first grayjacket. The statement was polite but clearly did not admit of discussion.

Konteau shrugged. He had been in close but unobtrusive custody from the moment he got off the express. He understood now that it would continue right up to the audience with the Vyr, and very likely beyond that. There was only one conclusion possible. Delta Five Eighty-five had indeed disappeared, and the Vyr was going to nail him for it.

7

Paul the Pious

The grayjackets escorted him in silence up an elevator to a check room, where he was strip-searched, x-rayed, and CAT-scanned.

The examiner in charge, a grayjac captain, was intrigued by the kron-man's cerebral scars. "Your personality implant was rejected?" he asked curiously. He passed the viso-plate over to his colleague.

Konteau grunted.

The assistant examiner, a sergeant, chuckled. "And look *here.* They tried a second implant on the *right* hemisphere. It was also rejected, and had to come out." He rubbed his chin. "Fascinating. He was a real problem child. Police record?" He studied the printout inching up in the computer terminal. "No. He's clean. And look—twice decorated in the Corps." They whispered together for a moment.

Konteau felt mildly guilty for having a perverse personality with no supporting criminal record. Was he visiting the Vyr under false pretenses? He called over to the two: "I kicked my third form teacher in the shins and was suspended from school for a week."

The captain looked back at him and frowned.

"Not good enough, eh?" said Konteau. "Well, I once ran away overnight with the headmaster's daughter. We. . . ."

"Hah!" said the sergeant. "What's *this?*" He was pointing

to the outline of Konteau's artificial eye on the CAT-plate.

"That's a suicide bomb," explained Konteau. "If I'm ever in danger of being bored to death by silly questions, I can take the easy way out. I blink in a certain way. The bomb blows and destroys everything within twenty meters."

"A real humorist," said the sergeant. He wasn't smiling. "How would you like a good-humored belt in the gut, funny man?"

"And how would you like his lordship to send you to the inqos for damaging his honored guest?"

The captain shot a warning glance at his assistant.

"Just being conversational, krono," muttered the sergeant.

The captain said quietly to Konteau, "Take it out, please."

Konteau popped the oculus out and handed it over.

The captain put it in the scanning cube and turned on the sonar net. The three of them watched the magnified holo of the left half-section slowly rotate.

"Sealed gas chamber, lower quadrant," intoned the sergeant.

"Gas analysis?" asked the captain.

"Ten helium, one neon."

"A gas laser?" the captain asked Konteau.

The time-man nodded.

"Interesting," mused the officer. He studied Konteau. "I've heard of them. It's the new thing for artificial eyes. How is the laser pumped?"

"Nuclear discharge."

The sergeant broke in. "Confirmed. You can see the scintillations . . . *there.*" He pointed.

The captain peered at the holo. "And insulated from radiation with an internal tri-molecular lead film."

The sergeant turned his back on Konteau and talked quietly with his superior. The krono caught some of the words. ". . . my brother works . . . prosthetics shop . . . fifty thousand silver jeffs."

They turned back to their guest. Did he detect a new respect? Or just a mild mix of puzzlement and uneasiness? Fifty thousand jeffs was more than the captain made in a year. Konteau hid a smile. He knew that Mimi had been budgeted at a cost of at least a hundred times the sergeant's estimate. But then Mimi could operate on levels the sergeant couldn't even imagine.

"Wait," said the non-com. He was peering closely at the oculus. "What's this?" He read aloud, slowly. "M . . . I . . . M . . . I . . . R? *Mimir?* You name the ancient god who guarded the waters of knowledge?"

Konteau sighed. He very definitely didn't want to get into a religious argument. "It's just an acronym for Multiphase Imaging Milliplex Interfacial Resonator. It's got nothing to do with the cult of Odin." He knew instantly he shouldn't have used the word 'cult'. Too late he realized that this moron was an adherent of that most improbable of theologic hybrids, the Norse branch of Kronos.

The sergeant's face went through various shades: pink, red, and now a bloodless white. He forced speech through knotted vocal cords. "You make a travesty of ancient truths! Odin gave his right eye to Mimir for the privilege of drinking the waters of knowledge. Blasphemer, you mock the very gods themselves!"

Konteau stifled an impulse to disclaim any sudden influx of wisdom from Mimi. About the most he could claim was a certain cunning in concealing his sundry stupidities. But even that seemed to have failed him now. "I. . . ." he began lamely.

The sergeant broke in, his voice trembling. "Next, I suppose you will take Odin's sacred spear, and impale yourself to Yggdrasil, the Holy Ash Tree, that unites gods, men, heaven, and hell? . . ."

Konteau's mind was whirling. How to get out of this? He tried desperately to recall the grisly Norse legend. All right, he had it. Now turn it around. "Would *you?*" he asked. "Sergeant, would you impale yourself on Yggdrasil, and die, and fly up to Valhalla? Would you follow the great Odin's shining example?"

The zealot was barely aware when Konteau took the oculus from his hand and gave it over to the captain.

The sergeant stared at the krono. "You dare ask? You are not even an apprentice druid! You must *pay!*" He doubled his fist and struck the startled kron-man in the stomach. The captain instantly intervened and pulled his assistant away.

Konteau's face writhed for a moment as he leaned over with his arms folded over his abdomen. Slowly, with a wary eye on his attacker, he straightened. The sergeant stood well away, breathing heavily.

Watching them both, the captain picked up the recording microphone and spoke in a hurried monotone. "Prosthetic eyeball. Designed by Bio Lab, Corps. Registration Number Four Twenty-eight." He looked over at the kron-man. "We'll hold it here during your audience." He was courteous but firm. "Pick it up on your way out."

Konteau shrugged and pulled his eye patch down.

The captain now called some unseen person on the intercom. "We're through. He's clear." A voice replied, "Send him around." The sergeant led Konteau down a short hallway and knocked at the door at the other end.

As they waited, the sergeant whispered to Konteau. "We know how to deal with smartbellies like you. You and I will meet again."

Konteau looked at the name on the noncom's gray shirt. "I can hardly wait, Sergeant Thor Odinsson," he said gravely.

A man in a white cloak blazoned with scarlet stripes opened the door and took the kron-man inside.

The two were alone in the room.

The cloaked man asked quietly, "Do you know where you are?"

Puzzled, the visitor looked about the room. It wasn't large, about the size of his studio back at Xanadu. Computer accessories lined the walls: receptacles for software, metallocards, discs. There were several CRTs and holo screens, a couple of chairs, a desk. Conventional stuff, thought Konteau. But in the room center stood the unconventional. It was a glass box, a one-meter cube, and in it floated something long and pink and ropy, evidently held in immobile suspension in air by anti-grav coils in the box support. From adjacent optical equipment, wraparound laser nets flickered back and forth over the suspended thing: two beams from the sides, one from overhead. They were, he reasoned, sending 3-D data back into the computer.

He gulped, and he wondered if the cloaked man was enjoying his discomfort. He was feeling just a little sick at his stomach, and he wondered if he had recovered fully from the scrgeant's blow. No, it was more than that. His reconstructed right cheek was twitching and throbbing. He was reacting to the thing in the glass cube. He wanted to run his hand over his face, but he refused to give his host the satisfaction.

Did he know where he was? He did. His answer was framed in the same monotone as the question. "Yes, I know where I am. Those are the entrails of some animal. Your computer is reading them. You are the augur. This is the Haruspex Room."

The other smiled faintly. "True. And my name is Tages. I am a direct descendant of that original Tages, the great grandson of Kronos."

"Indeed," said Konteau politely.

"You may know the history." But he continued without awaiting a reply. "My ancestor Tages taught divination to the Etruscans, who in turn taught the Romans. That's why the authoritative treatises are in Latin."

"Of course."

"I have parchment copies of the originals. There on the shelf, with the other software, including the twelve *Libri Haruspicini Fulgurales, Rituales.* Absolutely essential."

"I would think so." Konteau did not know how to deal with this.

His host continued. "As a science, haruspicy faded into the background for a time. The early Christians, you know."

"Oh? I hadn't realized. . . ."

"Oh yes. We were forced to use inefficient specimens. Birds, cats, rodents. Far too small, and statistically barely functional. You'd laugh at the size of the standard deviation."

Konteau wondered whether he should laugh quietly, as a simple courtesy. Actually, though, he saw nothing humorous in any of this.

Tages watched him for a moment. Then he said, "Let us

come straight to the point. I examine these entrails to determine the fate of 585. We know you are closely involved. I need your input."

"But I don't know anything. I *did* recommend triples. . . . I'm sure of that."

"You don't understand, Mr. Konteau. By input, I mean we merely want a laser readout of your face. It's perfectly harmless. You'll feel nothing. Would you sit over at the desk for just a moment?"

The time-man hesitated, then walked over and took the chair.

"Just stare at the little red light. Ah, that's it." The augur paused. "You lost your right eye?"

"Yes. A field accident."

"You have a prosthesis?"

"They kept it, out there."

"Mm. It would be much better if we had it. But, well, let's see how the reading goes without it. We'll start with some voice input. Your name?"

"James Konteau."

"Profession?"

"Kron-man."

"How long in the Corps?"

"Thirty-two years."

"Did your crew survey Delta Five Eighty-five?"

"Yes. And I recommended triples."

"Irrelevant." The diviner sounded impatient. "Watch the screen and listen carefully. We'll now try for some answers from Haruspex." He addressed the oversize CRT in the side wall. "Is Five Eighty-five lost?"

The word appeared simultaneously in the screen and in the voice synthesizer. "Yes."

"That's history, of course," said the augur softly. "Now we move to divination." He asked the computer, "Is Five Eighty-five retrievable?"

Konteau listened intently to the metallic voice: "Possibly."

The augur continued in slow measured tones. *"Will* Five Eighty-five be retrieved?"

"Possibly."

The diviner's jaw tightened as though he were determined to suppress any sign of annoyance.

"If retrieved, then by whom?"

"Perhaps by him who rides the strange iron cart. . . . Or perhaps not." The words were now coming out in hesitant disjointed groups, as though Haruspex was thinking in some ancient tongue, then translating into English.

"Iron cart?" Tages looked over at Konteau, who lifted his shoulders as though to say, this is *your* fantasy, don't ask *me*.

"Audio?" asked Tages.

They listened. *Click clack clickety clack clackety clack. . . .*

Something about it reminded Konteau of the little steam machine back in the game room at Xanadu.

"Do you recognize anything?" asked Tages.

The time-man shook his head.

The augur addressed Haruspex. "Who rides this strange iron cart?"

"Several. Or none. Perhaps a lover . . . an engineer . . . cadet to ancient West Point. . . ."

"*When* do they ride the cart?" pressed the augur. "What date?"

"Date? Date? Data . . . data . . . need more . . . what was in his empty eye socket? They cannot go, unless . . . unless. . . . How can you expect me to predict anything if you withhold vital data? Data! Data! Data!"

The augur strode up and down the cramped confines of the room as he swished his striped cloak in nervous impatience. "Damn them. They should have left that cursed false eye in your idiotic kron-head!"

Konteau wondered if he should express resentment or sympathy. He decided to keep quiet.

The entrails-master looked at his watch in a petulant gesture. "We don't have time. We'd have to make another printout of your face *with* the brass eye, another set of voice data. Kronos, what a fiasco. The Secretary will blame me, of course." He turned bitterly on his visitor. "Any ideas?"

Konteau made a strenuous effort to look blank and innocent. A flicker on the CRT caught his eye. "Something's coming in," he said helpfully.

They looked up at the screen. It had added (and the synthesizer was whispering:) *Terrapin sauce. Madeira, basil, thyme, marjoram, parsley, followed by murder.*

"Seems to me," Konteau said thoughtfully, "that ought to just about wrap it up. Incidentally, though what is this *terrapin?*" (And, he thought, who kills who, and why? Or was "murder" a typo?)

There was a peremptory knock at the door. "That'll be the First Secretary," said the augur sourly. "He'll take you in to the audience."

"A quick question?"

"Oh, all right."

Konteau gestured toward the thing floating in the glass box. "Sheep entrails?"

The augur finally smiled. It was an interesting smile, and seemed to suggest that no matter what tactical losses had gone before, he would have this last small victory. "Human guts, Konteau. They give the very best results. We have a contract with the prison."

The time-man felt cold. But the human detritus floating in the glass container wasn't even the worst of it. He thought about the mind that had built the program for Haruspex's computer, and his knees wobbled a little. He couldn't leave it like this. He had to try one last sally. "Have you predicted the next Overlord?"

The augur's eyes narrowed, and his smile changed subtly. "Tonight all this will be moved to the Great Hall of the Conclave, for audience by the entire assembly of Vyrs. A special, blood-fresh system will be used. Tomorrow the question will be put to Haruspex, and Haruspex will answer."

Konteau gulped. "A . . . special . . . system?"

"Taken instantly on death from a time-traveled mammal. They're the very best, you know. They're psychotropic. In the vernacular, they've got time in their very guts. It helps them predict."

Someone was pounding on the door, and calling out, but Tages ignored the summons. He said, "Oh, do not think it

ends here, Konteau, man-of-time." The augur's statements
were becoming as disjointed as those of his alter ego, Haruspex. "I tell you, I have already been appointed the official
Warden for the Conclave. I shall wear the Black Mask, and
I shall wield the knife, the holy *athame*, with which I shall
personally excise and install the sacred entrails. And through
my work, Kronos the God shall speak aloud to the assembled
Vyrs." The voice suddenly dropped to a whisper. "And Konteau?"

"Yeah?" The visitor shivered and backed away a few steps.

"Guess whose guts will be in that cube?"

"Guts . . . in the? . . ." His eyes shifted in alternate stupors
from the glass box to the face of Tages and back again.

"Entrails, Konteau. The very best. Absolutely the most
responsive. Twenty-seven feet, small intestine, and the large.
Twenty-seven, the perfect number. Three cubed. *Whose?*"

The eyes of the diviner rolled up in their sockets. Konteau
could see only the whites. He ran a finger around his collar.
He wasn't cold anymore. He was sweating. He actually felt
relief when the next detail of chancellory cohorts flung the
door open, said something unpleasant to Tages, and led the
kron-man out. The door closed on Tages' wild laughter.

His escorts took him down another corridor. This one was
carpeted, echoless, and the ceiling was a good five meters
over his head. He surmised he must be approaching the
hallowed chambers of Paul the Pious, Vyr of Delta.

He was met at the next doorway by a small dapper man
wearing a red silk jacket and velvet knee breeches. His hair
was lacquered black except for a single gilded curl over his
forehead. He looked at Konteau and sniffed. "Mr. Konteau,
I am the First Secretary. I assume this is your first audience
with his lordship. There is a certain protocol, an etiquette to
be observed. Immediately on entering, you will bow deeply,
and then you will await his lordship's signal to approach.
You will not speak unless spoken to. Do you have that?"

Konteau looked at him curiously.

The First Secretary sighed, rolled his eyes upward, opened
the great door, and announced, "Mr. Konteau!"

The kron-man walked in and surveyed the scene briefly

and dubiously. Near the entrance on the left was a great oaken credenza inlaid with polished black and white marble tesserae. In the center was the famous equine cluster, the ancient symbol of the Corleighs: the Four Horsemen of the Apocalypse—War, Death, Disease, Famine. Half life-size. Konteau looked up a moment, then passed on.

To his front, a good ten meters across the room, Paul Corleigh, Vyr of Delta, Defender of the Faith, sat on a golden throne, on a dais behind a great black desk. Behind the Vyr was a huge curving transparent panel, and through it Konteau could see the distant towers of a couple of buildings. He realized that this was the top storey in Delta Central's complex, the perimeter of which comprised the thousand traffic ports for Delta's thousand boros. In each boro lived five thousand souls. The Vyr's fief aggregated five million people. No, not quite five million. Subtract five thousand; for Five Eighty-five was *gone*.

Konteau stared across the room at the great man. The head was back-lit, the light glinted off the golden wig, and the features were hard to make out. The Vyr was talking to the woman seated on the nearby sofa. Did his lordship know he was here? Or perhaps he was being deliberately ignored, to put him in his place at the outset?

From the corner of his eye he noted grayjackets standing quietly in niches along the walls. He shrugged, then began walking toward the desk.

As he crossed the room, the deep iridescent pile of the rug seemed to move three-dimensionally beneath his feet, developing holographic patterns of ancient landscapes and prehistoric biota. Oligocene? He blinked as he seemed to skirt a rush-lined pond, and a pair of moeritheriums plunged massively into the water, scattering illusionary spray high into the air. Oh, well done! But he passed on, determined not to let these people know that he was impressed.

He could see the woman clearly before the Vyr's features came into good focus. The black-and-gold velvet robes of a Malthusian nun enfolded her. She was sitting there, silent, watching his approach with vague amusement. She wore earrings, jet black, that at first looked like grape clusters, but on closer inspection emerged as tiny replicas of the Corleigh insigne, the Four Horsemen. Death's scythe glinted as she turned her head to look at the krono. There was something strange about her mouth; in fact, there was something odd about her whole face and demeanor. It made him uncomfortable. He looked away, toward the Vyr. His host (he saw) appeared about as Konteau had expected. The face was the same as that on current Delta coins: the cheeks were soft clean-shaven pads; long false eyelashes bordered languid eyelids. He had watched this man deliver the Overlord's eulogy on the screens back at Xanadu. He was mindful of Demmie's warning. He hadn't liked him then, and he didn't like him now. And of course there was that crystal of the Norns (he still thought of them as three). The audience chamber of the Delta Vyr was simply not a safe place to be.

He noted then the planter on the near side of the big glass panel: it carried a magnificent mimosa, in full-scented flower.

The Vyr rose to greet him. "Welcome, Konteau." He smiled bleakly. "Thank you for coming so promptly."

I had a choice? thought Konteau. Unabashed, he returned the stare. By Kronos, those eyes! Elliptical, hard, glinting, hypnotic, reptilian. He nodded noncommitally. "Milord."

The Vyr waved a hand toward the woman. "Dr. Michaels, Konteau."

In the cold grace of this simple gesture Konteau saw not merely generations of aristocracy: he saw his own gaucherie flung back at him. To make it worse, the dual declaration wasn't even deliberate. It was something he figured out all by himself. But, actually, it didn't really matter, for there was nothing he could do about it. So he simply bowed politely.

"Dr. Michaels is our resident paleographer," explained the Vyr.

How do you acknowledge an introduction to a nun of the House of Malthus, who is also a doctor of something or other? Sister? No, no first name. Well, make it short and simple. He bowed again. "Pleasure, ma'am."

The woman inclined her head a little and grinned. The mouth was large, strong; the teeth sparkled. Konteau had the uneasy feeling that he had committed some incomprehensible faux pas. Well, let's get to it. "Excellency, how may I serve you?"

"We'll come to that, Konteau. First, let me say you were quite right. Five Eighty-five is gone, vanished. Second, we wonder how you knew? . . ."

"Milord, I was not completely certain. In any case, if I knew, I don't know how I knew."

"On that point, dear Konteau, perhaps we can help you."

What's going on? he thought. He looked about for clues. The mimosa? What could a fragrant undershrub have to do with his presence here? No. But what's that on the desk? A cubical glass case, filled with dirt and topped with a plastic lid. With some sort of tiny insects crawling around inside on the dirt? Ants?

The Vyr watched the kron-man's eyes, and Konteau thought for a moment the aristocrat was about to explain the cube. But the moment passed.

The Vyr said, "There is really only one rational way you could have known." The speaker paused and fixed Konteau with cold eyes. There was a sudden stillness in the room, relieved only by the rustle of the Vyr's gorgeous golden tunic. Then the bland monotone resumed. "You had subconsciously reassessed the risk. You made a redetermination at this late date that the boro would fail. You even decided *when.* Rather exactly, I might add. And you did all this subconsciously. There's no magic to it, Konteau, no psi, no parajunk."

The krono was silent. What was there to say? Every statement the Vyr had made was utterly ridiculous. But Konteau wasn't about to announce the fact. He pondered the Vyr and his background. He knew that in his early youth Corleigh had been selected for imprinting in the ways of government. Part by the chance of computer-draw, part by ancestral pressure. (His father had been third Vyr of Epsilon.) As a boy he had been educated by Malthusian monks, and of course had been indoctrinated with their gloomy views as to the significance of the human race.

The Malthusians claimed quasi-divine origins, even preceding No. Their charter was defined in a sacred interplay between a giant computer and the great Malthus himself. Techno-historians who pointed out the several-centuries gap between Malthus and the computers were put down by the very cogent observation that Malthus had asked the question in 1834, the year of his death, knowing the answer would have to await the mainframes of the twenty-first century.

Inconvenient anachronisms aside, Malthus's Question was: *What is man?*

The Malthusians have a number of publications dealing with the Question, the computer-structure, the comments and conjectures by wise men as to what the answer would likely be. (Konteau had read some of them.) The computer was "LC", the giant mainframe in the Library of Congress, nicknamed Elsi, and the seance took place there in the Main Reading Room, with the CRT and audio over the central hub.

The Question had evoked some initial misgivings. The Chief Data Compiler had protested, "Elsi, a man-made machine, will be looking at man. She'll be RAM-ing the man-made data collection. Man looking at man. She'll loop."

The Chief Designer pooh-poohed the objection. "We have redundant loop protection."

And then the speculations as to the probable answer were collected. Most seemed simply quotations extracted from ancient philosophers: *The Psalmist:* "You have made him a little lower than the angels." *Hamlet:* "What a piece of work is man . . . how like a god . . . the beauty of the world." *Gorki:* "How marvelous is man!"

Elsi had answered the Question, but her answer had not been anything like these panegyrics. Elsi's answer had started as a giggle, which progressed to a chuckle, then spilled over into a chortle, and finally burst into a guffaw. And then Elsi had literally exploded, hurling glass and parts all over the place.

The Malthusian Manual quoted the headlines in *The New York Times:* "GIANT COMPUTER CONSIDERS MAN. Laughs Self to Death."

Proving, the Malthusians claimed, that *H. sapiens* is nothing.

A famous techno-historian claimed Elsi knew something her audience didn't. Indeed, within the week, the buttons were pushed in the East and in the West, and No was on the way.

But back to the Vyr, and the present!

By now Konteau had integrated a series of very subtle impressions. He sensed that this very powerful man was covertly half-afraid of him, in the way a cobra might fear an inexperienced mongoose, or a rat might watch a half-grown terrier. But that made no sense at all.

He looked over to the side wall and the portrait hanging there: the late Overlord, peering out into the room with those sad gray eyes that seemed to say, "This hurts me more than it does you." Like hell it does, thought the kron-man. He turned his good eye back to the Vyr. "My team made the original survey. It was a good survey: a twenty-kilometer triangle in the Early Triassic, in the Chesapeake Sector. A good place to anchor a boro. But we also noted a tendency to time fractures. We recommended triple-duty stabilizers."

"Did you, now?" murmured the Vyr. But he would not look at his truculent, if uneasy vassal. "Triples? Very expensive."

"But necessary."

"Debatable."

"Not debatable. Look what happened."

The Vyr frowned, then sighed, as if forced by noblesse oblige to forgive the blatant contradiction. "We don't really know what happened, Konteau."

The time-man felt a sudden chill. It was like standing sweat-drenched again in that Message Center in Xanadu. "Milord, is my report still of record?"

"Of course."

"The *full* report?"

The Vyr looked blank for a moment, then flushed. He replied through compressed lips. "Theoretically."

"With the recommendation for triples?"

"Now about that, I couldn't say. By Kronos! Are you sure you made such a recommendation?"

"Could we see the report?"

"All that bother. . . ."

"Just Section 4, Conclusions and Recommendations."

The Vyr grunted impatiently, and then was silent for several seconds. "Oh, very well, if you insist. We'll order it up. May take a moment." He nodded to the First Secretary, who gave Konteau a haughty stare, then stepped over to a computer terminal near the portrait of the late Overlord. "Meanwhile," continued the Vyr, "let me show you something."

8

Ants

The Vyr pointed to the dirt-filled glass box on his desk. "See this? This is an ant farm. Did you know a boro is quite similar to an ant farm?"

"I'm aware that they have been compared," said Konteau cautiously.

"Both are rigorously structured," said the Vyr. "They have their food gatherers and processors, their propagative systems, messengers, service workers. There are dozens of castes, each with its own unique specialty. The ant colony as a unit is a self-sufficient entity or organ. No matter how large or how small, it has an underground life all its own. The five thousand inhabitants, whether ants or humans, operate under the same prime directive: exist. And yet, if they *cease* to exist, what then? Nothing, Konteau. The world sails on. It's as though they had never been there in the first place. As Mephistopheles told Faust, it all comes to nothing." He stood up, lifted the glass box carefully, and walked over to a side wall. "And what's the cube root of five thousand? About seventeen. Seventeen ants—or humans—on a side. Not very many, really." A panel opened in the wall and he dropped the box into the disposal chute. He turned back to his visitor, but still would not look at him. "Ants, dear fellow, a measly five thousand, more or less. Instantly incinerated. They felt nothing. You felt nothing. I felt nothing.

Nobody felt anything. The little creatures probably had distant cousins, in other ant colonies, and *they* felt nothing. Nobody cares, Konteau."

No, thought the kron-man. It's not that way. Pain and death *is* important. To me, to you, to an ant. The individual can hurt, and he can sense hurt in others. Bad thoughts! Proves my high PD. Actually, high *im*Permissible Deviation. Maybe I truly can't think straight. Misfit. Anachronism.

The Vyr interrupted his reverie. "Ah, here we are, Konteau. Section 4."

The visitor turned quickly and read the luminous lines on the great screen. Then he reread the lines, word by word, his lips moving. His heartbeat picked up. He fought off a tendency to wipe his hands on his trousers. He said dully, "They were there. Recommendations for triple stabilizers. And now they're not there. Somehow they got edited out. The builders must have installed singles. One or more of the singles failed. But maybe Five Eighty-five is still out there somewhere. Maybe they're safe. No *Homo* bones have ever been reported in Triassic drill cores."

"Quite true, but that doesn't mean they're safe."

"You have run a projection?"

"Of course. And it shows that Five Eighty-five almost certainly slid onto the Atlantic plate, which was subducting under the North American plate during the Triassic. Five thousand skeletons were carried down through four or five hundred kilometers of magma. Like the ant farm in the incinerator. They were all dead before any pain stimuli could travel up their nervous systems to their brains. Not a bad way to go, Konteau."

"With respect, milord, that's all theory. Have you actually sent a search team in to look for them?"

"Oh dear, no. A live search is so inefficient, so . . . *primitive.* Computer projections are much more accurate and comprehensive. Dr. Michaels can explain this better than I. Doctor?"

"We made several computer searches," said the woman. "The last report preceded you by just a few minutes."

Konteau stared at her. He realized that this was the first time she had spoken. The voice was modulated, semi-masculine, with a slight lisp. And her Adam's apple moved when she talked, which it shouldn't do, because women don't have Adam's apples. Dr. Michaels was a man.

He hoped he wasn't blushing.

'She' continued blandly. "Our search pattern was thorough, yet economical. We examined the Triassic first, then earlier, in the Permian and Carboniferous. Then finally forward, into the Tertiary. Ironically, our task was facilitated by the rather erratic and dramatic geologic history of the Delta area. This part of the Chesapeake has been drowned dozens of times, slammed at least twice by off-shore crustal plates, baked, frozen, and so on. In our search we simply skipped these unpleasant episodes. It's pointless to look for Five Eighty-five under a thousand meters of Atlantic seawater. Wouldn't you agree, Mr. Konteau?"

He shrugged morosely.

Dr. Michaels continued. "The Chesapeake Bay means water, of course, and the water line is critical. Presently, it's the drowned outlets of the Susquehanna and Potomac Rivers. It's sinking, and has been for centuries, at about two and a half centimeters per decade." She punched a button in her hand-carried control capsule, and the wall screen lit up again, this time showing a map of the North American east coast. The scene shifted to show an enlarged coastal area. "We can start here, in the Recent. As you see"—she pointed with her indicator—"twenty thousand years ago there was no Chesapeake Bay. It's all dry land, save for the giant Susquehanna and its tributaries, the Potomac, Rappahannock, Patuxent, York, and James Rivers. Sea level is low, one hundred meters below normal, because so much water is still locked up in the great ice caps. The local climate is cool, but not too cool. It's livable. So there we find Delta One, our first Delta boro." She stopped for a moment and smiled at Konteau. The krono glowered back. Michaels continued. "Going on backwards in time, the next safe and solid ground is one hundred thousand B.P., another interglacial. There we put Delta Two. Delta Three is at one hundred thousand B.P., during the Bemian interglacial. That's just the start. The computer has made complete searches, all the way back to Delta One Thousand, in the Silurian. We found nothing, not a trace. By ruling out all other possibilities, we have pretty well established what happened to Five Eighty-five."

"Subduction?" growled Konteau.

"Of course. The only reasonable solution. Five Eighty-five is neatly dissolved in magma several hundred kilometers beneath the North American plate. No mess, no pain, no bother."

The krono said something under his breath.

"You don't agree?" Dr. Michaels seemed amused.

Konteau did not reply. He was thinking, *you know everything; yet you know nothing, because you didn't go looking for it.*

"It's easily confirmed," said the transvestite. "Let's look at how it was, way back then. Starting with the Triassic, two hundred and twenty-five million years ago, Five Eighty-five was on solid ground. It sat on a low hill of Appalachia, still in the middle of the supercontinent, Pangaea. But Pangaea will soon start to rumble. The plates are shifting, and it is beginning to break up into smaller daughter continents, the two Americas, Eurasia, Africa, and Antarctica. Five Eighty-five sits on the tight rope of time. On one side, in the fairly recent past, is the collision of Larussia and Gondwana to form Pangaea and the Appalachians. On the other side, just a few million years later into the Jurassic, the Eurasian plate rips away from the North American plate, and a fair part of eastern Appalachia, including Five Eighty-five, will sink into magma off the continental shelf. And that's where Five Eighty-five is now. Or *was.*" The paleographer looked up at Konteau and smiled bleakly. "You really might have mentioned triples, my dear fellow."

The Vyr coughed delicately.

Well, thought the kron-man, while they're waiting to put me through the meatgrinder I might as well enjoy the view. He took a deep breath and, in a total disclaimer of courtesy and protocol, started walking toward the great circular glassed area behind the Vyr's desk. He noted from the corner of his eye that the guards in the corners of the room tensed and leaned forward, weapons at the ready. He ignored them.

As he passed the Vyr's desk he noted a golden plaque embedded in the side. Something about four hundred years old, certified C-dating. Less than one ten-millionth of the age of the Earth—yet a status symbol. The kron-man wondered what the peer was trying to prove. Perhaps legitimize nebulous ancestral roots with isotopes? To each his own. None of his affair. He walked on, but paused briefly at the planter, his brow wrinkling. Something was wrong with the mimosa: all of the tiny bipinnate leaves of the perfume-plant had folded up. A wisp of memory drifted across his olfactory receptors along with the subtle perfume of the flowers, but he couldn't hold it. Something recent? . . . Damn, he wished he had Mimi here. She'd tag it in milliseconds. Something to do with Demmie? No, not Demmie. Ditmars? What had the biopsych shown him?

He walked on. He knew the Vyr was frowning at his back, and he suspected proper decorum required that he should have asked permission, or at least stated what he had in mind. To hell with all that. Anyhow, he didn't have anything specific in mind. He just wanted to look out the window. Let them protest. Let them decide not to invite him back. He hoped!

He peered outward through the great glass expanse.

It was mid-morning. The sky was clear except for a couple of small clouds. The Delta Government Complex was the hub of a great wheel, the perimeter made up of one thousand arc-segments for the boros, each connected to the hub with fifteen-kilometer-long transit spokes for air and surface vehicles.

Within the Complex he could see Interport, where he had landed less than an hour ago; next to that the Prison, then the Kron-Temple. Beyond that should be Ratell Park, presently invisible. His one eye flicked back briefly to the Temple. He was well aware of certain rumors and reports. If you're in trouble, try for Sanctuary in the Temple. A good thing to remember, all things considered

His eye moved on. Here and there, just beyond the gates,

was a thin belt of mesquite, cactus, and sage: futile efforts to brave the radiation of the deadly deserts that reigned between the intermittent oases of surface colonies. A few millenia hence perhaps something hardy and green would finally conquer that wasteland. By then it would be irrelevant. In fact, poisonous radiation aside, it was already too late to return the land to the plow. With no ground cover, nine-tenths of the world's topsoil had already either blown away or had washed into the sea, making great muddy fans at the mouths of once-beautiful rivers.

The alluvial deposits of the Mississippi, the Rio Grande, the Alabama, the Trinity, and a dozen lesser streams had already converted the Gulf of Mexico into a swamp. The Gulf Stream had choked to a trickle and no longer crossed the Atlantic. North Europe was entering a new Ice Age.

He peered off to the northwest, where a long dark cloud blanketed the horizon. This was dust. Winds were sweeping away the ever-thinning layers of weathered sand from the Great Plains and dropping it in the Atlantic Ocean and on Iberia and western Africa. The dead topsoil had already vanished in this fashion, in the first centuries of "?". The phenomenon incorporated a curious irony: the wind was gradually cleansing the land of radiation, but was demanding for this favor a price that could not be paid. Millions upon millions of square miles of desolate bedrock were being laid bare beyond that horrid horizon.

Beyond the cactus nothing grew: no shrubs, trees, birds, mice, animals. Nothing was out there but swirling dust and ghastly networks of erosion.

Somewhere over the western horizon, of course, you could find the other eight North American colonies, with their own Vyrs, and their own rabbit-warren time-complexes—modern troglodytes, living in caves of time. And eastward, across the sea, Europe had returned to life, and they too had populations problems. And where to put the human overflow? The red planet? Yes. There was no other place to go. (He wondered whether Demmie had really delivered his report to the Directrix.) In each boro five thousand people lived their complete, safe, invariant lives. And these boros were located in almost exactly the same three-dimensional space. How can one thousand boros occupy the same space? By stacking them in different time epochs. Delta One is fixed in the present. No problem at all there. Delta Two stands in almost exactly the same place, but yet doesn't get in the way of Delta One, because Two is built in the Maryland of one hundred thousand years ago, when there were no people in North America, and much sea-water was still locked up in glaciers. The builders used the Ratell Time Equations. They built in Maryland when the Chesapeake Bay was high and dry, and the Potomac and Rappahannock were mere tributaries of the great Susquehanna, which rolled all the way to the sea. (You got that much right, Michaels.) The dwellers of Number Two couldn't get through the Ratell barriers into the prehistoric Maryland that lay outside their narrow estate, nor could the biota outside break in on Delta Two. All was well.

And so down the stairs of time to the Triassic and Delta 585, which Konteau's crew had surveyed and laid out a mere five years ago. Five Eighty-five sat on the edge of a crack in what was then Pangaea, the giant supercontinent of two hundred and twenty-five million years ago. In coming eons that crack would slowly widen. North America would split away from Eurasia and South America from Africa. Strange phenomena would accompany that break-up. The strangest would be cracks and fissures in the fabric of time. Intrusive disconformities such as Delta Five Eighty-five might find themselves ejected from the Triassic, forward into the Jurassic, or backward into the Permian—or into Kronos knows when. Such things had happened. But they could be prevented. The builders simply doubled or tripled the stabilizers, and the cost of the boro.

In the Catoctin Mountains, one hundred kilometers to the northwest, nestled Beta Colony, with its five million souls, and to the west, forty centichrons by metro, Alpha. In fact, in isolated radiation-free pockets, units of five million people had sprung up all over the country. Today there were forty million people in North America, and twice that in (and that's the word, *in*) the whole weary planet. Small wonder, thought Konteau, the Vyr is not too perturbed by the loss of a measly five thousand men, women, and children.

All this time-building had begun a hundred years ago, during the Yes Century. (There had been the Time of No, when it looked as though the human race had come to an end. Then the years of Maybe, now abbreviated to a simple question mark, '?', followed by Yes!, or simply '!'.) And then the population explosions. Where to put the people? Most of the planet was still radiation-poisoned. Underground? No, said the great Ratell, under *time.* Bury them in the Past. And he had shown how.

But people will have to behave, Ratell had said. Screen them. Set up limits. They should all be about the same, within a permissible predetermined deviation. The Permissible Deviation. The PD. Need a highly structured society. Aggression, innovation, independence, detect it at the outset. Turn it away at the door. Peace requires stasis.

Ratell, thought Konteau, staring far out down the strangely empty Five Eighty-five traffic-way, your own PD was so far out from the norm you'd be destroyed in infancy today. But look what you gave us. Time travel. Which was— what? A religion? A science? An art? A process? A business? A circus? All? None? It depended on how you looked at it, and what you expected to get out of it.

As he watched through the great window, the distant spires seemed to shift slowly to the right. For an instant he was puzzled. Then he understood that the tower room itself was slowly revolving. And as he watched, the characteristic traffic gates of Five Eighty-five came into distant view. These gates, he noted, were unique, quite atypical. The openings alternated with sections of solid wall, and at this distance the assembly reminded him somehow of something he had seen at Xanadu. Yes, the little ceramic incense burner: the open jaws of Kronos. Exactly apt, he thought. Kronos has indeed devoured his children.

He knew the Vyr had swiveled his chair around and was watching him. "There'll have to be an inquisition," said

Konteau, still looking out the window. It was half statement, half question. .

"Just a formality," said the Vyr.

"They will need a scapegoat."

The great man laughed almost absently. "Your cynicism is refreshing but a bit premature."

"I'm *it.*"

"Now, now, Konteau. You know we'll protect you."

Protection, hell, thought Konteau. Demmie had warned him. The Norns had warned him. I'm a dead man. He said, "It didn't have to happen. I put it in my report. Triple stabilizers."

"Let's not go into that again."

"When is the hearing?"

"Tomorrow, ten o'clock. In the Trial Room, Corps Central."

"Get them to postpone it. I have to start looking for Five Eighty-five."

"Now, Konteau, don't be difficult. In the first place, Five Eighty-five no longer exists. We've explained that. In the second place, you have nothing to fear from an inquisition. My own personal advocate will represent you."

Worse and worse! Konteau tried to think. Had the Vyr himself deleted the safety recommendations? Had the money saved gone into the peer's credit accounts? But it didn't make sense. The money saved wasn't all that much. But no matter how it had happened, or why, they could and would blame it on sloppy work by Konteau. And the consequences could be serious indeed. The statutory penalty was death—or (worse) life imprisonment. Prison. He thought of the grim gray building that bordered Interport.

The Vyr considered his visitor through heavy-lidded eyes. "Where will you stay tonight, Konteau?"

The krono shrugged. "Probably at Corps Overnight, if they have space."

The Vyr nodded to the First Secretary, who told Konteau, "A fleabag, my dear fellow. We recommend the Delta Arms. Your room is already reserved. Everything is paid for, including whatever, ah, company you like. Indeed, his lordship *insists*. Skitter waiting for you now at the chancellory entrance. We'll have your bag sent over from Interport." The little man put a hand on his hip, lifted his chin at Konteau, and sniffed haughtily.

So that's the situation, mused the visitor. They were going to hold him under surveillance until they could decide what to do with him. If they weren't actually afraid of him, at least he certainly made them all very uneasy. And it was quite clear they didn't want him to go looking for Five Eighty-five. They wished he hadn't discovered the disaster in the first place. Perhaps they regretted bringing him in from Xanadu. And absolutely, under no circumstances, were they going to turn him loose to search for the missing boro. Which meant that they were not one hundred percent sure in their own minds that the boro had been destroyed.

So what to do? For now, play along. He said meekly, "You said, everything paid for?"

"Everything," replied the First Secretary disdainfully.

"Meals? Drinks? Entertainment? Tips?"

The equerry's lips curled. "As I said."

"Well, fine. Of course. Thanks very much."

The Vyr smiled. "It's settled, then. Thank you for coming. Just be there in the morning."

"Yes." Well, at least they hadn't held him behind bars to await his trial. Very curious. And a bit unusual. But perhaps they had a reason. He sensed that these people—the Vyr, the paleographer, the First Secretary, and perhaps a few others not present at the moment—knew something crucial that he did not know. And he had been brought here under strict controls to make sure he did not find out.

He bowed, turned, and walked toward the door.

"Konteau."

He turned back, his face blank. "Milord?"

"Just one more thing. We know your loyalty, your dedication to duty." The Vyr was actually smiling. "We are aware that this dedication may persuade you to go personally in search of Five Eighty-five." The cultured tones hardened imperceptibly. "But we warn you, don't do it. Don't even think about it. Excessive ramblings about the halls of time can be quite dangerous, not only for yourself, but also for the time-scaffolds of the other boros. We cannot have you flailing about." And now the bland grin vanished; the voice became stern, metallic. "So we instruct you, Konteau, we *order* you . . . don't go looking for Five Eighty-five. Do you understand us?"

The hell you say, thought Konteau. But he nodded respectfully. "Milord."

The great man seemed to relax; he waved a hand in languid dismissal.

Konteau took a deep breath as the Secretary took him by the elbow and pointed him toward the exit. Very curious. Of course, they could still grab him in the check room. Maybe that was the plan. Wait and see.

The First Secretary tried manfully to suppress a sneeze as he ushered the kron-man out into the check room, where Konteau retrieved his artificial eye from the captain. As he reinserted the oculus he turned back to the First Secretary and clucked sympathetically. "You'll probably want to have the whole chamber resanitized and resanctified. Now it just happens my cousin Louie runs this shop, down in Eight Ninety-eight, in Los Padres Street, and he'll do both jobs for the price of one, rugs and drapes included, standard six-month guarantee, with ten percent kickback to you. . . ." He studied the frowning equerry. "Fifteen percent? Twenty? Look, they have to live. . . ."

The Secretary doubled his fists and trembled in ill-controlled rage. "Oh, you are so uncouth! You ruined the mimosa too, you know!"

Mimosa? The folded leaves? . . . By the krapulent krotch of Kronos, *that* was the key! He had it! And it had been staring at him all the time! He whirled on the little man so eagerly that the Secretary shrank behind the sergeant. "It's the great grandfather plant, isn't it? Seeds were taken from it for all the boros of Delta, right?"

The other three stared at him as though he were insane.

Konteau pressed on. "Including Five Eighty-five? *Answer!*"

There was no denying him. The little aide nodded through his fear.

The truth was battering Konteau's face like a sudden blast of sunlight. The endangered mimosas in Five Eighty-five had called out to the parent shrub in the chambers of the Vyr, and the leaves of the parent had responded by folding. But the parent leaves had not fallen. They had merely folded. So if you believed Ditmars and those bio-experiments, Five Eighty-five was stricken, but still alive—somewhere, some-*when.* And he had been right to send that urgent code to Devlin: "Assemble." Which meant, get me a surveyor and a rodman. It was just as well he hadn't simultaneously told Devlin the two crewmen could wind up extremely dead before the hour was out.

Already he was feeling a lot better.

Just one last thrust at the Secretary, whom he decided he detested. "Louie would probably do it for free, if you'd promise to recommend him to your friends."

The little man stamped his foot in total fury. *"Out!"*

Konteau grinned and walked away.

He looked up and down the corridor. No escorts for the return trip? They must feel very sure of themselves.

On the down elevator he pondered his problems further. Perhaps, he reflected, the Vyr'll have me killed anyhow. He can pretty well pick the time and place. The aristo must realize I'll testify I recommended triples in my original report. Then the inqo judge will have to decide who's lying. Since the Inquisitors report to the Vyr, no contest. But will the Vyr let me live long enough to testify? Why didn't he have me killed the minute I walked into his chamber? Was he afraid I'd mess up his beautiful holo rug? So maybe he's waiting until I step off this elevator. That, your excellency, would be downright inhospitable.

But is the Vyr actually the guilty party? The great man has absolutely no motive. And that human-swarm was his own people. But if he didn't do it, who did? The inqos, maybe? Or the Grayjacket General Staff? But that brings it back to *him,* the Vyr.

And then there was that horrid, gaping maw, the Kronos-

Gate. Those grinning arches raise some interesting questions in themselves. To look at them you'd think that whoever had deleted the recommendation for triples had intended from the beginning that the great god Kronos would gulp down those five thousand people. Had the gates been deliberately shaped to announce this most cynical of mythical ironies? Had some very high, very powerful prince of the temple of Kronos done this? Had he—they—designed this horror years ago, knowing the time-quake would come, and that Five Eighty-five would vanish? Is it possible? Great Kronos! It is indeed. Perhaps the Vyr suspects it, too. Perhaps that's why I'm still free. Perhaps he wants to see what I'll do, where I'll go. Perhaps he wants to see who will try to kill me.

And perhaps . . . perhaps . . . perhaps the time lines have finally addled me.

But suppose, just suppose, I'm *not* crazy.

Start over, Konteau, he told himself. Think it through, slowly, logically. Once more now. The pieces to the puzzle are all there. You just have to put them together properly. Try again.

A given: The Vyr had this insane ambition to be the next Overlord. Another given: firm rumor had it that the Vyr had done something remarkable, something that was sure to get him elected. And what was this remarkable thing that the Vyr had done? (I'm catching a glimmer.) The Vyr had downplayed the loss of Five Eighty-five. A mere antswarm, the Vyr had contended. So forget it, Konteau. Go away, Konteau. Five Eighty-five is over, discussion closed. Third given: he, Konteau, had been brought here just to be told he mustn't go looking for Five Eighty-five. Fourth given: the Kronos-maw—that obscene entranceway to Five Eighty-five. Somebody had *known* for years. Somebody had planned for years. Who? You, Paul the Pious, Vyr of Delta? Is it conceivable? Is it possible? Are you, Vyr of the Four Horsemen, lover of women-men, an absolute madman?

He passed a hand over his forehead. He didn't know what to think. Every time his mind seemed to be closing in on some vital essential conclusion, it veered off again. He could not bring himself to accept the unacceptable. He was hyperventilating and had to pause a moment to recover his breath. And what about Tages, and Haruspex, and those grisly pink and purple ropes in Tages' glass box? What did Tages know, or think he knew? He had to stop and get a grip on himself. He noted then that the right side of his face ached and that he was simultaneously shivering and perspiring.

He clenched his teeth and deliberately shifted his thinking.

Helen. She had a little office somewhere in this very building. He would drop in for a casual hello. Except, he couldn't. He clenched his teeth again. Kronos! What was he thinking of? She had absolutely no interest in seeing him.

Back to the problem. He had to break surveillance.

He got off at the next floor, entered another elevator, rode up a few floors, changed again, then merged with a group of visiting legates. He was about to get out on the first floor with them, but noted two grayjackets standing near a cluster of indoor shrubbery, watching the doors of his original elevator. Underneath those jackets he could make out the outlines of body armor. And the faces, hard, cold, blank. He shrank to the rear of the elevator, and stayed in it when it passed on down to the basement. He found an emergency exit at the rear of the building, walked casually out into the street, and hailed a cruising skitter.

"Where to, tembo?"

"West. I'll give you directions."

"Your brass, tembo."

9

The Temple of Time

"Tembo?"

"Yeah?"

"You know we're being followed?"

Konteau jerked. All that evasive effort for nothing! And so near the Park. Actually, just one square away. He twisted around and peered through the backport. A grayjac skitter, a hundred meters behind them. And what was this building coming up? Something public . . . couldn't tell exactly . . . but there had to be an exit on the other side. And then the Park.

"Stop here," he barked. He tossed a handful of clunkers into the farebox and hit the street running.

He was wondering about the doorway design even as he dashed up the stone stairs. Something familiar. Of course. Like gaping jaws. The maw of the time god. He had entered the Temple of Kronos. He had seen the dome from the Vyr's great view-panel.

Breathing heavily, he leaned for a moment against the vestibule wall. Get moving . . . find a rear entrance. It was dark. He brushed against fabric and almost cried out. But it wasn't a person. Just a robe, hanging on a peg. He grabbed it by reflex and began sidling along the wall, facing outward, and feeling the cold stones with his fingertips. Like a frightened mouse, he thought sardonically. He paused when he reached the arch-entrance to the central nave, where it seemed even darker and more forbidding. He essayed an I.R.-scan with his oculus. Outlines were blurred, but he could make out a central circular dais bordered by concentric circular benches, intersected by radial aisles. The shortest way to the rear was through the central aisle. He started carefully up the passage.

Something—a spark of light?—flicked in his artificial eye. *He* was being scanned!

And then a voice in his right ear. He stumbled as he tried to whirl around, and had to grab the back of the nearest bench.

No one was there.

"Pilgrim! Greetings!"

Of course. A unidirectional, narrow-beam audio.

"Pilgrim," continued the voice, "welcome to the House of Kronos."

A computer program was talking to him.

He felt stupid. It was all in accord with the secret reports. These were the first steps in the drama of Sanctuary. But *his* lines had to be done exactly right, or he would die before the grayjacs got to him.

He declared in a loud voice: "I claim Sanctuary!" The words echoed hollowly in the empty chamber: *Sanctuary . . . Sanctuary . . . Sanctuary.*

The response was immediate, and disconcerting. "Are you he for whom I wait?"

There was something wistful in the question. Konteau was reminded of a dog who could not accept the fact of its master's death and who met every stranger on the street, searching for that lost face. "No," he said, "I am not Raymond Ratell." Did the computer give sanctuary to all fugitives on the theory that the next one might be the great time magician?

"What is your name?"

"James Konteau."

"You are a krono?"

"Yes."

"So you have moved in time?"

"Yes."

"And perhaps you have met my master, he who made me?"

Konteau sighed. "No, I have never had the pleasure."

"But someday you will meet him?"

"Who knows?" (He did not think it advisable to explain that Ratell had been dead for two hundred years.)

The artificial voice seemed to join in his sigh, and then was silent.

"Can you provide Sanctuary?" persisted Konteau. "If not, I must leave, and quickly."

The calm voice came alive again. "At the moment all exists are watched. But you shall have Sanctuary for a time, and afterward you can leave safely."

"They'll come in?"

"Actually, just one man, I think. He approaches the front entrance."

"He'll enter?"

"Yes."

"And search the building?"

"He will indeed search the building. Indeed, we want him to come in. We want him to have a good look. We insist. And he will enter this sacred atrium, and he will laser-scan every cubic meter of this holy interior."

"So where shall I hide?"

"Within an illusion."

"Explain, please. Does he find me, or not?"

"Yes, James, he will find you, but no, he won't find you. Remember, I have given you Sanctuary."

Someone, sometime, wrote a gorgeous program for this building, thought Konteau. But I fear it has just crashed. Which way to that rear exit? He started up the aisle again.

To his horror, the central dais suddenly blazed up with light.

"Step up, James," commanded the voice. "Stand toward the front of the platform."

He stepped up onto the platform. "What's going on," he hissed.

"We have several Sanctuary programs," replied the voice,

"adjusted to a given pursuer or pursuers. We have, for example, a fairly effective sequence that we have used in the past on susceptible grayjackets of limited mental organization."

Most interesting. "But suppose a certain very powerful Vyr is searching for me for his own personal reasons. Would you? . . . *Could* you resist him and his agents?"

The voice seemed troubled. "You touch on a possibility that I thought had died out. Yes, James Konteau, this temple will resist human sacrifice though that be commanded by the entire Conclave of Vyrs."

What was he talking about, thought Konteau. Human sacrifice? How did *that* get into the discussion? Did this very well-informed program carry data not available to him, Konteau? Stay with this. "Five Eighty-five!" he blurted. "What really happened to Delta Five Eighty-five?"

"Don't get involved with Delta, James. Stay away. But no time to talk now."

"But. . . ."

"Don your robe, pilgrim! Quickly!"

"I. . . ." He shook the robe out and pulled it over his head.

"He's coming in," said the voice. "One man. A grayjac sergeant. Fold your arms into the sleeves. Try to look like a priest of Kronos."

Konteau gulped but followed instructions.

With the light showering him from above and all around him, he made a perfect target. He groaned.

"Silence," whispered the voice. "This man coming in is under thirty, with about four years' schooling, just elementary core. Thoroughly hypnoconditioned. Should respond well to fire, blood, and violence. Presently posted at the Chancellory. I read 'Vyr's Check-room.' "

"You're right!" whispered Konteau. "I met this kork this morning. His cult name is Thor Odinsson. They probably sent him on the patrol because he can identify me." He had a sudden thought. "I know just the thing for him. Can I give you some holo input?"

"Through your oculus?"

"Exactly. I'll work it out as we go along."

"Oh, absolutely. And perhaps I can add a few touches of my own. Careful now, here he comes."

The sergeant remained in the distant darkness, but Konteau could hear him walking slowly and tentatively up the aisle. Probably the man's laser-net reader was scanning the interior and by now had established that this black-robed figure was the sole occupant of the great chamber. Konteau could pretty well guess what was going on in the officer's mind. This robed figure was either (a) a true priest of Kronos, or (b) Konteau the fugitive. So let's find out which.

"Ready?" whispered Konteau mentally to the temple computer.

"Ready."

"Here we go. Should be very, very interesting."

The grayjac approached the edge of the dais, stopped, and looked up at Konteau. And even as he did this, the fugitive knew that the officer was seeing something beyond the krono . . . something strange and terrible. So far, so good.

With growing interest Konteau watched the face of the intruder. He knew, from images delivered by his occipital cortex to the unseen computer, that a remarkable holo image was forming on the dais behind him. He wanted to sneak a look, but he didn't dare. He had lines to say, and he would now begin. He spoke quietly and reassuringly to the officer. "Behind me you see a man, a Son of Time. He is impaled with a great spear through his heart, against the trunk of Yggdrasil, the immortal ash tree. This is the tree of Valhalla. Odin himself thrust this spear through the heart of the Son of Time. That is why the blood flows. There have been many Sons of Time, and there will be many more. One heart leaves, but another comes to take his place, so that the blood will flow forever."

Konteau realized now that blood was pumping in unceasing spurts from the heart-wound of the sacrificed man. He fought an urge to turn around and stare at his handiwork, along with the grayjac. But that might break the spell and could get him killed. He continued. "This is done because it is necessary. You would be the first to understand *that*. This sacrifice to Kronos is required so that the race may live."

He heard popping sounds, and he knew that the blood spurts were bursting into flame as they struck the floor. The flames traveled in tiny rivulets across the dais, between his legs (could he feel the heat?) and onto the floor.

"And now that *you* have come, *he* can leave," said Konteau.

He knew that behind him, the sacrificed human holo had grasped the spear shaft with both hands and was pulling it forward, out of his body. It clattered down into the pool of flamelets.

"Odin. Oh, my holy Odin. . . ." breathed the sergeant. "Look at that. . . ."

From the corner of his eye Konteau caught the slow sibilant sweep of great golden wings. Exactly as ordered! He watched the stricken eyes of the officer. "Do you see the face of that man?" he asked calmly.

"Yes." It was both a gasp and a monosyllabic question.

Konteau continued the relentless program. "Whose face has that man, who has now become an angel of Odin?"

"*My* face," moaned the officer.

The wings swung in beautiful languid arcs. The officer watched the holo-creature rise away from the dais and spiral in great leisurely circles about the vault, higher and higher. . . .

They both looked overhead, following the slow sweeping ascent. It was impossible not to look.

Far up in the center of the dome something began to move, and it was producing an eerie scraping and grating sound. Some sort of machinery? The dome ceiling was poorly lit and at first it was difficult to make out any details. Some sort of holo, he surmised, with explicitly realistic audio. The temple computer's own private joke. Certainly, none of this could be real. As the movement continued, glints and sparkles of light from unseen sources began to reflect from the thing making the noise. Teeth? marveled Konteau. Of course, teeth. The temple was capped by the great Maw of Kronos, and it was opening to receive this latest offering.

The winged man disappeared into the giant jaws, which

closed instantly with a clang that reverberated through the building and shook the temple floor. Konteau found himself shuddering in synchronization with the vibrations. For the sound of snapping jaws was not the only sound. Had he heard what he thought he heard? A shriek from overhead, shut off, swallowed up, engulfed by that overriding clangor that was still sounding and sounding and shattering his eardrums?

And what's *that?*

He watched the lorn holographic feather float down, gyrating crazily. It drifted off to one side, into the darkness.

Surely none of this was real! And yet, the sound and sight work were so skillfully presented and blended that he had to wonder if perhaps some small fraction was real. And if, with full knowledge *he* could be thinking this, what must be going through the mind of Sergeant Thor Odinsson? He realized then that he was panting and that the armpits of his gauzy black robe were drenched with sweat. Holy Kronos! He had to regain control. It wasn't over. He still had some very important lines.

He sensed the holo-spear in his hand. Back to the farce-drama! "Thor Odinsson," he said gently, "you have come to renew the god-pledge. It is right, and it is just. Come, Son of Time, walk through the fire. You are holy, and Loki the Fire God will protect you. Take your place against the ash tree, and bare your heart to the spear. You will suffer for but a year. And then your successor, the next Son of Time, will walk through yon door. Your face will change to *his* face, and you will take wing, and fly up and away, into Valhalla, where you will live forever, an angel of Odin. Come!"

The officer made several strange noises, then he whirled and ran. His legs were not well coordinated, and twice he stumbled. And then he was through the archway, and he was gone.

Konteau watched him go, and was thoughtful. How much of me, he mused, is real? How much is just a holo in the mind of some superintellect?

"And now back to you, James Konteau," said the computer voice. "The grayjac was not the one, and you are not

the one. You are a good man, though a bit foolish at times."
The Temple spirit paused, as though to reflect. "That was a
fine program, and I have taken the liberty of storing it for
future use. On the other hand, I have several that are even
more exciting, if you'd care to linger a few moments. How
about the One Hundred Konteaus destroying themselves in
battle royal? Or Konteau in the center of Ylem, the original
fireball? Starts the adrenalin flowing. Not to mention. . . ."

Konteau broke in. "No thanks. Really appreciate it,
though. Is the back exit clear now?"

"The back is clear. In fact, everything is clear. They've all
gone. If you care to, you can walk out the front. If you're
looking for the Park, the entrance is up the street and around
the corner."

"Thank you, friend, and goodbye."

"Farewell, James Konteau. When you see Raymond Ratell, give him my greetings, and tell him to go easy on the
terrapin sauce."

Terrapin sauce . . . the last words of Tages' Haruspex.
These computers must have their own secret society, a cabal
closed to human beings. What in the name of Kronos was
terrapin sauce? Or, for that matter, a terrapin? He'd have to
find a dictionary.

He left without replying.

10

Ratell Park

Laurenz Devlin was the only commoner (apart from his father) that Konteau addressed as 'sir'. Devlin had once been Konteau's crew leader. He had been a good man, and brave. But stupid things can happen to the very best. They had made a landing back in the Permian, down from Kappa, in Texas. The pilot-book had not shown the fault nor the resulting deep chasm. It had caught them all. The rodman had been killed. A tumble-suit will not protect you from a three-hundred-meter fall. Straight down. They left the body there. They thought Devlin had bought it too, but Konteau found him on a ledge, unconscious. The fault began to close up just as Konteau went down for him. The crew hauled Devlin up in good order, but falling rocks hit Konteau in the face and took out an eye. He was three months in plastic surgery. Devlin came out with intermittent lucidity. He quit. They all tried to convince him it wasn't his fault, but nothing worked. Konteau found him this job as gate keeper at Ratell Park.

"Hail, Dev!" Konteau grinned at the older man. "You're looking great." Actually, he thought the ex-leader had aged perceptibly since he had left him four days ago.

As always, the old krono was dressed in a tattered tumble-suit, as though once again ready to make that catastrophic time-jump down from Kappa. In fact, for Devlin the day's most dangerous journey was getting to and from his raffish rooms over the corner food shop. But Konteau did not smile. Every day was Kappa for the aging crew master. Every day he relived the chasm drop that wrecked his mind, his nerve, his body, his career. The park flora, thought Konteau, probably nurtured Devlin's hallucination that he lived in the Permian of two hundred eighty million years ago. In most other respects the older man was fairly normal.

The pale washed-out eyes squinted at the newcomer, then the face grimaced into a half-smile. Konteau relaxed. Devlin would be all right, at least for now. They shook hands.

Devlin said, "Good to see you, James. You're back early?"

"Yes, sir. Special job."

Devlin handed him his tumble-suit and chest pack, and Konteau wriggled into the suit and pulled the pack loosely over one shoulder. He turned casually for a look back toward the street. Nobody there.

Devlin caught the gesture. "Is someone following you?"

"No, I don't think so." Konteau faced the Park again and inhaled deeply. "Ah, this wonderful air! With genuine chlorophyll-generated oxygen! The real thing! You can't get it out in the planets."

Devlin looked puzzled. "It's just plain air."

"Yeah." Konteau wondered whether he should try to explain, but decided not to. He got down to business. "Did you find a crew for me?"

"Sure. No problem. Good experienced surveyor. She brought her own rodman."

"She?"

"Female."

"Oh." No! It couldn't be. And yet that's the way the fates work.

There just weren't that many women surveyors in the Widow. His heart began to skip beats. "Where? . . ."

"Take the path into the trees." The ex-leader paused, a troubled frown took shape on his forehead. "Now, James. . . ."

"Yes, sir?"

"You watch for surface irregularities. The Kappa time-pilot is a real botch."

"Yes, sir, I know."

"There's a terrible drop out there, James. It's not in the pilot. Half a kilometer, straight down the cliff."

Konteau's stomach was turning inside out. He said thickly. "Glad you told me, sir. We'll be careful."

"James?"

"Sir?"

"I'm all busted up." He spoke in a half-whimper. "They're waiting by the statue. Take over. Get them out."

"Don't worry, sir." His eye was wet, and bright with pain. "I'll take care of everything. He was glad to move off, and he felt guilty for it. "We'll leave by the far exit. Be seeing you." (But would he ever see his former leader again? Nice question. According to the Norns his subconscious had been quite specific: through the door, and then, D(Al)eth. Meaning, Death in Delta. With "Al."

He strode off down the flagstone walkway to meet his ex-wife and her current lover.

His pulse-rhythm became more erratic. He could sense the premature ventricular contractions. Oh God. This had to stop. Get his mind off her. Look around. He forced his steps to slow.

The archaic forest began just beyond the gatehouse. Giant ferns towered overhead. He recognized lepidodendrons, some nearly a hundred-and-fifty-feet tall, with their crowns of 'weeping' cone-tipped branches. Hyacinth-leaved bark curled in spirals around their trunks. Helen, ah Helen, revenant. . . . And sharing the sky, the Cordaites fern tree, with long lanceolate leaves on lofty branches. He had seen them many times in surveys in the Devonian and Permian. A few primitive struggling conifers were interspersed among the great Cycadeoid palms, with their six-foot fronds. Enormous club mosses flourished. The path wound along shallow ponds scummed with ancient algae and filled with Calamites, giant scouring rushes. A delicate rankness filled the humid air. Vegetation was growing and dying at a tremendous rate. In the real world, way back there in the Carboniferous, these wonderful green monsters would eventually transmute into coal—black gold—for which nations would (a few hundred million years later) attempt to destroy each other. The names of some of the more striking specimens were stamped on metal rods stuck in the ground. He noted particularly Hornea, an humble little plant, rootless, leafless, from the lower Devonian. He had brought that one in himself. It was, so the paleobotanists told him, the first, or one of the first truly efficient plants that took carbon dioxide from the atmosphere and returned it as oxygen, thereby initiating an oxygen-containing atmosphere and starting a whole new system of evolution of oxygen breathers that led eventually to mammals and man. Hornea and its cousins would lead step-by-step to the truly modern greenery of the Upper Mesozoic, and we would have fruits, nuts, grasses, cereals, and vegetables for some very interesting mammals due shortly on the scene of the Tertiary.

All these flora had been brought here with great care. Each plant had its own Historical Impact Statement, so that nothing would be done in the Past that would change the Present in any way. (But it's all so silly, thought Konteau, because how would anyone know?) He had a recurring ironic fantasy: one day the paleobotanists would bring up a tree, say a ginkgo, from the Cretaceous. Unbeknownst to them the original tree-shrew ancestors of the entire hominid line would be hiding in the branches of that tree. At what point in time would lemurs and gibbons and baboons and chimpanzees and gorillas and human beings vanish? And who would know, or care?

As he walked, he checked his chest pack. His mental checklist carried over thirty variables and constants. Everyone of them had to be exactly right. Theoretically, there had been no changes since he left the pack in Devlin's locker four days ago. But you never know. It was safest to check, starting with the primary caesium clock. 9 192 631 770 periods per second. He punched in the number, memorized long, long ago, along with h, the quantum constant; then pi, e, and the log of 2 to the base 10; all to ten places. And then the fudge factors for leap seconds (plus, minus), then as you really start going back, leap minutes, leap hours, and leap days. Next, the hydrogen standards, the iridium sensors (absolutely essential for leaving the Paleocene and entering the Cretaceous). Then the quartz crystals—the faithful workhorses of the pack. At once the best and worst of the system, for quartz aged with time and with use and with a general contrariness specific to each crystal. Fortunately, he had the best, sawn from magnificent oversized prisms he had personally chopped from a Proterozoic pegmatite ten years before. He had got age/use/drift variations down to one part per billion per month, some sort of record. Synthetic crystals, even grown from natural seeds, were nowhere near that good.

He walked on slowly. The silence was eerie. He had been in Mesozoic forests where the din was ear-splitting. Once a pair of very stupid, very love-hungry duck-bill dinosaurs searching for each other in a nearby swamp had kept him awake all night. But no animals were permitted here in Ratell; no archaeopterices, no insects, nothing.

The unnatural quiet was relieved bit by bit as he approached the statue and the ring of fountains, which were now becoming pleasantly audible.

Ratell Park—one square kilometer of manicured greensward—was practically empty. And with good reason. The Park was reserved for government officials with at least a nine-hundred rating. Even *they* were rationed to a quarter day per month (non-accumulative) which they were generally too busy to use.

He walked on. The great bronze statue of Ratell lay just ahead, in the center of its circle of little fountains.

The marble obelisk that supported the statue once carried a plaque on the entrance side with the names of kron-men lost in service. But the First Secretary (so the story went), wandering here one day, had seen the plaque and ordered it taken down as too depressing. Actually, it hadn't mattered one way or the other. Nobody seemed to care. Somewhere, thought Konteau, was there a place on the other side of life where someone *did* care about kron-men? Interesting. He was a krono. Plural, kronos. You could argue that the god Kronos was simply the collective of kronos, living and dead. By the Four Horsemen, we are the God of Time!

And. . . .

There they were, on the benches, looking up the path, and waiting for him.

He had a sudden sense of shattering disorientation, almost of falling, very like that sheer drop in Kappa, when he had lost an eye, Devlin had been broken, and the rodman had died.

This woman. The mother of his son. Helen ex-Konteau. He still went to sleep dreaming of her. But she had left him, and he could never understand why. And now, through Devlin, he had put out an urgent call for a contract-crew, and she had responded. At least to the extent of meeting him here. She had known it would be he; yet she had come.

They stood, silent. They looked at him, he looked at them. Especially at her.

Kronos, she was beautiful. *Helen, thy beauty. . . .* Get thee behind me, Edgar Poe!

His mind, his treacherous endocrine system, were without pride or integrity. For a brief instant he merely pawed her with his eyes; mentally he fondled her face, arms, body. Not enough. He contemplated rushing to her, ripping her tumble-suit from her white-hot body, covering her mouth, neck, breasts with kisses. He stiffened. This was no good.

She shifted her body as though to pull away from his excoriating eye, but without moving her feet. It was an astonishing maneuver, and he wondered how she did it. The moment passed, and she remained, standing there, twisting a hyacinth curl with her right index finger, in the old familiar way, and looking at him, but not looking at him.

Helen, the navigator-surveyor. She could bring them through a tortured maze of time to drop through a mere fraction of a centimeter onto a Precambrian plateau. And the youth with her: Albert Artoy, the rodman. Konteau knew him only by reputation. In his late twenties, but already with four boro surveys on his record. Good routine work. But this project is definitely not routine. He tried to visualize this man in the face of death. Would Artoy crack under extreme pressure? Think ahead. Say they find Five Eighty-five, and say the three of them are trying to hold it in place until it has recrystallized. They need the power of all three packs. If they fail, nobody would have enough reserve power to get back into the Present. They were tied together like mountain climbers. If Artoy panicked and cut the links and left, Konteau and Helen could die. Unless Helen and Artoy left together. Which of course, she might well do. It all came back to the basic question: if Artoy became sufficiently fearful for his life, would he cut and run? Maybe. But was this an objective appraisal? Could he be fair to Helen's paramour? Perhaps, he thought, I'm cutting him down because I'm jealous. After all this time, am I still jealous? He grunted in indecision. He should tell them to leave, go away, not risk their precious hides. But where to find another crew? There was no time. So be it.

All together they made a neat triangle, a ménage à trois. He thought of the three corners of the Five Eighty-five base triangle, and he almost smiled. The Triangulators. In the field the triangle was the only sensible geometric figure for surveyors. All else is built on it. And likewise the boro-plats. The triangle was the easiest polygon to stabilize. But when you tried to apply the triangle to human minds and human flesh, it collapsed like withered reeds.

They waited as Konteau approached.

She made the stilted introduction. The youth ("Just call me Al") moved to meet him with assurance and grace. Konteau could see how Helen might find him interesting. He shook hands briefly with "Al," then got right into it. "Delta Five Eighty-five dropped a few hours ago. The Vyr admits he didn't install triples. Claims I never recommended them."

"Phil?" Staring, she jerked the question out.

"He's still in Lambda. I checked."

She relaxed and turned half away. "I thought triples were in your report."

"They were. Somebody changed the report."

"Krappokronos!" She looked squarely into his face.

"There's a hearing tomorrow," said Konteau.

"You can testify you recommended triples," said Artoy.

Konteau smiled at the youthful face. So innocent, so trusting. No easy way to explain reality to him. "I doubt that I will be permitted to testify."

The rodman stared at him. "But . . . how can they stop you? It's your right. It's in the regulations."

Konteau sighed. "We can't get into that. The question now is, what to do about Five Eighty-five?"

"Have you run a projection?" asked Helen.

"The Vyr has. His paleographer says the computer puts Five Eighty-five on the subducting Atlantic plate."

"So they're all dead," she said curtly.

Konteau shook his head. "So *maybe* they're all dead. And maybe not." He pulled a pilot guide from an inner fold of his jacket and turned to the map in the inside front cover. "I don't know whether you've seen this. I recommended triple stabilizers because my team found signs of a latent time fracture, near what today would be the western edge of the Chesapeake Bay. About right *there.*" He pointed.

"I'm not sure I believe in time fractures," grumped Artoy.

"Time does funny things," said Konteau patiently. "Two hundred years ago, before Ratell and his equations, we knew very little about time. We didn't know it had most of the attributes of light, of electromagnetic radiation. We didn't know you could reflect, refract, and polarize time." He had a sinking feeling that he was not going to be able to convince them, and that in the end, he'd be walking down that exit path alone. He needed time to organize his thoughts. He looked up at the patinaed statue. Could you persuade them, Raymond Ratell? Ratell at thirty. The sculptor had caught almost exactly the same shifting cunning in face and eyes that one sees in holos of the great man. An odd one, indeed. Today, thought Konteau, your incredible Permissible Deviation would exclude you from all boros, all professions, all academies, all government posts. You're the original wrong-thinker. The inqos would instantly hang, draw, and quarter you. The great Raymond Ratell—vanished in mid-career. And perhaps it's just as well. Killed in a kron accident, some said. Body never found. Traveling out there in time, somewhere, others said. After two hundred years, still alive? Impossible! Not impossible, Ditmars had once explained. There was a thing he had learned to do with his body, total time control. Ratell may be immortal . . . silly thoughts!

Back to earth!

He continued. "There are several ways you could get a time-quake. For example, the universe is presently expanding. This happens because the eleven dimensions of space-time are expanding. But the expansion isn't smooth, continuous, and gradual. It moves in quanta, in jumps and jerks. To use Ratell's term, time stretches, and then it fractures. He explained time-quakes that way. Theoretically there are millions, perhaps billions, of such fractures in the galaxy; indeed, in every galaxy. And by crazy happenstance, Five Eighty-five is—*was*—sitting on just such a fracture. That's not the only theory, of course. As a matter of fact, Five Eighty-five was sitting on the edge of the North American segment of Pangaea, just before Eurasia, South America, and Africa broke away. The split-up might well have sent shock waves back into the Triassic and into Five Eighty-five. Thirdly, the great meteorite of sixty-three million B.P. might have fragmented stretches of local time. We don't really know. However it happened, let's say time cracked. The gate into Five Eighty-five shifts. Not the whole boro, just the gate. The exit up into Delta's present perimeter moves out; not much, say only a few meters and/or years. But now nobody can find the gate. So far as Five Eighty-five is concerned that gate no longer exists. Delta Five Eighty-five is marooned in the Triassic." He thought about other, less pleasant possibilities for time-quake victims. Burial in molten magma, according to the Vyr's paleographer, that very strange Dr. Michaels. Or perhaps Five Eighty-five had been translated back into the middle of a granitic monolith, where they had all died instantly. Or perhaps the terminal site was no longer even on Earth, but was instead a million miles away in space . . . where they still are, diminutive freeze-dried human asteroids in complex orbital minuet around and about Earth, moon, and sun. He was aware of one theory, provable with tensors, flexors, and other exocomputer tools, that lost people were moving backward in the Sea of Time, toward the beginning of the Universe, and that they would eventually move into the Mother Fireball. If so, they would be making *that* journey unaware and quite painlessly, since they would be moving at the speed of light and therefore time does not move for them, and they could not have any sensory experience. A nice way to go.

"So," said Helen. "What do you want from us?"

He looked at her with his crooked smile, and he shrugged. "In Widow history, eighteen crews have encountered fractures—quakes—breaks—whatever. Twelve came back."

They stared at him. Suspicion had crystallized into foreboding certainty.

He said evenly, "I'm going down. I'm going to find the gate to Five Eighty-five and link up the exit again."

Artoy's laugh was short, incredulous. "You're crazier than Devlin."

Konteau would not look at him. In a way, he envied the rodman. Al Artoy still had sense enough to be afraid. You lose that after a time . . . and then you start taking chances without even knowing you take chances.

"James," said the woman firmly, "you should go underground immediately. Run. Hide. We'll help."

"And always be looking over my shoulder? And what about those poor suckers in Five Eighty-five?"

"Not your fault," she said hurriedly. "Feel bad? Guilty? Is that your problem? Take a little loss therapy. I'll lend you a cassette. You'll get over it in a week. Guaranteed."

Cut it short. "I'm going."

"I'm not," she said curtly.

"Me neither," said Artoy. "You're dead, Konteau."

"Yes." He smiled at them both, pulled the pack tight against his chest, and adjusted the straps. He turned and started off down a side path. He didn't bother to look back, but from the sounds he knew the two were following him. Once he thought he heard low curses. He smiled again.

11

The Passage

At the far exit he turned. "The grayjackets are watching all gates, including the Five Eighty-five portal. We'll have to make a few detours."

"That's just great," muttered Artoy.

Helen asked, "What's your final destination?"

"To wherever Five Eighty-five broke contact. We'll head for the original site and start the search from there."

"Needle in a haystack," complained Artoy.

"Worse," agreed Konteau genially.

"We have no way of knowing whether Five Eighty-five's time fracture is still active," said Helen uneasily. "If it's still expanding we'll be caught and swept in."

"That's right," added Artoy. "You can't detect a time fracture until you're in it, and then it's too late. It's worse than quicksand. This is getting sillier and sillier."

Konteau grinned. "I thought you didn't believe in time quakes."

"Well, maybe, sometimes. . . ." The rodman added bitterly, "You're going to get us killed. We're all going to die."

"Everybody dies, sooner or later," said Konteau philosophically. "Meanwhile, though, we'll take this gate down to one of the side tunnels, then a conveyor car over a secret access tunnel to Five Eighty-five. It's not on the Delta general plan, and I don't think it will be under surveillance.

First, though, let's synchronize. I've been away." He asked Helen, "Any pilot changes for the late Triassic, the last four days?"

"One. It's minor. I'll plug it into your pack." She handed him the line. "Instrument Control has disconnected the time check against Pulsar P5R. They say a minuscule variable has been detected, probably caused by passage of the pulsar's radiation through the sine wave path of the sun through the galactic plane."

"Can we switch it to gross-check? I'd hate to lose it altogether."

"Sure."

Kronos! He loved the sound of her voice. "Everybody ready? Off we go!"

The subterranean corridor was poorly lit. They came suddenly on the terminus, closed by a heavy bronze panel. Konteau's heart beat faster. Had he been here before? That door looked oddly familiar. A case of déjà vu? No. He knew now that this was the big door in his dreams. D(Al)eth. But he couldn't stop to think about it. Dreams were just subconscious wishes and fears, not facts, not genuine predictions. And the door of course *would* look familiar, because this was the routine design for close-offs in Delta sub-corridors. He had seen the type before. A neat question, though, who will the dead man be?

Konteau watched as Artoy searched along the wall and found the 'Open' button. He punched it. Nothing happened.

"Damage extends all the way up here," muttered Helen.

"Maybe," said Konteau. "But more likely, the contacts are simply corroded." He found the handcrank in the door itself and tugged at it briefly. Nothing budged. "Stand back." They retreated a dozen meters while he took the explosive from his pack, set the timer, and then rejoined the crew. They turned their backs. The flash came seconds later, then the roiling dust and smell of blue-hot metal. Then silence.

They approached the gaping hole cautiously and shone beams out into the heavy grayness beyond. Still no sound.

Konteau leaned over, extracted his artificial eye in an

expert gesture, and tossed it out into this forbidding unknown. The little globe hovered there, a few meters out, flashing and beeping.

Helen frowned. "That signal will bring the grayjackets."

"Can't help it. We'll have about ten minutes." He ordered the oculus into a standard search pattern, a series of widening circles. Like the dove, thought Konteau, that Noah tossed from the ark, and with the same question. Would the oculus return with some sign of life? Some fragment of Five Eighty-five?

Artoy watched, fascinated. "I've heard about your Mimir. What do you have to do to get one of those?"

"It helps to have an accident that takes out one of your born-eyes," said Konteau dryly. The rodman did not pursue the subject.

They waited.

"Ten minutes," said Konteau. "It hasn't found anything." He called it back to his hand. "Triangle, please."

They took the corners of an imaginary two-meter equilateral triangle.

"Hook on," he said.

They pressed the connector buttons and luminous blue lines, wavering, hazy, sprang up between their chest packs, linking the three together with immensely strong lines of force.

Artoy peered down the corridor behind them. He said nervously, "I think somebody's coming."

"A grayjacket," said Konteau evenly. "Relax, Al. I'm setting the entry at the exact center of Five Eighty-five's period: two twenty-five million, the Triassic."

A beam of blue-white light suddenly shattered the blackness of the corridor. A megavoice boomed out at them: "Freeze! Arrest! Arrest!"

"He's going to shoot," cried Artoy.

"Real unfriendly," agreed Konteau. He set the controls on the oculus the way Ditmars had taught him. All he needed was thirty seconds delay. He aimed the little instrument at the distant infra-red image. The sights locked in. He pulled the little trigger. A blue line formed ahead, then instantly vanished, along with the grayjacket, who had just bounced into the past of thirty seconds ago, which put him way around the corridor corner, out of sight. Konteau tossed Mimi back through the hole in the portal. "Let's go!"

The linkage squeezed tight as they clambered through the gap and out into the silence. As Konteau stepped through, he looked back, just in time to catch that piercing shaft of blue-white light. He wondered whether the grayjac had any memory of shining that search beam thirty seconds ago. He smiled. There was no way to know, and he didn't really care.

Each of them had stepped into space-time on past occasions, and Konteau felt no difference in this jump. But as always, he had this strange sense of falling; and not merely falling: falling upside-down, helplessly, as one falls into the stifling blackness of a nightmare. Worse than weightlessness on an interplanetary. He always had to fight incipient nausea. He wondered what the other two would think if they knew their leader was such a weakling. But they were probably too involved with their own immediate problems to reflect on his.

He folded the star screen out from his chest pack and peered 'down' at it. The counters were dutifully clicking off the precessional intervals, every twenty-five thousand years, as they went back, back, back. . . . He watched as the pole star oscillated between Polaris and Vega, faster, faster. And now just a blur. But still able to get a fair time check from the Big Dipper: Alpha and Eta not part of the local group, and moving swiftly up and away. The millenia whirred. Change automatically to stars with good measurable proper motion: Bernard's, Kapteyn's, Groombridge. Follow positions with hydrogen chronometer. When last calibrated, accurate to plus or minus three seconds per 10^{15} seconds. This is less than two minutes since the birth of the solar system, and every bit of this accuracy is needed. Ammonia was the old standard, superseded by caesium, and now hydrogen, the best of all. But double-check everything. Take two, three fixes. Earth rotation slowing at one millisecond per century. Take a rotation reading.

Seven million B.P., and the first 'bump'. "Got it?" he called.

"Check," the two voices came in.

Actually, Number Seven was barely detectable, and it wasn't even buoyed. Nemesis, the sun's dark companion star, in its eternal twenty-eight million year orbiting cycle, had passed through the Oort Comet Cloud eight million years ago and had dislodged a few small comets. Oort lay as a comet-speckled shell well outside the solar system, at some ten thousand A.U. from the sun, and the dark star's passage through the cloud on this last occasion had been unusually inconsequential, geologically speaking. The cometary impacts one million years later had created very little havoc on Terra, and the dust thrown up had pretty well settled out of the atmosphere in a couple of centuries, a mere blink in the eye of geologic time. Indeed, Kron-parties were always glad to meet Number Seven. It meant they had made a proper entry through the time gate. Just now Nemesis was at aphelion, 1.4 light years away, its greatest distance from the sun. It would not make its next foray through the Oort for another fifteen million years. For the present, except for the idiocies of its dominant life form, the home planet was relatively safe.

Some of Nemesis's prior passages had not been so temperate. Number Thirty-five was buoyed. Here there had been several impacts. Nearly thirty-six million years ago Nemesis had broken out a number of big ones from the Oort, and they had not arrived simultaneously. Their impacts were strung out over intervals of hundreds of millenia. Konteau had listened to their cosmic cannonade many times. His awe increased with each exposure.

"Thirty-five," he said laconically.

"Thirty-five," answered Helen.

They waited.

"Al?" demanded Konteau.

"Well . . . yeah, check for thirty-five. But. . . ."

"All stop!" barked Konteau. "But *what?*"

They hung there in time, oscillating in and out of the late

centuries of thirty-five million BP. "What's wrong?" demanded Konteau.

"My pack's gone haywire," said Artoy plaintively. "I'm getting a premature reading."

"Of what?"

"Sixty-three."

"Impossible," declared Helen. "We're only at thirty-five."

"I know. Therefore I've got a serious malfunction." He added anxiously, "I'm going back."

"Al," said Konteau, "are you wearing a platinum ring?" He heard Helen's muted gasp.

"Ring? Yes, I have a ring, so what?"

"Throw it away with all your might! *Fast! Now!*" Konteau's voice was a rapid metallic guttural.

"No! That ring cost seventy-five jeffs. You're crazy."

Helen's urgent whisper broke in. "Listen, Al. Jewelry platinum carries ten percent iridium. In normal wear, the ring loses some of its weight every year. Those trace amounts affect the iridium sensors in your pack. Your pack thinks it has reached the iridium layer of the Cretaceous, at sixty-three B.P. Al, throw it away!"

"Damn it all, Helen, you could have told me. You know I've never been below the Miocene before. All right, it's gone, and I hope everybody's happy." The snarl was icy, savage.

Konteau just shook his head. Every piece of metal on a kron-man and in his equipment was deliberately required to be Ir-free. The manuals spelled it out. The schools taught it. And then every once in a while you would find somebody like Al Artoy, who had neither read nor listened. So now, added to his search for Five Eighty-five was the additional burden of not letting Al get them all killed. Artoy would never receive his Hourglasses. If he stayed in the Corps much longer he was going to do something extremely stupid and get himself killed, and probably others with him. Maybe not on this project. Maybe not the next. But eventually.

Well, he had been warned, so he couldn't really complain. His subconscious—the Norns (bless them/her)—had spelled out the danger. Delta equals Daleth equals Al plus Deth.

He said tonelessly, "Al, now do you check thirty-five?"

"Check," said the rodman sullenly.

"Helen?"

"Ready."

"We go," said Konteau. "Watch it, now, everybody. Next buoy, Sixty-three."

And now they had to start being very, very careful. At sixty-four million B.P. Nemesis teased a ten-kilometer iridium-loaded monster out of the Oort. And then what happened? Nothing, at least right away. (Time flies, but in a very unhurried fashion.) Monstro bade farewell to his brother comets and began his long and leisurely journey into the vacuum. The rest was inevitable. One million years later—at sixty-three million B.P.—he crashed into Terra (some say into what is now the South Pacific). He made a crater two hundred kilometers wide and he filled and chilled the skies with iridium-laced dust for a hundred thousand years and utterly altered the ecology of the entire planet. He ended the Mesozoic and the reign of the dinosaurs. Human ancestors survived because they could burrow and because they could eat almost anything (including the rotting reptilian corpses) and because they were no longer hunted.

Ratell's mythic R-culture aside, human beings owed their existence to Monstro. But for the big comet, thought Konteau, the scalies would be the dominant life form today, living in great cities, and probably raising us mammals for food.

A matter to ponder, but not too long, because now they are entering the outskirts of Sixty-three.

Your chest pack knows, and it watches for iridium in the top layer of Cretaceous clay, which it estimates by neutron activation analysis. In that clay layer Ir is typically six parts per billion, as against one-tenth part per billion in the general crust. You can pick up the warning with great precision if you are totally Ir-free and if your n.a.s. is perfectly calibrated. Otherwise, you have a fine chance of being caught in the shock and killed.

Ah, there's the warning buoy! Everything's working. His chest pack brought in the three repeating beeps loud and clear. Translation: *"Danger! Stand clear!"*

"Got it?" he called.

"Yes . . . yes," returned the muffled replies.

He couldn't see them, but at least the other two were still there. In fact he couldn't see anything. It was like driving down a boro side-street at midnight with no lights. Or groping down a dark stairwell. You do it by feel, training, and knowledge: slowly, carefully.

And so on through Sixty-three, and now they can speed up just a little.

Time passed, and the remaining buoys went by predictably, one by one. There would be eight altogether. Some signaled mere bumps, some announced cosmic catastrophe. At the next to last, at one hundred eighty million B.P., it was customary to slow to a crawl and proceed once more with extreme caution. And this they did.

There would be one more warp buoy, Number Two Twenty, in the late Triassic, at two hundred twenty million B.P., just before the Five Eighty-five site, where another great guest from Oort fell, threw up its deadly sunshade of dust, and killed one-half of the then existing genera of land and marine creatures. Indeed, Konteau believed this cosmic catastrophe might well have been responsible for shattering the orderly flow of time at the Five Eighty-five site.

"Two Twenty coming up!" he called. "Ease away!"

They gave the time-zone a wide berth; even so, Konteau could feel his spine trembling in the residual turbulence.

Only triples could have protected Five Eighty-five against this monster. Had he truly recommended triples?

YES!

"Soundings!" he called. "Helen?"

"Two twenty-one and counting."

"Al?"

"Two twenty-one point five."

"Slow now. All switch to vernier. Helen?"

"Two twenty and point five one."

"Al?"

No answer. He called again. "Artoy, do you read? You should be getting a visible."

The reply was a nervous croak. "Yes . . . well . . . I. . . ."

Konteau smiled grimly. The rodman had never been in this deep before; he had touchdown fever. He would firm up after t.d. He switched to his ex-wife. "Helen? Can you hold, and give us a reading?"

"Point five one six. Holding at point five one six."

"We're within twenty-four hours of foundation. That's close enough. Al, Helen, set for point five one six five. Got it?"

"Yes." She was first.

"Al?"

"Yeah . . . got it."

"Slow drop," said Konteau.

Any second, now. . . .

Ah!

The ground was solidifying under his feet. Squishy, but in its own way, firm. At least the landfall was fair enough. No drop into jagged rocks or into a boiling thermal spring, either of which would have been a crazy challenge to even the best tumble-suit.

And where was Mimi? He'd half-expected to find his oculus waiting for him here.

Pitta-pitta-pitta. . . .

Rain!

He looked up. No enclosing dome. They stood on bare ground, empty and desolate, stretching out to horizons edged with green. Overhead was nothing but mist, fitful rain, and one bright patch where the sun was trying to break through. No matter. He knew they were where they should be. The time-fall was precise and accurate. Always exhilarating to find you have hit it on the button. Because, sometimes, you don't. Good navigation, Helen. But she would be suspicious if he told her.

The other two stood nearby, at corners of the line-linked triangle.

"We're here," said Konteau. "Disconnect."

Artoy was looking around in dazed wonder. "Five Eighty-five is gone! The whole damn boro! Five thousand people!"

"Quite so," said Konteau, almost absently. "I'm standing exactly where Stabilizer Number One should be. Used to be, I should say. You can see the bench mark. No way to tell whether it was a single, double, or triple. Anyhow, take this fix as one corner of the Five Eighty-five triangle. Helen, will you and Al please locate the other two apices. We need to know whether the other two stabilizers are missing too."

The woman pulled the portable transit from her chest pack and motioned to the youth, who energized his anti-grav and started floating off to their left, over thin puddles. As she continued sighting, Al turned back from time to time. Konteau watched him through a telescope. Finally, at her motion, Artoy stopped and dropped to the ground.

"It's here!" the youth phoned back. "Stabilizer Number Two. And it's merely a single!"

Ah, thought Konteau. And who's surprised? So it was singles all around. His original survey report had been gutted. Slaughter by deliberate editorial revision. No mere sloppy routine murder; this was premeditated and refined, with an elegant if macabre finishing touch. Murder down an exquisitely designed Kronos-Maw. And by whom? What one man had the power to do this thing? Paul, the Pious. Was the Vyr the killer? It made no sense. "Ask Al to get a fix," he told the woman somberly. "Make sure the unit hasn't shifted."

She motioned. Artoy pulled out his telescoping rod, and after a few preliminary jabs, held it steady. A yellow light began to flash at the top of the rod.

On target, thought Konteau. She was damn good.

Helen waved the rodman on, and within another ten minutes they had found Stabilizer Number Three, exactly where the designers had planted it five years ago. And of course, also just a single. As though to congratulate them, the sun came out, and suddenly they had shadows, stark and black. Helen and Artoy pulled down sunshades.

"Shall we come in?" Helen asked.

"Wait just a bit. Let's check around."

The question now was, where was Stabilizer Number One?

He suspected *that* was where he would find Mimi. With his good eye he peered out over the landscape. He phoned over: "They cleared out a one-kilometer dead-zone in a peripheral strip, but beyond, you can see the forest." He studied the distant green band carefully. "Conifers, ginkgoes, some palms. Fern undergrowth, with mid-size scouring rushes. Nothing deciduous, so far as I can tell. Definitely early Triassic, Two hundred and twenty million B.P."

He pondered the epoch. In the Triassic Terra seemed to pause and take a breather. What had Terra (and/or Ratell— or whoever) accomplished so far? It depended on who was writing the judgment. Man hadn't appeared. In fact, not a single mammal was on the scene as yet. Nor even the mammal-like reptiles that started the order of mammals. Those creatures awaited the Jurassic, which lay twenty or thirty million years into the future. And yet, Terra had already spent nearly 4.4 billion years as a bio-functional planet, over ninety-five percent of its life. What does it have to show for this prodigal expenditure of time? Konteau answered himself. It has produced lands, and seas, and air, and marvelous creatures to dwell in these domains. It has set the stage for later, more competent genera, including *Homo,* who, almost as soon as he arises from all fours, will begin to totally befoul that beautiful stage. Perhaps the Malthusians had a point.

Helen and Artoy pulled out glasses and peered at the horizon.

"So it's the Triassic, so what?" complained Artoy. "We don't really know any more than before we came in."

"That's not the point," said Konteau. "We're here, exactly *here,* at this time and place, because that's where we programmed the packs to put us. But Mimi *isn't* here, and that is the point. She's not here because she's sitting on Five Eighty-five, or on the Number One Stabilizer, or maybe both."

"You don't know that," said Helen.

"You're right, I don't know," said Konteau slowly. "But I do believe she has found *something.* Shh!" He held up a finger to his lips.

Through binoculars they watched him curiously. He

heard Helen phone a whisper to Artoy: "He's got a sensory coming in. I think the tracer is trying to make contact."

"It's pretty faint," said Konteau.

"You're not sure, then?" said Artoy. His elation began to fade.

"Well, I'm sure it's Mimi, but I'm not sure *when* she is. It's almost as though she's calling back from the, let's see, the nineteenth century? As best as I can make out, she is saying, find the stabilizer, hook it into position, then the whole boro will come together again, at the right time and place. Five Eighty-five and its five thousand people will be *here* again, and all channels to Delta Central will be open again."

"She said that?" asked Artoy. "It, I mean?"

"Yeah. Well, I think so."

"James," said the woman calmly, "I say this with the greatest respect. You're insane."

"Doubtless. Nevertheless, I will ask that we try to put it together just as Mimi recommends."

"Whatever that is." She sighed.

Artoy's voice twisted anxiously. "So now what, Konteau? Where . . . when . . . is the tracer?"

"I'd say, somewhere nearby, near what used to be early Baltimore. But not in our present—not in the Triassic."

"How do you know?" Helen demanded.

"I'm getting an interference pattern, like intersecting ripples from two stones tossed in the water. This means two different time sources. When I cancel out ripples from our own time, the other time source remains. I get a fair reading of signal strength and direction, and Mimi confirms the input. Twenty-three kilometers southwest of ancient Baltimore."

"That's only *where,*" objected Artoy. "*When* is she?"

"I'm getting it. Let me tune the date a bit finer . . . about 1825 to 1830. Still tuning. Ah, I makc it 1830. August 1830."

"Baltimore?" asked Artoy. "Was that A.D. or B.C.?"

"Kronos!" groaned the woman. She phoned over to Konteau. "So what are you going to do?"

"I'm moving out to find Mimi and the stabilizer. Don't

worry. I'll be back before you know it. You'll sense me as I return. When you do, will both of you turn on your packs. *My* pack may be drained, or nearly so, and you may need super strength to close up with me."

"But that may drain us—Helen and me," protested Artoy. "We might not have enough power to get back home to Delta Central."

"Quite so," replied Konteau equably. "On the other hand, if we use it all up in fully restoring Five Eighty-five, we can all take the next shuttle out to Central."

"How long should we, ah, wait?" asked the rodman hesitantly.

"You mean, how long before you can reasonably infer I'm dead?" Konteau chuckled dryly. "Give me two hours. That'll be"—he looked at his watch—"until fifteen hundred. After that, get the hell out."

"But. . . ." started Artoy.

Helen hissed. "Shut up!"

Konteau looked around where he had been standing in the mud. Funny, he was leaving tracks just like some Mesozoic animal. Perhaps someday an enterprising young scholar would saw out a section of this lithified imprinted mud and do a thoroughly researched paper, "Konteau's Last Steps."

He watched the man and woman and muddy plain vanish.

And he was falling, and gasping, and crying out.

Small wonder, for he dropped a good two or three meters, into a little group of people, and onto something clattering along metal strips. His tumble helmet was ripped away, and his head hit something. Someone cursed. A good English curse. That at least, is some comfort, he thought as he lost consciousness.

12

※

The Train

He groaned, opened his eyes, and looked up. In the dim light several faces were looking down at him. He noted that he was lying on a makeshift cot in some sort of primitive shed. He could see rough-hewn boards overhead. A small window with glass panes admitted a shaft of daylight inside. An obviously inefficient portable device provided interior illumination: a glass-cased oil lamp, he surmised.

"How do you feel?" asked one of the faces.

He had trouble with the accent, but the concern seemed genuine, and he was grateful. He touched the side of his head. "I've felt better. What happened?"

"You took a nasty knock on the noggin. I'm Dr. Wright. Just let me have a look at your eyes. Ah, eye, I should say. Well, that's out. Can't compare size of the irises, now, can I? Any nausea?"

"No. Help me up, please."

"I wouldn't recommend. . . ."

"Doctor, it's a life-and-death emergency." He sat up. Bones all there. There would be bruises. He ran a hand over his chest pack. It seemed intact. How long had he been unconscious? He pulled back his sleeve and looked at his watch. Someone gasped. They had noted the radiant dial. Fourteen thirty. He had been out an hour and a half. Thirty minutes to go. Get moving Konteau. But first, get the facts. "What happened?" he repeated.

The reply was grim. "What happened? You set steam back one hundred years, that's what happened!"

"Huh?" He looked up at the speaker, a bespectacled man with a garland of gray whiskers running under his chin from ear to ear. "Who're you?"

"My name, sir, is Peter Cooper."

"And mine is James Konteau. What about 'steam'? Kindly explain, Mr. Cooper."

"You want the whole gruesome story?"

"If you please."

"All right then. You shall have it. With my own money I built a new locomotive, the Tom Thumb. The men of the Baltimore and Ohio Railroad Company were skeptical. For several years now they've been running horse cars between Baltimore and Ellicott's Mills, thirteen miles up the Patapsco Valley, changing horses at Relay, at one and a half hours the trip, and four trips a day. Gentlemen, I said to them, Tom Thumb can make the trip in half the time. On straight stretches, my little locomotive can develop eighteen miles per hour. Show us, they said. Race a horse train on parallel rails. So we did, and I was winning, until you decided to jump aboard, just a few miles out, as we were coming in to Baltimore. You knocked the fan belt from the blower. We couldn't replace the belt properly. The blower wouldn't work, and without a blower we couldn't get adequate draft in the boiler. Steam pressure dropped, and we lost power. The horse—their best gray mare—came up from behind." He concluded sadly, "We lost. Steam locomotion lost. A great pity, Mr. Konteau."

"I'm truly sorry, Mr. Cooper. I'll try to make amends. But before we deal with your problem, I need some input for mine."

"Input?"

"Information."

"Oh? Such as?"

This was going to shock Mr. Peter Cooper, but there was

no good way to avoid it. Somewhere, not many kilometers away, Mimi was hovering over the Number One Stabilizer. She had (he hoped) been broadcasting a continuing fix into the receptors in his chest pack. He would soon know. He punched the mapmaker keys, and a sheet of paper began to roll out from a slot in the pack. All around, in the semi-light, jaws began to drop. He tore the paper off and spoke to Cooper. "There's a very heavy black box here"—he pointed at a ridge between two rivers—"Do you recognize the location?"

"Of course. That's Ellicott's Mills—between the Patapsco and the Tiber. And from the looks, right smack dab in the middle of the new station the B and O is building."

A stroke of luck! And now he had to think. He could go anti-gravving along the tracks, up to this Ellicott's Mills. Thirteen miles—twenty-one kilometers. Too slow. At ten kilometers an hour it would take over two hours. And when he got there alone in the middle of nowhere, would he have trouble with the locals? Suppose the militia was standing guard over the stabilizer? He could kill them all, of course. No he couldn't. It was unthinkable. He said quickly. "I have to get to Ellicott's Mills, fast. How do I do it?"

"First horse car's at seven this evening," said Peter Cooper.

Konteau looked at his watch again. Five minutes lost since he had regained consciousness. Suppose he was late, would Helen and Artoy wait a bit? Why should they? They would be entitled to assume he was dead. It would be very dangerous for them to wait. Another timequake could shake the Five Eighty-five site at any moment. No, they wouldn't wait, and he wouldn't blame them.

He said: "We're taking your steam locomotive back to Ellicott's Mills."

"Can't do that, Mr. Konteau," said one of the men respectfully. "The blower's out. The belt won't stay on the pulley. Remember?"

"Who're you?"

"Horatio Allen, sir, engineer."

"And this chap?"

A fourth man stepped forward. He said proudly, "Ross Winans, Mr. Cooper's assistant, sir, and general factotum."

Konteau noted a fifth man in the dim background, standing beside Dr. Wright, a youth, perhaps just over twenty. The stranger was about five feet eight inches tall, with an expansive brow that sheltered alert, deepset eyes. And somehow he looked familiar. But the youth remained silent, and Konteau decided to ignore him.

The time-traveler stepped to the shed door and looked out. The Tom Thumb sat on a turntable a few yards away. He walked over to it and inspected the machine critically. The group pressed behind him. He traced the pipes with his eye. "You used musket barrels for steam lines? Very clever!"

"They work fine," acknowledged Cooper modestly. "And they're cheap."

"Any more in the shop?"

"Several hogsheads full."

He sensed possibilities. What did he know about steam locomotives? Not much. Just what he had picked up while watching the little steam model in the game room, back at Xanadu. Clickety clack clickety clack. He grinned. It was all coming back. He knew how to do this. He would now violate the prime directive and introduce a bit of modern technology into the Past. "Musket barrels. We'll need a couple more."

"Winans, . . ." began Cooper.

But the assistant was already off to the shed. He returned quickly with an armful of musket barrels.

"What are you about to do?" asked Cooper uneasily.

"We'll pipe exhaust steam from the pistons directly back into the boiler. Should give a fine draft. You won't need your blower."

"But we'll have to find the blacksmith, fire up the forge. It'll take several hours."

"No it won't." Konteau pulled the cables from his chest pack and quickly electrowelded a steel musket tube to the piston exhaust. This he heated and bent into a curve. Not long enough. He welded another to the end, and so back to the boiler grate No time to toot for leaks. A few wouldn't matter anyhow.

They watched him in awe.

Cooper recovered first. "We've got water, but we'll need some cordwood."

"No. I can furnish the thermal."

"The what? Oh, the heat."

"Gentlemen," said Konteau. "Can we turn it around, now?"

All five heaved at the turntable. It rotated a hundred eighty degrees, and the little locomotive now faced outward.

"You're not from these parts, are you?" puffed Cooper.

"No." Konteau did not elaborate. It would just make things worse. He fussed with his chest pack a moment, inducing a good electro-thermal in the firebox. There, it was glowing, and he could hear the water beginning to burble and boil.

From behind them the quiet young man with the expansive brow pressed forward to watch. This time Konteau stole a good hard look at him from the corner of his eye. There was indeed something disconcertingly familiar about the youth. Have we met? wondered Konteau. Impossible. And yet. . . . His heart began to pound. He thought of the holes back at Xanadu. He had seen . . . he had listened. *He knew this man!* How to handle this? He addressed the group casually but quickly. "This is going to be quite a trip. We need a writer, someone who can prepare a report for the weekly papers. I don't suppose? . . ."

The young man stepped forward. "Sir, my name is Edgar Poe, of Richmond. I have literary aspirations, though as yet I haven't published much. I'm presently en route to West Point—just stopping over here in Baltimore. I'd like very much to go along and report the trip to the papers."

"Of course, Mr. Poe. Pleased to have you with us." Konteau shook his hand gravely. He tried to recall. A couple of years before, the youth had published one very thin book, *Tamerlane and Other Poems.* No one had taken any notice. But that was all. *To Helen* lay ahead, along with everything else: nineteen years of misery, exultation, devastation. He could not, would not, tell the poet anything of this. He stepped back, looked at his watch, and said without expression: "Time check, please."

Somewhere a bell began to chime. He counted. "Three in the afternoon?" Fifteen hundred. The deadline. Helen and Artoy had his permission, even his orders, to leave.

Cooper pulled out a gold watch and peered at it through his steel-rimmed spectacles. "More or less. The Baptists like to jump the gun a bit."

"We're ready," said Konteau. "All aboard, everyone. Stand where you can hold on to something. Grab a rail, there, Mr. Poe. Let's go, Mr. Allen."

The engineer took the throttle bar and slowly pulled it back. The machine shuddered. The piston rods moved out slowly, and the wheels began to turn. The cylinders exhausted dead steam into the boiler with a puff. They watched a cloud of vapor blast out of the smoke stack, gilded by mid-afternoon sunlight.

Tom Thumb began to clatter along the rail ribbons, slowly, then faster and faster. It became quite noisy. And we're off, thought Konteau. "What's your top speed?" he shouted to Cooper.

"Designed for eighteen miles an hour on straight track. A lot less on curves. We follow the river and it winds around a lot."

"Steel rails?"

"Some steel, some iron."

Fair enough. He could hold the curves by magnetizing the wheels. "Faster!" he shouted to Allen. "Give it all you've got!"

"No, no!" cried the engineer. "She'll derail . . . the curves!"

"No she won't!"

"But the boiler'll blow! We'll all be killed."

"It won't blow. Your plates are strong. She can take twice the pressure!" He seized the throttle from Allen. "Grab the railings!"

Horatio Allen looked to Peter Cooper for help, but found none. Quite the contrary. The great entrepreneur, drunk with the incredible motion of his hurtling iron demon, was actually helping the stranger with the throttle. The engineer then looked at Edgar Poe, who looked back at him, grimly philosophical, as though one more disaster in his frazzled life was hardly relevant. Allen moaned and muttered something about caring for his widow.

They passed blurred farms; fuzzy half-seen shapes Konteau took to be trees; long patches of gray granite outcrops. Cliffs and escarpments echoed back the madness of their passage.

"The town of Relay coming up!" Cooper cried to the wind.

A cluster of rail-side buildings hove into sight and was instantly gone.

Relay? thought the time-man. Yes, that's where the horse-trains changed teams.

The upward slope gradually increased. They were approaching the fall line, the geologic rim that divides piedmont plateau from tidewater flatlands.

"Mr. Cooper!" shouted Konteau.

"Sir!"

"We'll be there soon, not much time to talk. Could I make a few suggestions?" Just a few more violations of the Prime Directive!

"Yes!" cried Cooper.

They clattered around a narrow curve. Konteau looked back to make sure they hadn't lost anyone. Allen stared at him white-faced, beseeching. The time-visitor ignored him and turned his attention back to the designer. He lifted his voice. "The boiler, it's vertical. That's wrong. Build it horizontal, that'll lower the center of gravity, make for better stability on curves, and cut wind resistance."

"Good points," bawled Cooper. "What else?"

"Superheat your steam to reduce condensate losses in your cylinder."

"And?"

"Build a cab to keep Mr. Allen out of the weather, especially in winter."

"Go on."

"Add a separate car, right behind the engine, to carry wood, or better yet, coal."

"Fine, fine. Oh oh! We hit something."

"A cow!" cried Allen.

"Bolt a big wedge onto the front of the engine," said Konteau loudly. "It'll shove stock aside, maybe without hurting them."

"Slow down!" called Cooper. "Coming into town!"

Konteau eased the throttle back. "And they don't know we're coming?"

"No."

"You could add on a steam line for a whistle. A certain number of blasts could mean, here we come."

"Excellent, Mr. Konteau. But slowly, now, slowly. Dear me, quite a crowd at the station."

"Good!"

"Why good?"

"That means my stabilizer is still there. They're gathered around it."

The locomotive clanked to a halt. "Time check," said Konteau.

"Eight minutes after three?" Cooper shook his watch, then held it to his ear. "Oh dear, I'm afraid it's damaged."

"Your watch is quite correct. It *is* eight minutes after three, local time."

"But . . . thirteen miles in eight minutes. Nearly a hundred miles an hour!" Cooper was appalled. "That's quite impossible, Mr. Konteau!"

"Let's just call it non-reproducible," said Konteau dryly.

And now he was going to break the rules again. He faced his fellow voyagers and singled out the youth. "Mr. Edgar Allan Poe?"

"Sir? How did you know my middle name?"

"No time, Mr. Poe. One question. I have to know. *Who was Helen?*"

The poet-to-be stared at the intruder. "Who are *you?*"

"I can't explain. . . . I don't think you'd understand. Please answer. Quickly please, who was Helen?"

"But I haven't yet published *To Helen*. There is no way you could know."

"Please, Mr. Poe. It means a great deal to me."

The group watched this in astonishment. Allen looked at Cooper, who shrugged, as though to say, they are both mad.

"If you know that much," said Edgar Allan Poe, "perhaps you have the right to ask. Helen was Jane Stith Stanard—the mother of a boyhood chum, back in Richmond."

"She had hyacinth curls?"

"Yes, and strange, naiad-like airs. . . ."

"A classic profile?"

The word-imager gaped at him. "You knew her, Mr. Konteau?"

"What happened to her? To Mrs. Stanard?"

"She died insane, four years ago. She was very young." Poe spoke with infinite sadness. "She lies buried in Shockoe Cemetery."

The message echoed and re-echoed within Konteau's consciousness. Insane . . . insane. . . . A hot iron was cauterizing a part of his Helen-wound. *His* Helen. Like a blaze snuffed by a blast of dynamite, had his gnawing anguish been finally subsumed in the catastrophic mind of this latent derelict? Was it over? Was he healed? Did he *want* to be healed?

He said heavily, "Thank you, Edgar. Go with God." He turned away. "And now I have to go see about my black box."

Trailed by his companions, he walked across the tracks and paused at the doorway of the unfinished train station. A crowd had gathered all around the outside of the low granite walls.

The black-cased stabilizer sat in the approximate center of the dirt floor. Mimi hovered a meter overhead, blinking ominously.

A tall man with musket, silver badge, and a tremendous handlebar mustache barred the newcomers at the door. He picked out Konteau immediately. He drawled, "This your property, mister?"

13

The Sheriff

"Yes," Konteau said warily, "it belongs to me."

And now began the eeriest conversation of his life.

"Son," said the sheriff, not unkindly. "Exactly how late are you?"

Konteau was stunned. "About ten minutes."

The other said quietly, "Will they wait for you?"

There was something implicitly marvelous in the question.

Konteau stammered, "I don't really know. I ordered them not to."

"So you may be in real trouble, huh?"

"Yes." The monosyllable wobbled.

"A local stretch?"

"Stretch?" he repeated stupidly.

"You know, time fracture, quake, fissure. Your team can't hang around too long, or they'll lose their coordinates. They won't be able to get back. You know."

Konteau looked at this man, then one by one back around at the faces of Peter Cooper, Edgar Poe, the train crew, the gathering populace of Ellicott's Mills. A great glaring fact had just hit him in the head and had knocked him semi-senseless. As soon as he came to. . . .

"You can lose an entire village in a time-flaw," said the sheriff calmly. "Boro, I mean. I believe that's what they call them now. And I'll betcha that's what happened. You lost a whole damn boro. You went back looking for it. And now you've found the stabilizer, and it's just a mono, and you should have used doubles, maybe even triples."

"I recommended triples. But they installed monos anyway."

"*Oho!*" Dirty work there, somewhere. Anyhow, now you're going to put it all back together . . . set up a stable triangle? *If* your other two people are still out there, waiting like good little elves?" It was a question.

Konteau stared at the weathered face . . . magnificent drooping mustache . . . glinting black eyes . . . hawk nose. I have seen you before! Many times. In pictures, holos, even statuary. He tried to match up this face with the benign visage on the statue in Ratell Park. There was indeed a resemblance.

Was *this* the man who wrote the profound *Philosophies of Time,* who conceived the Nine Equations (so intricate, yet so devastatingly simple), and designed the machines to use them? Did that mustache camouflage the face of that elusive genius, long ago reported dead, who established the first boro, far back in the Permian, thereby changing forever the face of civilization?

It was not possible. This man would have to be nearly three hundred years old. And yet . . . and yet. . . . How about old Zeke Ditmars's theory that Ratell had truly conquered time, and that Ratell had discovered how not to age. But what would the great man be doing *here,* in this nineteenth-century American backwater? He had read something. . . . There was another side to the historic Raymond Ratell, an exuberant side, a side that denounced the lock-step order his own work had wrought. The rumors were right. Ratell the free spirit. Ratell the river-boat gambler, Ratell the outlaw, Ratell the gourmet, Ratell the gun-totin' sheriff.

If you *are.* . . .

His good eye searched, and found, the great oversized golden cufflinks, enameled with a black hourglass insigne, and bordered with gem clusters that danced in the sunlight.

"*Are* you? . . ." began Konteau.

"Now, sonny, let's not get carried away. Let's go over

behind this wall, where we can talk private-like. 'Scuse us, folks, got to interrogate the prisoner.'' He guided the traveler into an alcove, first flushing out two boys and a pig. "We'll finish this little building next year," he said matter-of-factly. "And it'll be the first railway station in the whole U.S. of A. All granite. It's going to last for about four hundred years. Came down when they razed the whole area to start Delta."

"Mr. Ratell, . . ."

The sheriff held up a hand. "I can see you're in a big hurry. Well, so am I. But we got time enough for a little talk. You know why I came back here? To this place, at this time?"

"No. Why?"

"It's the food, boy. You took me away from a most sumptuous dinner, over there at Ellicott's Hotel." With a jerk of his head he indicated a handsome granite-block building across the street. "They take everything right out of the Bay. Not your twenty-sixth-century Chesapeake. I mean the nineteenth-century Bay, before pollution killed it. You know, you can go out in a skipjack and lean over with a frying pan, and the rockfish fight to jump in. You bring 'em in, along with a few buckets of crabs and oysters. Ah, my boy, broiled rockfish with butter and chopped parsley, garnished with scraped horseradish. Along with deviled crab—you mix the meat with milk, mustard, green pepper (hold the cayenne), butter, bread crumbs. Carefully brown in a hot oven. All of that's after the fried oysters and clam fritters."

"Mr. Ratell, . . ."

"Don't interrupt, son. We started, of course, with oyster soup. For that, you mix in onions, cloves, some slices of ham, then some flour, cream, egg yolks. . . ." He sighed, and his great mustache drooped. "Lucky I at least had the soup. 'Fraid the rest of it's stone-cold by now. You know what you did, boy? When you come right down to it, I mean?" He fixed Konteau with a cold eye.

"What?" Konteau said uneasily.

"You traded off a measly boro—a few thousand faceless morons—against a genuine eighteen-thirty Maryland dinner, complete with terrapin sauce in Madeira. That's what you did."

"Well . . ." (*Terrapin?* Where had he heard that before?) Konteau was flustered. His crimes were accumulating faster than he could deal with them. Another reason to cut it short! "But how did you get *here?* I thought the entire millennium since 1492 was proscribed."

"Oh, that's true, all right. But I have an outlaw license."

And just what did he mean by *that?* Konteau thought it best not to inquire. He took a deep breath. "Mr. Ratell, it's been wonderful, meeting you, but if I'm going to have any chance at all, I've got to leave immediately."

"You're right, so let me say it quickly. There's a way to make up your lost time, most of it, anyway."

Konteau's eyes widened. "You're sure?"

"Fairly sure. Nothing's one hundred percent sure in this life, boy. Actually, though, you don't have a lot of choice."

"And I can get the stabilizer out?"

"That too. Just one little bitty problem."

"Which is?"

"If it don't work, you're adrift in Time. You'll never get to *any*where. You'll probably go crazy from the loneliness, if you don't starve to death first."

"As you said, Mr. Ratell, I don't have a lot of choice. What do I do?"

"Several things. Recover your tracer, throw a tractor line on yon stabilizer, and punch in a special double combo, for retro-time and space co-ords. Like so. And now one small piece of advice."

"Sir?"

"Son, you were bushwhacked, back there in twenty-six hundred whatever. Have you ever heard the myth about Kronos eating his children?"

"Well, sure."

"Some of the Vyrs—especially the Malthusians—have sort of expanded on the idea. With them it's not exactly a myth. Stay away from the Vyrs and their inqos!"

What could he say? This was simple confirmation of his worst suspicions, but he had no time to discuss it even with this great man. "I get the message," he said simply.

"Now, son, a few final comments. You've got this idealism

streak—a rotten flaw in an otherwise well integrated personality. No matter. I can overlook it. Nobody's perfect. So just let me conclude with a recommendation. It won't cure your personality defects, but it may do you some good in another direction. You want to hear it?"

"Of course."

"All right, this is it. If you ever find yourself in a distant land, with a gorgeous but undecided lady, try melting her heart with a Chesapeake Bay dinner. Results guaranteed. Don't forget!"

"No, I won't. But. . . ."

"And if you ever decide to leave the Widow, come back here. What with the railroad coming in, and crime a-doublin' and triplin', I'm going to need a good deputy."

"Thanks. I'll remember that. And now let me say goodbye to my new friends."

"Yeah, sure."

Konteau popped Mimi back into his eyesocket, threw a line to the stabilizer, then waved farewell to the puzzled, wide-eyed Peter Cooper, Edgar Poe, Horatio Allen, and to the assembled gaping Ellicott's Millers. And then he pulled his pack switch.

14

D(Al)eth

He came through grayness as solid as dark felt, dragging the stabilizer behind him. Were they still there? They had every right not to be. The waiting time had long passed. They might well assume that he was hurt, lost, dead . . . that he would never return. She had left him once before. So why not now? Hold on . . . he was picking up something. A great flash of relief swept over him. He sensed, rather than saw, the man and the woman at the far corners of the Five Eighty-five plat.

Ah, Helen with the hyacinth hair. Namesake of a nineteenth-century madwoman. You'll never believe whom I met. Nor will I ever tell you. So now, I ask myself, is the wound sterilized, stitched, and cauterized, or is it worse than ever, like trying to smother a fire with pentane?

He called on the phone: "I'm back! Pull me in! Link up! Hurry!"

The woman's tensor locked in to his pack instantly.

But no action from the rodman.

"Artoy!" he cried. "Get your link over here! Hurry! I'm loose! I'm slipping!"

No answer. "Helen," he called, "what's wrong with Al?" Damn! He should never have brought the youth. Couldn't take the stress. But how could he have stopped her from bringing him? It was loverboy or nothing.

"Al!" cried Helen. "Don't move! We're hitting your pack with our own side-links. James?"

"Got it." His line snaked out, hooked into Artoy's pack. Good show! If Artoy wouldn't send lines out to them, they'd throw their own lines over to him.

They listened to the rodman scream. "No! I'm cutting out! We're all going to die! Don't link with me! Stay away!"

"Helen!" shouted Konteau. "Make him stay put! Otherwise I'll have to override him! We need his pack. We've got to have the power. Steady, Al . . . don't move. Just a few more minutes. See? Feel *that?* The stabilizer is pulsing nicely. The walls are lining up. Look. . . ."

"No!" howled Artoy. "I'm going!"

The indicators on his side-link to the youth told Konteau that the rodman was trying to dissolve the connection. He had to override this man, or the boro would be lost forever, and overriding a panicked man was risky. Always, at the instant of domination, the sympathetic nervous system is affected. The neural waves and the override waves impinge on each other. They garble, they foul, they can even cancel each other totally. Take the worst case. If the person is in panic, his vitals—heart, respiration, neurals—may simply stop and never restart. Artoy, of course, had also known all this, and it had compounded his panic. It could kill the youth. Her lover, thought Konteau. He knew what she would say. You did it out of jealous spite. His finger was on the override button, but it was paralyzed. He could not will it to move. They were all going to die. He wasn't sure he really cared any more. If only the rodman would stop screaming. . . .

Artoy's wail was suddenly chopped off.

There was a moment of dead silence.

"Al?" called Konteau nervously. No answer. "Helen? Anybody, come in!"

"Override," said the woman dully. "I used full power."

She had known, but she had taken the risk, and she had killed her lover. Why? Certainly not for *him*, Konteau. The ghost of that past love never rose up to haunt her. Why then?

For five thousand lives? No. For their son? No. Philip was nowhere around and was irrelevant to this operation. A sense of duty? No. He didn't know why she had done it, and he doubted that he ever would. Perhaps even she didn't know. In the final analysis, perhaps there wasn't any reason.

It was pointless to ask *her*. In the first place, in her mysterious oblique way, she would not perceive 'why?' as asking her to explain why she had killed Artoy. That would not be the right question for her. 'Why?' to her would mean, why had she left him, Konteau? And he could predict that, in her quixotically direct way, she would answer, 'Because.'

So why *had* she left him? What did she *really* want? He was finally beginning to understand. She wanted to be free. From her husband, her lover, her son, her daily routine. So now, here was freedom, delivered up on a platter of death.

He stood there, numb. Oh hell, Helen. . . . I'm sorry . . . sorry.

And now he sensed the booming clangs as the time walls came together. Everything was working. Just give things a moment to solidify completely.

And it was over. At least this part of the problem. And he suspected that most of the several thousand souls who dwelt in this dungeon of time had never even known there had been a problem.

He found himself in the middle of a little park, with walks, benches, swings, slides, gym bars, and several dozen very noisy children. Across the way was the outer wall that kept Triassic biota out of Five Eighty-five. The wall was lined with mimosa trees. Even from this distance he thought he could smell them.

He recognized a white durostone building not far down the street: the Teknikron Institute, perhaps the Widow's best trade school. Apprentices came here only by invitation. Last summer he had taught the course that used the new descent simulator, a lightless gray-fogged anechoic chamber that was supposed to help the time-students resist panic. He sighed. If Artoy had attended that seminar he might be alive today.

Five thousand lives saved, one life lost. So how did he feel? Not heroic. No, he didn't feel heroic at all. He felt miserable.

How would his Widow-comrades remember him? They would probably always wonder if he had really recommended triples. Would they think he fouled it up, and when he tried to straighten it out, he got a crewman killed? He took a deep breath. If he lived through this . . . if the Council ever really got interested in a Martian colony . . . maybe he could change his name, disappear into one of the survey teams. He'd be happy to go along in a minor capacity . . . apprentice rodman, something like that. But there would probably never be a Martian team . . . not in the foreseeable future, anyhow. So forget it.

He called the woman surveyor on the phone. "Helen, I'll handle the body. Did you know his parents?"

She didn't answer.

He continued. "There will have to be certain arrangements." He added almost as an afterthought: "You go on. I'll meet you at the main gate. The grayjackets will probably be waiting there." With a little luck, he might be arrested before he had to face her again.

As he walked through the streets of Delta Five Eighty-five to claim the dead youth, he envisioned a scene with D, sitting cowled and faceless at the chess table.

K: She was sublime. Why did she do it? I do not understand her.

D: Naturally. The comprehension of women is not given to you. Nor would it become you.

✳

15

Prison

The grayjackets kept him in a cell in Delta Prison overnight. He assumed Helen was detained similarly, somewhere in the same building. He began the night by dozing fitfully, and thinking. I should be afraid, shaking and sweating . . . if not for myself, at least for her. Poor Helen. He had brought this on her. His guilt was not bearable. Because of him she had pushed a button and a man had died. Not to mention that for hours her life had been at risk, and indeed it still was.

And what (he thought) do I feel? A massive sorrow that deadens my mind, body, spirit. He thought of his son. He had set a horrible example for Philip by being in the Black Widow. Devlin's Law: "Any man worth a damn in the Widow won't stay. He'll apply that intelligence to getting out." Not very flattering!

Sometimes he felt that life (or Kronos, or himself) was doing a transcendental number on him: like pi, it went on forever and kept getting more and more refined, but never really settled down to anything definite. Some mysterious asymptotic fate awaited him out there. And he was sure he wasn't going to like it.

Sometimes he thought he grasped the entire time flow, from the Big Bang right through the three novas in sequence that made the stuff from which the sun and planets had formed. But formed to what end? Was there truly some magnificent purpose behind it all? Or was the whole scheme just an awkward accident, terminating (so far) in man? Just thinking about it made it worse. His vision of Time but deepened the Great Mystery.

He was suddenly alerted. The floor was . . . tingling? He could feel it in the soles of his feet. No, not a message from some lost boro. He knew what it was. A ship was landing at nearby Interport, and the tarmac was trembling. In fact, he guessed it was the twenty-one hundred express from Xanadu. The ship would change crews, refuel, take on cargo and passengers, and take off again in half an hour, headed back to Xanadu. Ah, Xanadu. Why had he ever left that distant sanctuary?

Helen . . . Helen . . . Helen. . . .

He exhaled slowly and closed his eyes.

As he drifted off, he found himself once more at the chess table with the cowled figure.

K: Our last session, D. Let's wind up the game.

D: You seem to be in a hurry.

K: Why drag it out? You've had a winning position for the last ten moves. Why don't you go in for the kill?

D: You know why.

K: Because you'd have to show your face?

D: . . . .

K: D for Death. Remember? The Norns told me all about you.

D: Perhaps D is for Demmie. Or maybe for Deimos, the moon of Xanadu.

K: Don't hand me that. D is for D(Al)eth. That man is dead . . . dead . . . dead.

D: One died, or five thousand. Which was it to be? She did it so you wouldn't have to. She took one hell of a risk. They could kill her for this.

K: I don't want to listen to that. I'm tired. All I wanted . . . all I ever wanted . . . was peace. With Helen and Philip. And now I've killed her, and I'll never see him again.

D: So Mephistopheles was right. It all comes to nothing.
K: No. There's got to be a meaning. And you have to have
a face.

He slept.

In the morning the grayjackets came again, and he and
Helen were taken together to the hearing room. He looked
at the woman with his good eye. (They had confiscated
Mimi. He didn't even have a patch to wear over the empty
socket.) He could see that Delta prison had left its mark on
her but had not been able to destroy completely that marvelous grace and beauty. She was semi-groomed. Eddie Poe
might not have approved the hair, though.

She looked at him; in her eyes there was no anger, no
accusation, just a simple grave regard. But he could not meet
those eyes. He turned away. She hides her feelings well, he
thought. Actually, she probably detests me. Because of me,
a man is dead and she's in jail.

"Where are you taking us?" he asked the two-striper jac.

The non-com looked at him wearily. "Shut up."

"Fine. That explains everything."

The leader motioned, then turned and led them down the
dungeon corridor. They were flanked and followed by more
jacs. Are we really so dangerous? thought the kron-man.

And then up racing elevators, and finally through other
corridors and into the ornate vaguely-lit chamber.

A diminutive black-robed man sat behind a big table on
a dais against the far wall. Konteau recognized first the
forehead curl, then the cruel smile on the face, then the
looming disaster. The magistrate was the Vyr's First Secretary. All in the family. If it weren't for Helen, this farce
would be almost funny. Behind the little man a couple of
inscriptions were inlaid in the wall. Konteau squinted with
his good eye as he read:

Kronos is God and Malthus is his Prophet.

Under that,

I have scant faith in the capacity of the human race to regulate its numbers by the exercise of prudence and restraint.

Thomas Robert Malthus (1766–1834)

Konteau suppressed a shiver. But what had he expected? The Vyr had been educated in a Malthusian Monastery.

A couple of recorders and clerks sat at adjacent tables. Other men and women sat in benches at the far left. Konteau recognized several important Deltas: the Chief Engineer, the Prime Surveyor, the professor of paleobotany, and the Vyr's transvestite paleographer. They were all going to testify—against him.

He gritted his teeth.

The little man behind the big table smiled. Once, back on a trip into the Mesozoic, Konteau had encountered a megalosaurus, and the great reptile had smiled down at him in just this way. He remembered the teeth, like Roman short-swords. He had barely got away. He wished he were back there now.

The First Secretary nodded to the guards, and the jacs shoved the prisoners down onto the front benches. "This is a preliminary hearing," said the Secretary. "At this time our purpose is simply to decide whether formal charges shall be brought." (The recorders scribbled busily.)

The speaker continued briskly. "In accord with the traditions of a benign jurisprudence, I now ask the prisoners, as a duo or singly, whether they wish to confess their crimes here in open inquisition, thereby inviting clemency, and also saving much valuable Delta time, manpower, and money." He glared sternly at Konteau, then at Helen. "No? Then we proceed. . . ."

"Now wait just a minute!" Konteau sprang to his feet. "What's the charge? You haven't stated. . . ."

The Secretary banged his gavel. "Silence! Sit down! I will have order, or I will have you both put in audio-cells."

The kron-man sank down on the bench, muttering under his breath.

"We have here," said the official, "a report from Delta Engineer to the effect that Delta Boro Five Eighty-five did in fact, on July twenty-five of this year, disappear for twelve hours, more or less. The Engineer further reports that Five Eighty-five lies in a time-fracture zone, and that the disappearance occurred when a time fracture struck the boro, throwing out the Number One Stabilizer. The report further states that at least double stabilizers should have been installed as part of the original equipment, and that had this been done the boro could have withstood the fracture." The Secretary laid down his notes and peered across the table toward Konteau. "Mr. Konteau, do you disagree with anything I have so far stated?"

There was something unreal about this. Early yesterday morning, at four hundred hours, in his bed on Xanadu, he had awakened from that nightmare. Only a day? It seemed ages ago. So here he was again, with another nightmare. Back to square one. He had come full cycle.

He became aware that his guard was punching him. His head jerked up. What had they asked him? Damn, this was no way to save Helen's life! Ah, it was coming back. The question was, did he disagree with the Secretary's statement. He replied: "I certainly disagree with the implication that my original survey didn't report that Five Eighty-five lay in a dangerous fracture zone. And let the record show that I recommended triples, and somebody deleted the recommendation and nearly killed five thousand people."

"*Aha!*" The interrogator peered back at him craftily. "Who did this, Mr. Konteau? Whom do you suspect?"

The kron-man shrugged. "It's not so much a question of who *actually* did it. The big question is, who *ordered* it done? Who had the final say? Who benefited, and how?"

The magistrate's voice now became very low, almost gentle, but it held an ominous edge. "Mr. Konteau, do you contend that one or more persons in high office are responsible for the lack of triple stabilizers? Answer yes or no!"

Konteau sighed and thought a moment. They were going

to try to destroy him one way or the other. Perhaps he should consider himself lucky that he was permitted to answer this very basic question. He said, "Yes."

"I see." The First Secretary's frontal curl trembled slightly. Then a smile took shape between his rouged cheeks. In a frozen, lacquered way, he looked almost happy. "Well then, this august inquisition regards your answer as a full confession, for yourself and for this woman, your fellow conspirator. We can therefore dispense with the formalities of charges and trial. Sentencing is automatic. I sentence you both to death. You and the female criminal will be returned to your respective cells to await execution. May Kronos and Malthus have mercy on your souls. Guards!" He banged the gavel, and the grayjackets seized their chains and dragged and pushed the two of them out of the chamber.

Half an hour later Konteau was pacing in his cell; pacing and thinking. I've got to get Helen and get out of here. But how? *How?* Start with Mimi. I'll. . . .

Someone was coming. He sat down quickly on the stool in the corner of his cell and looked up. The guards were unlocking the great metal door. Execution so soon? No, something else. Something altogether different. He realized that as soon as his visitor entered, preceded by four guards with weapons pointing at Konteau's chest.

The prisoner peered at the newcomer with his good eye, but the cell was dark, the guards kept their lights on him, and it was hard to see the man's face. Even so, there was something familiar about him. The man was tall, regal in his gilt-fringed, faintly luminescent robes. An aristocrat, certainly.

Yes. . . .

The Vyr.

Courtesy now required that Konteau rise and bow deeply. But he didn't feel courteous. He simply sat there, looking up noncommittally.

"Oaf," muttered the great man. His nose wrinkled in disgust. From the folds of his cloak he brought forth a bottle of scent, sprayed a little in the desolate air, then made a slight gesture toward the guards. Two of them left and soon returned with a portable throne and dais, and the ruler of Delta shifted his robes, sniffed, and took his seat. And now came whispered instructions to the guards. To Konteau's surprise, they left, closing the cell door behind them. Konteau could hear them just outside. What was to stop the condemned man from leaping up and strangling his guest? As he pondered this possibility, the Vyr answered the question: a weapon glinted in his right hand, which rested in the folds of his robe.

And now Konteau felt again that growing tingle in his feet. He looked up quizzically at his visitor. "The noon express to Xanadu?"

The Vyr coughed. "Exactly so."

"And it takes off again in an hour?"

"Right again, Konteau." He smiled agreeably. "In fact, you and the lady are booked on it. You have the best private compartment on the ship."

Interesting, but sinister, since he could realistically assume that neither he nor Helen would be on the flight. "Where *is* my wife?"

"Next door, my dear chap."

So near, yet so far.

"I gather the booking is more form than substance," said Konteau.

"True. Makes it simpler to explain things to the Corps, in case they come looking for you." The Vyr coughed again. "But arranging your theoretical exit isn't the problem. Actually, I came here to discuss something else."

There was a long silence. Finally the Vyr said, "Aren't you interested in why I am here?"

"Must you kill the woman too? She's completely innocent. You know that, don't you?"

The great man showed his irritation. "The woman is irrelevant to this discussion. We have other plans for her. Now listen to me. I'm trying to do you a favor. Some men die without knowing why. You, at least, will know why."

The prisoner essayed a sitting shrug. It didn't come off too well.

"Before you die, Konteau, it is important to me that you understand the enormity of your crime. The time is short, but even now, it is not too late for you to repent."

"And not die?"

"We'll come to that."

"How about Helen?"

"I told you—irrelevant."

Konteau hesitated. Any deal would have to include Helen. "Say on," he said quietly.

"Yes. Now, there are two basic social philosophies abroad in the world today. Unhappily, these two philosophies are in direct conflict. One is absolutely right, absolutely rational, absolutely sensible. The other is absolutely sick, absolutely irrational, absolutely wrong. Do you know what these two concepts are, Konteau?"

"I've heard about them. One says, control population by making the death rate equal to the birth rate. The other says find more and more room for more and more people."

"Well spoken, Konteau, although I have grave doubts that you know which doctrine is correct and which is error."

So now he knew . . . but he wanted this bizarre intellect to tell him . . . in so many words. "Tell me."

"Konteau, you must have some inkling, some hint, that this conflict of concepts has spread into the highest circles of religion and state; that indeed, religion—as represented by the Vyrs, and especially by the Malthusians—has united around one idea and the state—as represented by the Council—around the other. This confrontation of ideas has been brought on, as I'm sure you know, by the current lack of phenomena that once kept our population within acceptable limits. I refer, of course, to the Four Horsemen: Death, War, Pestilence, and Famine. In the distant historical past, these measures served us well. But no longer. The world has been at peace for three hundred years, and during that time we've fed all our people and very few have died of disease. Lacking these historical controls, both sides look to other means for solving the population problem." He paused and peered over at the kron-man. "You recently filed a feasibility report on a Martian unit. Right?"

Konteau frowned, then nodded. Face it, the Vyrs had the best spy network in the solar system. Maybe even Demmie. . . . No, he just couldn't believe she was an inqo agent.

The peer continued. "You—and the Council—would find space in the Martian Proterozoic for an overflow of five million people? And that would be just a start?"

"That's the general idea."

"Perhaps you are not really to blame for your errors, Konteau. After a time, the mind of a kron-man becomes altered. It's the stress of passing through the lines of time, backwards, forwards. . . . The cortex is deranged in subtle ways, particularly in the mind's ability to function syllogistically." He shook his head in genuine regret. "Can't you see how wrong you are? Think about it! Let's say you fill up Mars; after that, where will you go? It has to stop sometime, somewhere. Let it be here, and now."

Something was coming to him. Fragmented puzzle pieces were coming together. At this moment, frozen in time, Konteau finally understood everything. He gulped. The horror was beyond imagining. *"You."* The word came out as a metallic gurgle. "You planned it from the very beginning. You had the architect design the Five Eighty-five entrance gates to look like the maw of Kronos. You grabbed my survey report on Five Eighty-five. You had the compiler delete my recommendations for triple stabilizers. You knew . . . you deliberately planned the murder of those five thousand innocents." He wanted to explain to this creature the outrage he felt . . . but there just weren't any words for it. Especially since the Vyr just sat there on his jeweled portable dais, smiling as though basking in sincere and well-deserved admiration.

"Quite so, quite so," agreed the other. "At least that was the intent. And what a magnificent sacrifice it would have been to the great Kronos! An astounding precedent, you know. And a sure way to handle future overflows." He smiled in thoughtful appreciation. "The Greeks had it as a myth: Kronos ate his children as fast as Rhea bore them: Zeus, Hestia, Demeter, Hera, Hades, Poseidon. Other ancient civilizations had it as a reality. The Philistines had their tophets, great hollow bronze statues of Moloch, where they burned children alive. The Moabites after the siege of Nebo sacrificed seven thousand captives to their god Kemoth. The Persians also used human sacrifice. If one human is good, a dozen are better, and a hundred better still. The Aztecs were among the very best: thousands of human offerings in a ceremony that lasted for days. Hearts cut out, heads chopped." He surveyed the prisoner critically. "Nothing I've said has made the slightest impression on you, has it?"

"Oh, not so, Excellency. You have indeed made an impression. And you have made several things very clear."

"Not a total loss, then?"

"No. But a couple of things still puzzle me."

"Yes?"

"Why didn't you have me killed immediately?"

"Easily answered. As you may have conjectured back in the chancellory, we needed a scapegoat to parade before the public. We had to have a live Konteau for the trial."

"You were going to give the public one version, and the Conclave quite another."

"That's it exactly, Konteau. You see, I have to operate on two political levels: one with my Vyr peers and the coming Conclave, and the other before my five million faithful, innocent, unsuspecting subjects. I need two levels of truth, each diametrically opposed to the other. My lay public sees me rooting out and destroying the evildoer—you, Konteau, whose negligence killed five thousand people. The Vyr Conclave sees a spectacular sacrifice to the God Kronos, and the next Overlord." The Vyr rubbed his chin and studied the ceiling over Konteau's head. "These were not our only concerns in our decision not to kill you immediately. For example, we feared that your prompt execution might have been construed by the Council and certain other narrow-minded lay intellects as a belief on my part that Five Eighty-five was still salvageable. And of course, we never dreamed you could retrieve the boro. That was an extraordinary achievement, Konteau." He paused and heaved a long sorrowful sigh. "And yet it is very sad. In rescuing Five Eighty-five you defeated a project that would not only have solved a great social problem, but would also have assured my election as Overlord. With my election, it would then be only a question of time before a beneficent theocracy would rule the solar system. Now we'll have to try something else."

You're breaking my heart, thought Konteau. He said, "But how could you be so sure the stabilizers would fail just before the old Overlord died?"

"We were not absolutely certain, of course. Michaels gave us a probability, plus or minus a month. It worked out pretty well."

"But suppose the boro vanished while the Overlord was still alive?"

"He would have died soon after." The unblinking serpent eyes stared back at Konteau.

"I rather fouled it up," said the man of time.

"You did indeed. But that's not the worst of it."

"It gets worse?" He was genuinely surprised.

"You have gravely offended the inquisitors and me personally, Konteau. But we are magnanimous, and can accept your death as a full apology. Your offense to the God is however a different matter." He leaned forward and his eyes bored into Konteau's one good orb. The aristocrat's mouth twisted into a half-snarl. "You still do not repent?"

"For saving five thousand souls?"

"No word-games, Konteau! The Defender of the Faith is not here to play games."

"But just exactly what did I do that requires repentance?"

The accusation tumbled around him like falling rocks. *"You stole from the God."*

16

Breakout

"I *what?*" cried Konteau.

The Vyr's reply evoked images of distant thunder. "You stole! There's no other word for it. You struck from the god's very mouth a bountiful sacrifice. *My* sacrifice. For a theft so sacrilegious you must pay. Not with death. Mere death is nothing to Kronos. No, after you die you will go to Hell, where you must endure eternal pain."

Konteau shook his head in bewilderment. "But Kronos is just a *symbol.* You're talking as though there really is a god Kronos, a thing of intellect, with the power to order destinies."

"And so there is!" The Vyr was shouting. "Kronos is Time and Time is Kronos. And what is Time? Time is Light, but more than Light. Time partakes of, and unifies all dimensions. Time is the Great Universal Father and Mother. Did Time exist before the Big Bang? Of course it did! And that's *all* there was, and all that needed to be, to produce all that followed. For Time is indeed ALL: Space, energy, matter. Time was, and is, and ever shall be. Time is eternal. So what is Time? Time is the great god Kronos! May he flow forever!"

"So what happened to Jehovah, and Jesus, and Allah, and Brahma? . . ." asked Konteau.

"Nothing at all. They remain as they have always existed, aspects of Kronos, the one true god."

"You really believe that, don't you?" marveled Konteau.

"Of course. And you, too, can believe. You *must,* if you are to die painlessly. And you *can* believe. Tell yourself, Kronos *is.* Repeat it, again, and again, and again. Do this, and in your mind, he will exist. The necessary dendritic neural changes will automatically occur in your cerebral cortex. Belief becomes permanent and irradicable. And when you believe, you can understand. From faith, comprehension will flow. And who knows, perhaps Kronos will forgive your theft. Perhaps you will not burn forever in Hell."

One thing was sure: the longer this lunatic talked, the longer he, Konteau, would stay alive.

He said respectfully, "Milord talks as though he has actually seen the god."

"Of course."

"And the god came to you personally and ordered that you destroy Five Eighty-five?"

"This is most perceptive, Konteau. How did you know?"

"Under the circumstances, milord, a most logical deduction. Please tell me more. Perhaps it will aid my comprehension."

The Vyr rested an elbow on his throne arm and gathered his thoughts. "I can give you the substance of our first contact."

"That would be most edifying."

The elliptical eyes peered into the past, and the voice became soft. "Many years ago, on the night before my coronation, the god came to me in a vision. Paul, he said, I will make you great. I, Kronos, will exalt you above all other Vyrs. You shall rule the Solar System, and Beyond."—Konteau watched the man's eyes roll up until only the whites showed.—" 'Great Kronos, God of Gods,' I replied, 'I am nothing, an insect, not even yet a Vyr. How can I enter so great a destiny?' 'Plan now, my son,' he said. 'Offer to me a sacrifice. A boro.' 'A boro, my lord Kronos?' I said. 'A boro. Render up to me five thousand souls, and win my love, and the awe, respect, and admiration of your fellow Vyrs. They will make you Overlord, and then you can destroy the Council, and you alone will rule.' "

Reality slowly reclaimed the peer. He fixed his eyes once more on Konteau. "And so, with the help of the god, for a full generation I have held this miserable colony together by vision and brute strength. I acknowledged my debt by delivering up one full boro: Five Eighty-five. Indeed, the god and I planned this from the beginning. I knew Five Eighty-five lay in a time fracture, and even before you returned with your original report, even before you recommended triples, the god and I had already designed the exit mouth. Already, we had ordered mono stabilizers. In the simple, ordinary, inevitable march of events these facts would have sufficed to make me Overlord."

This creature was talking to him in an alien language; indeed, the Vyr was from another world. The abyss between them was unbridgeable. It was as though the Vyr stood on the opposite cliff shore of the great Martian Valles Marineris, seventy kilometers away, shouting unintelligible imprecations at him. And why, thought Konteau, does he bother to explain all this? Why doesn't he simply kill me here and now and forget the whole silly business? Does he feel he must do and/or say something to placate this nonexistent god? Except, of course, to *him*, the god is real. To him, Kronos *is*. Maybe that's the answer to my continuing, if brief, existence. This madman has to get it all properly explained, to himself, and to his god, before he pulls my switch.

He could see that the Vyr was absolutely sincere, that the man's convictions were total, without room for the slightest discomforting doubts. Whereas he, Konteau, was never totally certain of anything, was always ready to listen to opposing viewpoints. The Vyr knew he was right. That obsidian exterior wasn't just a veneered facade: it was monolithic, solid stone all the way through. For one brief flashing instant—a silhouette in sheet lightning—he was able to see himself by the eyes of the Vyr: to the Vyr, he, Konteau, was irrational, perplexing, an enigma utterly perverse and unreasonable. It was unsettling. Suppose, just suppose, thought Konteau, the *Vyr* was right? His reaction to the possibility was a prolonged shiver.

But he quickly recovered.

No.

NO.

He fought an urge to shrink away. The Vyr's convictions were so strong they might be contagious! On the other hand his visitor's arguments sounded a great deal like Devlin's harangue on how to accept the continuing risk of death. You have to arrange your mind, Devlin had said.

He watched the man's mouth, and half-expected it to begin foaming. He suppressed an insane giggle. If he started laughing, he'd never stop. He got his larynx under semi-control. And just now he had to be very serious. He had to think of Helen. "You mentioned an arrangement, whereby I don't die."

"Did I?"

"What's the deal?"

"Oh, that. Simple, Konteau. Come over to us, and we forgive everything."

"Come over? Then what?"

"Fight the Council, of course. You'll be our first Kronman. A Glasser with clusters. Quite a prize. Come over, and live!"

"And Helen?"

"Forget the woman, Konteau. Can't you understand? She's irrelevant."

Helen, irrelevant?

They must have something extremely unpleasant in mind for her.

"No deal," he said calmly. "So go ahead, kill me."

The Vyr was genuinely astonished. "You choose to die painfully, with certain Hell to follow, when you could live, and lead a happy productive life at court?"

Konteau looked up at him contemplatively. "You know, Paul, you saved a lot of money when you installed monos instead of triples. Just about enough to buy those black jade earrings for Michaels?" He met the Vyr's glare placidly.

As if making a categorical rebuttal, the peer called out a name over his shoulder: "Tages!"

The Haruspex adept sidled into the cell, holding his hands

under his scarlet-striped robe. He nodded diffidently to his master, then looked over at Konteau and smiled. It was a happy smile.

The kron-man stood frozen, like an ice statue. The presence of this man was telling him something, something extremely unpleasant, something his mind refused to let him think about. Yet, when he spoke, he noted with a measure of satisfaction that his voice was strong, well-modulated. "Greetings, O reader of entrails."

Tages bowed slightly.

"If I am a firm believer in Kronos," continued Konteau, "my guts are more likely to give an accurate prediction in the Haruspex?"

Another bow.

"Presumably in favor of our noble Vyr?"

"Of course," rumbled Paul the Pious. "Not that there could be any real doubt. But I do believe, Konteau, you may have misunderstood Tages' presence here."

There was something jarring in the statement.

What? . . . He was afraid to ask, afraid to verify his sudden sickening suspicion. "What do you mean?" he whispered.

The question seemed to amuse the Vyr. "Tages claims, other things being equal, a time-traveled female is better for divination than a male." He nodded to the man in the striped cloak. "Chief Augur, would you kindly enlighten Mr. Konteau? Just the basics."

"The intestines will be cut out while she still lives," said the diviner in honey-smooth tones.

Konteau's heart went cold with fear. His ancient facial wounds were suddenly laced with excruciating pain.

"And without anesthesia, I think you mentioned?" said the Vyr.

"Yes, sire."

Konteau turned back into the corner and retched. Kronos! He had read of would-be assassins of royalty in ancient Europe, where the criminal was hanged, drawn, and quartered. Shortly after hanging, the still living body was cut down; then "drawn"—which is to say, his belly cut open, his intestines drawn out and thrown in his face; and then the body was mercifully hacked into four quarters and spaced around the city walls.

He turned back. "Don't do this to her," he said huskily. "I'll do anything you want. Take me. I'll be your man. I promise. . . ."

They ignored him.

"Tages?" said the nobleman.

"Sir?"

"The Conclave opens in one hour. Return here with guards in thirty minutes. Bind him well. I want him to watch as you . . . prepare her."

"Of course, milord!"

Konteau put his head down between his knees. He had to stop this nausea. He had to find Mimi. That Xanadu-Express, just beyond the walls. How to rescue Helen and get on it? He had minutes to beat this. Otherwise they were both dead.

Mimi. He thought back. He had been dashing for the express, there on Xanadu, and Ditmars had been shouting something after him, something to do with Mimi. Use time to polarize matter, and then pass through. 'Polar-X.'

Of course! It was all coming together.

First, though, get these sadistic loonies out of here.

He addressed the Vyr. "You know, Pablo, if you cut a hole in that throne and put a bucket underneath, it'd make a fine indoor privy. Now, it just happens I have a bucket. . . ."

"Oh!" The Vyr glared in near shock at the blasphemer. "You are hopeless! Guards!" He swept out with a contemptuous flounce of his robes. Tages was close behind, followed by the guards, who carried the dais and throne.

Konteau got up, stretched, and waited until all footsteps died away.

Back to Ditmars. "Polarize time, spray matter . . . experimental . . . use only in life-and-death. . . ."

Mimi.

His precious oculus was probably sitting on a dusty shelf behind locked wire-meshed doors in some off-corridor property room, perhaps occupied by a lone grayjacket clerk, snoring, with his scuffed boots propped up on a battered wooden desk.

He flung the thought out: "Mimi?"

The response was immediate. She was not far away, perhaps a couple of hundred meters.

"Did they lock you in?"

He caught an affirmative radiant.

"Knock on the door. Throw in a few scratches."

In a moment, he sensed that whatever door held her was opening slowly. "Careful now, Mimi. He's going to shoot at anything that moves. Zip out, just past his nose."

Movement, very fast. "Good show. He thought you were a bat. Now come on down and around. You'll find some stairs and corridors, but no more doors."

He had hardly finished when something bronze and brilliant flickered through the bars of his cell and began to spin around his head like a lapsed halo. It finally bleeped to a stop in front of his nose.

Konteau grinned. "And I'm glad to see you, too, Mimi. Welcome home." He took the oculus between thumb and forefinger and inserted it into the empty orbit. "Now let's get to work. Not much time. They'll trace you here. First, Mimi, I want you to dip into your data bank and retrieve Ditmar's instructions, something he called 'Polar X.' Ho! Hold it, there . . . start again."

His mind listened.

Matter is mostly empty space. Only about one trillionth of the volume of an atom is occupied by protons, neutrons, electrons. The rest is simply a great void. You can polarize this matter, and you can polarize the atoms of your own body, and things in contact with your body, and then you can pass through. It's like polarized light passing through a calcite prism. The vibrations have to be parallel, of course. Your oculus can line it up for you. Extremely close-packed material, such as crystals of covalent, cubic habit, may cause problems. You have about 3 times 10 to the 28th atoms in your body, and 15 billion brain cells. For proper passage,

Mimir has to be given complete control of all of that. She'll make all those atoms oscillate in the same precise harmonics as you go through. It's all in the control of *time.* Remember! Step 1, fire Mimir at the objective. Step 2, turn yourself over to Mimir and *move!* If you linger, you'll solidify before you get through.

And die, thought Konteau. He thought of reports of early survey crews, when men had materialized in crystal granite, half in, half out. Kronos, what a mess. He looked at the bars of his cell. In his fantasy he could see bars piercing lungs, heart, and skull, holding him triply impaled. He smiled grimly. The grayjackets would never be able to figure it out.

He thought back. "Crystals of covalent cubic habit?" What did Ditmars mean by *that?* Just how serious. . . .

He heard running footsteps, shouts, harbingers of doom! Kreeping Kronos! It was too late to pass through the door bars and out into the corridor. He couldn't get into Helen's cell that way. They would see him.

There was another way, even more direct.

He popped the oculus out, sprayed the atoms of the cell wall, then quickly reinserted it in his empty eye socket. Then, hoping Mimi had taken over and had full control, he hurled himself at the wall.

He was through, and in the adjoining cell. He had knocked the inmate to the floor. "Helen?" he cried. Gasping and cursing, she began wobbling up on hands and knees.

"Helen? It's me!"

She stared at him in utter disbelief. "How? . . ."

"Now listen to me." The urgency in his voice held her in startled thrall. "The Xan-Express pad is on the other side of these walls. The ship will take off in a few minutes, and we're going to be on it."

She whispered, "You are mad."

"Shh!" He put his hand over her mouth as grayjackets flashed by his cell. He listened to the muffled clang and scrape of metal as they unlocked his door. Then the shouts and questions rose in considerable volume.

"They'll be in here next," he grated. "I don't know whether this is going to work, but we've got to try it." He grabbed her by the hand. The warm damp flesh was somehow reassuring. It made him think that maybe they truly were one flesh. Was that essential for matter passage? He would soon know.

Where was Mimi? Oh, still in her socket. He took her out and sprayed the back wall of the cell. And the grayjackets were now at Helen's cell door. He heard the key turning in the lock. He heard the command to freeze. "When I say jump, jump with me!" he told her. "We're going through that wall."

"Oh God," she groaned, but did not resist.

They jumped together, and they were through.

The great ship stood half a kilometer away, tall, radiant in its immense power and stunning beauty. At this moment the antigravs cut in, and the tarmac began to vibrate. The noon sun shone almost directly down on the vessel, pigmenting the gleaming sides in soft wavering yellow.

It took his breath away. Just one problem: the doors were closing. He managed to gasp: *"Run!"* He pulled her along, stumbling, falling, protesting.

Oh? What's this?

Out of nowhere a miniskitter was zipping over toward them.

The driver . . . long gray mustaches. By the kroaking kraw of Kronos! *"Ratell!"*

"Git in, sonny. Carry the lady, she's fainted. Pick her up, boy! I've just come from the ship. They'll wait a minute or so, but that's all."

"But how did you know we'd break out?"

"Wasn't completely sure. Chances looked good, though. Everything depended on whether you could recall Mimi in time. If you messed up, I had a fall-back, but it wasn't nearly as good."

"Lucky Helen was next door."

"It cost us a bundle to arrange that with Cell Assignment."

"Oh." Always wheels within wheels, plots, counter-plots. "You finished your dinner, back there in Maryland?" Konteau was uneasy but hopeful.

"Son,"—the voice was heavy, resigned—"let's face it. You have appointed yourself a committee of one to disrupt the best Chesapeake Bay dinner since George Washington said farewell to his troops. It took me a while to see this, but now I see it, and I accept it. So be it. Kismet."

Konteau was greatly abashed. "I'm truly sorry."

"I forgive you. On the other hand, it wasn't very smart of you to come back. You should have stayed in Ellicott's Mills with me."

"Yeah, I guess so. But all those people. . . . I had to try. I saved five thousand lives. But nobody would listen to me. I trusted the system. And now they want to kill me."

"Never trust the system, boy, unless you run it. I tried to tell you, but you're very difficult to instruct. I'll have to lead you by the hand, like a child."

"I guess you think I'm pretty stupid."

"No, son. Naive, maybe; and ignorant. And perhaps a bit too idealistic. But stupid? Definitely not. If you were, I wouldn't be here now."

"So why *are* you here?"

"I want to have a little talk with your friend the Vyr."

"Isn't that a bit dangerous?"

"Not at all. I'm a man of peace."

It was clear to Konteau that the time-magician would explain nothing.

They were at the ship-steps. The doors had opened again, and an attendant was staring down sternly. Helen was now semi-revived and was leaning against Konteau. Ratell tapped the shoulder of the fugitive. As the krono looked back, the older man handed him an envelope. "Your tickets. The First Secretary reserved a private compartment for you and the missus. He never dreamed you'd be using it." His eyes became hard, and there was a subtle change in his voice. "There's also a note. It's very important. Read it as soon as you're inside."

A note? thought Konteau. What's all this about? But he

knew he couldn't ask. He said, "Will we see you at Xanadu?"

Ratell shook his head. "I've just come from there on this very ship. Go on. Everybody's waiting for you. And for me."

And what, thought the krono, did he mean by *that?* Why did everybody have to be so damned mysterious?

They went on in, past the glowering steward.

Helen was essentially ambulatory by the time they reached the central passenger chamber. She said, "I'm going down the hall. My face is a wreck." He looked at her hair—straight, unbrushed, bedraggled. Where are now the hyacinths? he thought. They parted as strangers part, with barely a nod. He did not expect to see her again during the flight out. And, indeed, she would probably continue to avoid him after they reached Xanadu. And then what? Nothing. She wanted nothing more to do with him. Nor did he blame her. His middle name was Disaster. Maybe that's what 'D' really stood for. The Vyr must know by now we've escaped, he thought, but it's a problem he'll probably put aside for a while. He has other things on his mind. He wants to be Overlord. He has to put in an appearance at the Conclave and get himself properly and legally elected.

Now, Ratell's note. He opened the little envelope. There're the tickets, all right. Compartment A-1, straight ahead, at the end of the open seat section. Ah, here's the note. He unfolded the little piece of paper and read slowly:

Killer on board.
No description.

17

Second Honeymoon

An assassin, lying in wait. His neck muscles tightened into quivering knots. Would it never end? Well, perhaps he should have expected it. The Vyr was a careful man, with contingency plans.

Helen? He had to think of her first. Fortunately, for the moment she was probably fairly safe. She had disappeared up-cabin, headed for the ladies' lounge. In half an hour the Conclave would go on screen in the ship's club-room. The passengers would begin to settle down. The assassin would logically strike during the next thirty minutes, while people were still moving around.

And now he had to concentrate. He had to plan his defense. He considered his options. Wait until the killer finds him? No, the advantage would lie with the assassin. Also, if he delayed too long, the agent might go after Helen. The ladies' lounge provided no real safety.

It wasn't the first time he had been hunted. He had dealt with carnivores, reptilian and mammalian, in a dozen prehistoric periods, not to mention Sergeant Odinsson in the Temple. On the other hand, never before had he been required to defend in the narrow confines of an express ship. But the constraint changed nothing. If anything, it emphasized the basic three-step tactic: hunt the hunter . . . surprise . . . kill.

There was something revolting about the idea of killing a

human being. It tore him up inside. On the other hand, it had to be done. On this ship there was no place to hide. And there was the question of how best to protect Helen. He didn't want to have to warn her. Hopefully, leave her out of it altogether. She had gone through too much already.

All right, he thought, *I* go looking for *him.* No description. Actually, I don't even know whether the assassin is male or female. So how will I recognize him? Interesting problem. Will he stop me as I go down the aisle, and say to me, I'm the one? The First Secretary sent me. Will he say that? In a sense, yes.

Fascinating.

"Mimi," he told his oculus, "let's get an odor check."

"You'll have to tell me what to look for. Or sniff for. What does an assassin smell like?"

"I wish to Kronos I knew. Just stay alert . . . anything odd. . . ."

He wandered casually down the aisle, looking at the faces. All standard types. He'd seen the same pattern a dozen times. Vacationers, mostly, headed for Xanadu's dubious delights. Singles, men and women. In-ship vendors. ("Souvenirs sir? Tapes? Books? Masks? Can't get these on Terra!") Salesmen, commercial travelers. He passed a Priest of Kronos leaning over a couple and expounding on the advantages of the true faith. The expoundees were looking up, red-faced and embarrassed. Can the Priest be the one? thought Konteau. No way to tell. Not yet, anyhow. "Anything?" he signaled Mimir. "Nothing," she replied.

On down. Must be two hundred people on this flight. Here's a cluster of newlyweds . . . honeymooners. They seem to collect in one section. Up ahead are the private compartments. His—and Helen's?—is first on the corridor. Maybe the killer is inside, waiting.

Somewhere behind him among the honeymooners someone was playing a brassy wind instrument. He thought he detected strains of ancient wedding songs and marches. A medley of Wagner's *Lohengrin* and something from Mendelssohn. There was a sudden swell of chitter-chatter, as from a band of simians in an ancient rain forest, followed by an eruption of raucous laughter, and a cloud of something rose up and clattered toward the wall over his head. Some bounced off his jacket. Rice grains, he surmised. Not real rice, of course. Actually, just syntho-rice—tiny glass beads: a eutectic of calcium, sodium, and magnesium silicates. The new fertility symbol.

"I have a coincidence," his oculus reported calmly. "Behind you. Stop, but don't turn around just yet."

He stopped, almost casually, as though he had finished his stroll, and was wondering what to do next.

"It's the yellow wig on the Tolstoyan bride," continued Mimi. "The odor is an exact match for the wig on that newly-wed . . . *person* . . . back at Xanadu."

"Lots of yellow wigs," thought Konteau.

"This one is synthetic hair made of a polyamide fiber, dyed with picric acid. Scalp perspiration has partially hydrolyzed traces of the wig materials, and this gives a unique. . . ."

"All right. All right." Konteau thought back. Yes. That little butterfly auction. It was all coming together now. That pair of newlyweds. Was *she* the killer? Not just her. They probably worked together as a pair.

The muscles of his right cheek began to flicker and throb. Slowly, he turned around and started back up the aisle.

He remembered how they had stared back at him, on Xanadu. Back there they had been dressed in long flowing nuptial robes. Now, though, they were both dressed in Tolstoyan wedding garb: the man in the loose belted tunic over roomy trousers stuck in black boots; she in flowing blouse and multiple skirts. All the fabrics were gorgeously embroidered with designs in gold and silver threads.

He was alongside, now, and he could check the facial profiles.

The man: hard, square face. The woman: harsh blond hair, baggy eyes. Oh, I know you, he thought. A second honeymoon, so soon? Interesting cover. But he mustn't kill the wrong people. Make *sure*.

Meanwhile, the two suspects had swiveled their seats around in his general direction. But they weren't looking at him. In fact they seemed to be looking everywhere *except* at him. And that in itself was interesting. He noted now, almost by way of parenthetical afterthought, that they were both sprinkled with grains of white syntho-rice. At least, he thought, you will die with dreams of fertility.

Though they never once looked at him, yet he knew they were intensely aware of him. They were like two foxes concealed in the underbrush, scenting an approaching rabbit.

So far so good. He did not think they would try to kill him out here in the open. Too many possible witnesses.

He stopped in the aisle and spoke quietly to the man. "Excuse me, sir?"

The youth's head jerked up. His hands made a quick, unobtrusive motion that seemed aimed simply at concealing his cuffs in the folds of his tunic. Konteau was ready for a weapon, but there was no further movement. During this brief interval the time-man noted that the bride's face seemed even harder and more muscular than that of her spouse. In fact, the thin dusting of white powder on her cheeks failed to conceal completely her need for a shave.

"Sir," Konteau repeated, "there's a Priest of Kronos coming down the aisle, button-holing everybody. See him up there?"

The groom nodded without taking his eyes from Konteau.

"If you and the lady would like some privacy, you can have my Compartment—A-One, first one toward the rear." He smiled. "My wedding gift."

There was the barest pause, as the two seemed to consult with each other, then rapidly reach agreement. The groom spoke tersely. "We'd like that very much . . . but we're not really accustomed to such things . . . our first time on a real space ship. Are you sure you don't mind?"

"My pleasure."

"Well, then, could you please show us how things work in your compartment?" He essayed a sheepish grin. "How you let the bed down, and so on?"

"Of course. Come along, both of you."

The "woman" had remained silent. That was smart, decided Konteau. Again he sensed the crackling excitement passing between the two. He knew what they were thinking:

this stupid little rabbit is standing outside our open jaws and asking our permission to walk in.

Suppose I'm wrong? he thought. Suppose it doesn't work? No, no use thinking like that. Mimi, old friend, are we ready?

The cortical response was loud and clear. *Ready.*

He opened the compartment door. He noted that his permissible ten-kilo valise was there, strapped in the overhead rack. He hadn't seen it in . . . how many hours? Think of all the bureaucratic rerouting it had survived! He would be lucky if he himself could do as well.

But back to business.

They were all inside now, and the door was closing behind the bride. The eyes of the assassins were on him and ablaze with triumph. The "lady" was standing slightly behind the man, and Konteau realized she was opening her handbag. In her next motion she'd simultaneously pull the weapon out, aim, and fire. The man in front would simply provide shelter. They had it all worked out.

Konteau ducked—*fast,* but with head up, the way he had once dodged a swooping pteranodon on a littoral of the mid-Cretaceous. From his oculus a cone of faint blue light sprayed upward for one millisecond. The man in front instantly polarized and was translucent. As Konteau pushed him backwards into the "woman", the groom's chest felt like sticky gelatin.

The krono stood back and surveyed his handiwork.

They were both dead, the body of each grotesquely solidified within the other. The "woman's" lifeless eyes were peering wide at Konteau out of the tunic of her late husband.

Pensively, rubbing his chin with the back of his hand, he pondered this grisly thing, floating free in this tiny chamber, released finally from all cares, human and inhuman. Yes, a true marriage, in the fullest sense of the ancient English common law, where husband and wife were considered one person. Tenants by the entireties. By Kronos, a very successful wedding!

Just let me tidy up a bit, and then I'll send you on a honeymoon such as you never dreamed of.

He looked about the room. Overhead floated a dart gun.

There was a faint acrid odor in the little room. Great Kronos. "She" had got off a shot after all. Damn, she was fast! Or maybe he was slowing down. Or both. He recalled dimly that something had zinged past his ear as he ducked. He looked behind him. Yes, there it was: a needle capsule in the wall padding. It could still kill somebody cleaning the room. Very carefully he worked it out with thumb and forefinger and dropped it into the man's tunic pocket, followed by the gun.

Next he polarized the duo-corpse and a section of the ship-wall and began pushing the chimera out into the icy garbage dump of space. As the thing traversed the ferro-titanium plates, there seemed to be a brief hitch. Something snagged. He gave the monster an extra shove. It then cleared the plates and disappeared. Simultaneously something small and sparkling floated free across his line of vision. And there goes another! Two of them! A couple of last-word killers? He threw his arm over his face and leaped back. Why hadn't these things polarized and gone through? "Scan 'em, Mimi," he gurgled.

"I have. Identical. Circles of element seventy-nine, bordered with close-packed crystals of covalent cubic habit. Dr. Ditmars warned you there might be problems with such crystals. These baubles are quite harmless."

Konteau captured one as it drifted past his ear. Blood flooded his cheeks as he held it at arm's length. It was a golden cufflink with a black enamel hourglass design. It was circled with clusters of diamonds, and. . . .

"It can't be. . . ." he whispered.

"Check the engraving on the inside," advised Mimi.

"No. It can't be. . . ."

"You keep saying that. Oh James, what a coward. Do you want *me* to. . . ."

"No. I have to do it."

He brought the little artifact up toward his good eye. His lips moved slowly as he read the delicate engraving.

> James Konteau
> Kron-Corps
> 2645; 2650

In a slow dreamlike gesture he captured the other one. He held them both, and for a long time just looked at them, turning them over in his fingers, believing, yet not believing.

Possession by the Vyr's agents had not defiled them. Nothing could defile them. They were as pure and chaste as the day the Widow had presented them. I think he must have had them back on Xanadu, mused Konteau. I remember a sparkle. . . . Yes, affirmed Mimi.

He placed them carefully on the little fold-down credenza, removed his jacket and shirt, and punched holes in the cuffs of his shirtsleeves. He fastened the links in the cuffs, replaced his shirt and jacket, and admired his newly recovered finery in the vanity mirror.

"Kronos . . . Kronos. . . ." he mused. "It's almost enough to make me a believer. "Meanwhile, Mimi, we really do have to get back to the club-room. I have a feeling all hell is about to break loose at the Conclave. We don't want to miss it."

He stepped out into the corridor and was turning the doorknob dial to "Do Not Disturb" when he felt a hand on his shoulder. He stood up slowly to face the Priest of Kronos. "Brother," demanded the cloaked man, "are you saved?"

"Just barely." He shook off the hand and passed on down into the club-room, where he found an empty seat and strapped in. The screens lit up a moment later, revealing the center of the great crowded Conclave hall, where someone in a full black face mask stood next to—and here Konteau gulped—the Haruspex apparatus. *Tages!* The masked acolyte called out in a sonorous voice: "O valiant Vyrs! My lord governors! Are ye ready? Shall I begin the divination?"

The response was a thundering "Aye!"

Konteau's heart was pounding like a trip-hammer. Not *my* guts, he thought. Not Helen's. Whose? *Anybody's?* That *voice. . . .*

The acolyte continued. "Haruspex awaits! On this occasion. . . ."

The ship passengers leaned forward. Konteau was shamelessly foremost. He tried to recall the exact timbre and modulation of Tages' voice. Something . . . not quite right. . . .

"We add certain reverential touches to our time-honored selection processes," continued the acolyte. His mask puffed out with every word. "For example, today, for the first time ever, our selective process is being broadcast to the general public. Your loyal vassals and subjects in outlying colonies, on Terra, the far planets, and in ships at sea and in space are watching us at this very moment." He paused and looked about for effect. The great Conclave room was incredibly silent. Not a throat was cleared, not a shoe scraped. "But enough. To start, we need a volunteer. Which among you is the noblest, the most steadfast, the most modest, loving, most reverent in the service of the god? Let him come forward."

"That'll be the Warden of the Conclave," whispered one of the passengers behind Konteau. "He'll activate Haruspex. It's a very honorable function. They've already chosen Delta, of course."

From his ornate box in the front row, Paul Corleigh, Delta Vyr, arose, smiled, bowed modestly to the right and left, and stepped forward. He was alone, with no competitors.

"Ah, milord," crooned the acolyte, "a most excellent, logical choice." From a tray at the side he pulled back a white napkin and lifted out an oversize syringe. "If milord will kindly roll back his right sleeve." He held the needle up to let a drop of liquid run down the side. "Please? . . ."

"But. . . ." sputtered the Vyr. "Nobody mentioned a hypo."

"*No anesthetic?* Milord! Never in my career have I encountered such courage. This is absolutely *magnificent!*"

"Anes . . . thetic?" gurgled the aristocrat. "Courage? What are you talking about?"

"Why, the surgery, milord. As the best and noblest and most reverent of all the Vyrs, your—shall we say, *system*—goes into the glass box, to be read by Haruspex for the instant designation of the next Overlord!"

"*BUT!* . . ." howled Paul. "The *woman!* You were to provide a *woman!*"

"Oh, such bravery!" breathed the functionary. "Are you ready *now?*"

"Never!" cried the Vyr. "And you'll hear from me!" Livid, he stomped back to his box.

The attendant wrung his hands. "Oh dear. Perhaps there was a misunderstanding. Someone else, perhaps?" His eyes scanned the sea of faces. "Anybody?" But no one would look at him.

"Oh noble Vyrs, must we now break a time-tested tradition? Are we to be driven into the despicable democratic process of simple majority vote?" He seemed on the verge of tears, and stopped to wipe his eyes with his mask, thereby exposing a long gray mustache on one side of his chin.

I might have known, thought Konteau. He blocked out thoughts of what had happened to Tages. He wished Helen were sitting here with him, so they could share the show. But she had exiled herself, and perhaps it was just as well. She might ask questions, and there were certain things he could never bring himself to tell her. This world was a savage place.

He looked up. Action in the Conclave. "You have rejected your finest tradition," moaned the imposter acolyte. "In my sorrow, my shame, my degradation, you leave me no choice. Haruspex must go—forever. I will personally destroy the machine. And not only that, I resign my ancient and honorable post. I leave you in favor of your noble brother, Harold the Holy, Vyr of Houston, Grandee of Galveston, and Baron of Buffalo Bayou. All of you know Harold. He needs no further introduction. His lordship will now come forward and he will take nominations for Overlord from the floor. He will serve you as clerk-chairman and will handle all further procedural matters at this gathering. Milord Harold!"

A thin-faced man sitting next to Konteau clucked in disgust. "No respect for tradition," he muttered. "They've used haruspicy for three hundred years. It's safe, accurate. . . . And now look, all down the drain. What's the world coming to?" He glared at Konteau. "Don't you agree?"

"It's all very sad," said Konteau tactfully.

On screen, a portly man stood up in the midsection and walked down the aisle, bowing and touching hands with the well-wishers. Was it all prearranged? Konteau wondered. Or does Sir Mustachio know these people so well he knows exactly what he can get away with?

Ratell the acolyte vanished through the rear arras, driving the motorized Haruspex ahead of him. Was the time-wizard finally on his way back to that Chesapeake Bay dinner, thought Konteau, or had he truly given it up in defeat? His own stomach was growling. In fact, he was ravenous. He suddenly realized he hadn't eaten since he left Xanadu. He wished *he* could have that Maryland dinner!

At least the twenty-first Overlord selection was off and running, and it would be a long time before anyone would try another selection by Haruspex.

A young man was tugging at his sleeve. It was the steward. "Mr. Konteau, we'll be landing soon. Will you come with me, please. You are to leave the ship by the crew exit."

That worried him. Was he to be arrested *again?* Or worse? Maybe they were going to shoot him as soon as they got him free of the ship.

The attendant saw his hesitation, then grinned. "Sorry, I forgot to give you this." He took a folded note from his shirt pocket.

Konteau read it quickly.

Relieved to learn your safe arrival. Please join me in the Conference Room as soon as you exit.

—Demmie

He relaxed. "Milady Helen comes with me."

"Madame has already made other arrangements within the Mall, sir."

"Arrangements?" He was confused.

"Something to do with new apparel and hairsetters, sir. I don't really have the details. We made certain appointments for her. She's leaving the ship alone, by the regular exit."

Of course. The cosmetic shops, modistes, and couturiers of Xan were touted the best in the solar system. He wouldn't dare interfere with Helen's refitting operations. He suddenly felt shabby. Forget those rumblings in his stomach! Did he have time for a shave, a shower, clean underwear?

Soundless jars and jolts answered him.

"Landing, sir. This way, please."

18

D

The escort takes him down the special West Wing corridor. He is suddenly uneasy. This is territory reserved to the Council. He has no business here. What are they going to do to him? Probably nothing pleasant. No matter. At least Helen is safe. Theoretically she's shopping in the Mall. He hopes.

He is full of forebodings when the last door whistles open and he is ushered into a vaulted chamber.

The next instant he is standing at the end of a big oval table. Several men and women are seated around the table, and they are staring at him expectantly. (Hey, there's Zeke Ditmars! They exchange nods.) In front of each of them seem to be documents of some sort. Opposite him, at the far end, and next to an empty chair, stands a young woman, evidently in charge. He jerks as he recognizes her: the lady who was his four-day companion on this orbiting madhouse, Demmie . . . who now wears the blouse and tunic of Demeter, daughter of Kronos, and Directrix of the Council.

She smiles, and addresses him in those well-remembered resonances. "Welcome, James Konteau. Do you know where you are?"

He bows slightly. "I presume, Madame Directrix, that I am in the Council Chamber." His voice rises a little, so that his response is actually a question.

"Quite so, James. And may I present the other members

of the Council? Dr. Ditmars you know already." She sounds off the rest of the names, and one by one they rise and bow to him. He can't keep all the names in his head at one time. They all smile. Some say things . . . which he can't quite grasp. All of it is over his head. She sees he is being overwhelmed, and she tells him to be seated. She adds, "Just one more of us, James. Our Director Emeritus. And him you know already."

There is suddenly someone sitting in the chair beside her. The great mustaches wobble as the man grins broadly.

"Ratell!" gasps Konteau. "But . . . but. . . ."

"You're looking at a live holo, dear boy. You see me, I see you. But actually, I'm still down there, winding up affairs at the Conclave. Just at this moment they're casting the final ballots for the next Overlord. Your old friend Pious Paul was never even nominated."

Konteau nods, and Demeter resumes.

"The Council acknowledges with gratitude your rescue of Delta Five Eighty-five. We don't really know how to render payment. We thought you might have some suggestions."

He frowns. "I didn't do it alone. Without the help of my ex-wife and her friend, it would not have been possible. In any case, though, we didn't do it for payment."

"Of course you didn't. But at least you have our assurance that it will not happen again. On Terra at this very moment, the social order is being forcibly restructured. You have seen some of our program in progress, at the Conclave. Certain people in high places are being, shall we say, demoted. But we need not go into that."

She stops suddenly. She is staring at his sleeves. At his cufflinks, actually. She looks next at his face, accusingly. He returns the stare blandly. It is all very funny. She knows he didn't have his hourglasses on Xanadu, and no way to recover them during his perilous peregrinations of the past thirty hours. And yet here they are. Well, that's one on you, Demmie old girl.

She recovers gamely. She looks at him quizzically. "So then, James Konteau, have you nothing to ask of us?"

"I do indeed have a couple of questions." But he isn't

looking at her. He is looking at the holo of Ratell. His eyes are fixed on those of the time-magician. He begins almost tentatively. "You were not born a couple of hundred years ago, Mr. Ratell. Your own equations prove a man cannot move forward in time, beyond a certain point. And yet I know—and you state it yourself—you were at the Conclave. Presumably you are still there. Now, another thing. Our current technology is incapable of originating the great time transmitters, chest packs, stabilizers . . . or even my false eye, Mimir. With all respect, Zeke Ditmars, not even you could do it. You, Mr. Ratell, brought all this in from the future, from your own birth-time. Perhaps the very far future."

Ratell sighs. "It is so."

Konteau asks, "Your friends here. Do *they* know?"

"The Council is well aware."

"When are you from?" asks Konteau. "What century?"

"Almost five up the line."

"I suppose we have other . . . visitors?"

"No. So far as I know, I'm the only one. Actually, son, I did in fact derive the nine equations—what you call the Equations of Time—and I did in fact design and build the first machinery. And then I left my home-time. If anyone else breaks in here, they'll have to reinvent the equations and the equipment. But I don't think it will be done." He peers across at the krono. "You ever hear of a chap named Parkinson?"

"No, I don't think so."

"Not surprised. He flourished in the twentieth. Formulated a famous law: A man rises to his level of incompetence. Applies not just to individuals. Works with populations, races, entire animal species. Well, as a species, *Homo sap.* achieved his top level of incompetence in the thirty-third century. You think things were bad in the time of the Question-Mark, or even now? You should thank your gods you didn't make it to the thirty-third. I came back to see if I couldn't make history take a different turn. Maybe I did something useful, and maybe I didn't. We won't know for sure until the thirty-third rolls around again." He smiles at Konteau. "Does that clear it up?"

"Almost everything."

"But a few loose ends? . . ."

Konteau blurts, *"She's your daughter!"*

"Demmie?" Ratell laughs. "Just as the mythic Demeter was the daughter of the mythic Kronos."

"Kronos?" stammers Konteau. "No! There's no such creature!" If Demmie . . . then, the others?

Unacceptable.

But the names, the names are coming back. *Zeke* Ditmars? Try *Zeus*. And this Madame Herald. *Hera*, maybe? Admiral Poside? Rather, *Poseidon*, complete with trident insignia on his lapels. And Mr. Haydon. *Hades*, perhaps? And this chap Hestace. Read *Hestus*. The six children of the god Kronos. Naturally. Had he really expected to escape all that crazy mythic theology *here*—in the sacred chambers of the Council? In the final rational domain of the great Ratell? The irony is too much for him. He chokes back a crazy chuckle. Actually, in a way it makes sense. Perhaps the names are synthetic, assigned simply to identify ministries and functions. Not that sense really matters. Look at that! As he watches, Ratell's holographic hands reach out from Ratell's holographic body, and they take the report lying there, and pull it back toward the holographic chest.

Konteau's one eye bugs out. He wonders whether he dare send Mimi over to investigate this, but decides he'd better not, especially since none of the others seem to be particularly concerned. But things are really not quite right, and they really ought to explain . . . if he could just find the right questions. He begins, "Now wait just a minute." (Too loudly, he realizes.) "I'm entitled. . . ."

But Ratell's holo is fading. The man, the report, everything. The smile is the last to go. Wasn't there something once in an ancient book about a smile . . . on a cat?

Konteau sighs. The mystery is just too deep.

The Directrix has remained standing all this time. "You were saying, James?"

"No, nothing."

"Then I think we can proceed to the next order of business: your Report and Recommendations of the twenty-fifth July, James."

The brochure lies in front of her. The original. And that's what the other Council members had—copies of his report. He had signed it and had given it to Demmie to deliver to the Directrix for him. To herself, as it turned out. Not two days ago? It seemed more like twenty years. The report had never left Xanadu. And why should it? The Council was here, had been here all along.

She says with calm certainty: "Within two years we want . . . *we must have* . . . a full colony, five million people, on Proterozoic Mars. Starting now, for reasons of budgeting and planning, the new colony will have to have a name. We had thought to name it in honor of your rescue of Delta."

Konteau smiles uncertainly. A nice gesture; he can't object!

She continues. "We can't call it Delta, of course."

He shrugs.

She says, "What would you think of just the initial, 'D'?"

His heart begins to bounce crazily, and he is turning a greenish ivory.

She watches him in sudden concern. "James, are you all right?"

He manages a mute nod.

"You don't like 'D'? You want something else?" She puts her hands on the table and leans toward him.

By the Kryptic Kraw of Kronos! D is not a man. D is not Death. D is not Daleth, or Delta, or Disaster. What *is* D? D is his favorite project! D is the first Martian colony! Kronos has finally smiled on him. He declares firmly: "I like 'D'. 'D' is exactly right!"

At last he is getting to the bottom of the great mystery. So much for 'D'. Now, how about the cowled chess player? The man on the other side of the chess table is still waiting for him.

So the game isn't over, but at least he isn't afraid anymore.

Demeter says, "Very well, then. How soon can you start your surveys?"

"*Me?*"

"You."

"But I work for the Widow. You'd have to talk to them."

She holds up a blue envelope, bearing the hourglass insigne. "We have made the necessary arrangements. It's all here. You have a year's leave. More if needed."

It is all coming together. But this time he wants absolute control. He bores into Demeter's eyes with his one good orb. "Not so fast. You, the Council,"—his accusation shifts now to Dr. Ditmars—"and especially you, Zeke . . . you planned this, all of you. You set me up. You *used* me. Why should I do you any favors?"

Demeter replies evenly. "We picked you because you were the best. You had the knowledge, the science, and the experience. You are resourceful. You have an extremely high survival index. You have dealt successfully with at least two assassination attempts. You were motivated. And you were here. Yes, we used you. People always use other people, James. It's the human condition. You used Helen, and you used Albert Artoy."

He takes a deep breath, then lets it out slowly. He can't fight this anymore. Besides which, she was absolutely right. He *was* highly motivated. He wants this project with all his mind and heart and body. No point in letting these people know how badly he wants it, though. He grumbles, "I'll need a good crew—two people at least, a navigator, rodman. . . ."

"They're already here. Waiting for you in the game room."

The chess table is in the game room; he fights a sudden chill. He shakes his head. "I want to pick my own team. This is dangerous work. I have to have the best."

"These two *are* the best. The navigator-surveyor was brought to our attention by a highly experienced traveler. The rodman is an expert on Martian Proterozoic terranes. He has just completed his doctoral on oxygen sources of the Valles Marineris, a billion years B.P."

"Oh gods! A paperhead."

She smiles faintly. "At least look them over. The time gate opens in two days, but we can postpone it if necessary. If either crewman is unacceptable, you can hire your own. That's a promise. Deal?"

"Well. . . ."

"Excellent! You'll find your itinerary in the survey packet. And would you please check back with me before you leave." She stands back from the table, and the others rise.

Konteau gets up, grumbles something about "Pretty damn cavalier. . . ." But he can't really complain. After all, these people, with a little help from Ratell, saved Helen's life. Not to mention his. So he is polite. "Madame, Council members. . . ." He bows and leaves.

He looks into the game room, and his heart begins to jump and bounce, like a skitter out of control.

Seated at the chess table, a bare three meters away, is a man wearing the dark blue jacket of a krono apprentice. The jacket is hooded, and the hood is pulled up, concealing the face.

Play it to the end, kron-man. He runs his tongue around his lips, and he peers at the chessboard. He is close enough to make out the position. The mystery player has the black pieces, with a passed pawn on his fourth. In four more moves he will queen. White's king is locked in. The queening move will be checkmate. White must lose.

He mutters in an inner monologue as he studies the seated figure. So, not-so-great Death, it is not over. You come to me in the form of this apprentice. Do you know so little, that you must seek instruction from *me*? What can *I* tell *you* of the ways of danger, of terror, and of the only ultimate calm? The end has come. Or is it the beginning? No matter. At last, I shall look upon your face.

His guts are beginning to tingle. Odd, he thinks. A warning? Something to do with *time*?

The figure is now aware of him; indeed, probably has been aware ever since Konteau stepped into the entrance way.

Konteau stalks over to the table, and he commands in a harsh guttural that speaks from behind granite walls: "Lift your cowl!"

The seated figure, who has been watching him from the anonymity of his overhanging hood, stands up and pulls back the gray folds in a gesture of breathtaking grace.

No. O God no.

Konteau's viscera dissolve within him as he looks upon the face of his son. So proud, so icy, so elegant. He staggers back half a step. He wants to melt into the tiles of the floor.

The youth takes it all in. The smooth mouth curls in a smile so sudden, so luminous, that Konteau's heart skips several beats. He says feebly, "I didn't expect . . . you. Is there . . . some mistake?"

"No."

The older man struggles to gain control of his mind and body. He walks up to the table, but makes no effort to touch his son. Oh, those beautiful blue eyes, just like his mother's. He stammers, falters. "I didn't know you had entered kron school. This is . . . a bit of a surprise."

"I didn't tell you. I didn't tell anybody. You would have got me thrown out."

"Yes, I would have."

"It's too late now. You can't do anything about it."

That, thinks Konteau, is not entirely true, and he knows it. But I'm tired. I can't fight him anymore. He fixes his born-eye gloomily on his son's expectant face, and he frowns. "But I still don't understand. There's something browned-off helical here. I ran a locator on you two days ago. You were somewhere in Lambda."

"Just a plant, to throw you off, in case you came looking. I wasn't in Lambda at all."

"But you had to be in a kron-academy *somewhere.*"

"Quite so. I was in Delta."

"All the time?"

"All the time."

"Which . . ."—Konteau swallows noisily—"boro." It wasn't even a question. It is as though he is telling his son.

"Five Eighty-five," says Philip Konteau. He watches in curious silence as little beads of sweat begin to sparkle on his father's forehead. "I was in the Teknikron. They're new, but they're supposed to provide the best training in the East." He adds, "When Five Eighty-five began to skid, I called for you. Telepathically, I guess you would say. And you came. And mother." He shrugs, that delicate expressive gesture, where the left shoulder lifts barely perceptibly.

The Teknikron, thinks Konteau. He was in that very building. "The Widow assigned you yesterday?"

"Actually, the Council. I came out on the night express."

"Does your mother know you were in Five Eighty-five?" Konteau asks softly.

"No, of course not."

They smile at each other in sudden secret masculine communion.

Then Konteau *père* looks down at the chessboard, not really studying the position; just thinking about how his son happened to be sitting here, at this exact spot, at this exact time. By the Krafty Kranium of Kronos! He sees here once again the fine hand of the master conniver, the man of many times and many faces. He looks up again. "Philip," he says, "have you seen an old geezer around here, an odd-looking chap with a big handlebar mustache?" He holds up the index fingers of both hands at the sides of his mouth to model the mustache.

"Oh, you mean Ratell. He and I came in together on the express yesterday, but he left again this morning. And funny you should ask. He spent a few minutes in here, setting up the chessboard. He claimed it looked bad for white, but that actually, white had a win."

Konteau thinks about that. Ratell . . . even into his chess game fantasy. Which meant the time-master must have access to his psycho-records. Oh, well. At least look at the position. A win for white? The only way white could win would be to capture black's passed pawn immediately. Which meant that white's pawn at B-5 must be able to take it en passant. Of course! Black's pawn must have moved two squares on black's last move, a so-called 'phantom move', and is therefore presently vulnerable to capture en passant. Always a question of Time! There was a great lesson to be learned from this position. It's the Past that sets the Future in concrete. But it's the Present that reconstructs the Past. The rules of the game are the rules of Time. White wins because white understands Time. Ratell wanted him to understand this. Everything is beginning to make some sort of crazy sense.

Konteau grins at his son. It is a spontaneous, happy thing. "He was right!"

"You've solved the position?"

"Yes. Pawn takes pawn en passant."

"By golly, you're right. Well, in that case, I can give you the rest of his message."

It is Konteau's turn to show surprise. "Oh?"

"He said he gives up on dinner, whatever *that* means, and to give you this."

His son hands him a transpack of nested trays. The pack has been sitting on the other side of the table, but Konteau had not noticed it. "Something he called 'seafood'. What is seafood? What are you supposed to do with it?"

Konteau cracks the seal a little and sniffs. Still warm! "Mm. . . ." Rockfish, crab cakes, fried oysters, buttered cornbread muffins, a little wooden tub of terrapin sauce? . . . A dreamy look steals over his face. "Did he seem annoyed?"

"No. Just kind of sad, as though he accepted something inevitable."

We all have our roles to play, thinks Konteau. He says, "Why don't we page our navigator? We can share this fine dinner and go over some of the messier points of the assignment. I think I've got his name here somewhere. Have you met him yet?"

"Yes," says Philip dryly. "He's a her."

"A woman?" Konteau is suddenly uneasy again.

His son's face is carefully devoid of expression. "She volunteered."

Ratell once more? thinks the kron-man. Well, well . . . maybe. But he is cautious. He is not getting his hopes up. Wasn't it supposed to be all over? Jane Stith Stanard, Poe's hyacinth-haired Helen, died in a Richmond insane asylum in 1824. From across the room he hears the clickety-click of Tom Thumb on the circular track. He listens a moment. No, it's not all over. For him, it had never come to an end. He wants her. He wants her more than he wants to breathe. He gets control of his voice. There is only a slight rasp. "Experienced?"

Philip grins. "You heard Demmie."

Demmie. This boy gets around. Let's jump to the bottom line. "Your mother?"

"Sight/time zero." His son is watching him.

Konteau gives Philip a smile that seems to grow and grow, and then nicks him on the arm in the manner of teen-age chums. "When we pick her up, I'll grab some cutlery and a couple of liters of white wine at the bar. And then I'm going to give you old kronos the best dinner you ever ate!"

The new rodman looks at him with level gray eyes. "Dad, I can't join you. I'm really sorry. I have a briefing with Demmie. It'll take several hours."

"Oh. Of course. It's all right."

He watches his son walk away and out into the West End Corridor.

He is let down, abandoned. Should he set out, carrying a food case, and looking for a surveyor-navigator who hadn't the slightest reason to dine with him? Darn it, Philip, you might have found her and persuaded her.

Courage, Konteau. He looks about the crowded arcade.

A woman is entering the room from the Mall corridor. She stops by one of the big central pillars, and her eyes search the room. She finds him, and she looks at him evenly. She puts a hand on her hip, and bends a knee slightly, so that her pelvis dips. She leans against the pillar and her eyes never leave him. In the half light her face is enigmatic alabaster, pale, fey.

Now this pillar is the one shaped like the lepidodendron, and its bark is carved with those typically curled scales.

Helen? Is this Helen? She seems so young. A mere girl, exactly like the one he had possessed in that forest of the Upper Carboniferous, over three hundred million years ago. The purple denim work-suit . . . the jacket with pocket flaps that button under tabs like hyacinth petals . . . the dark hair, in hyacinth curls. He imagines he can smell the tiny florets.

This woman, this naiad, this fantastic beauty, is his once-wife. He is stunned. He does not dare blink. She might vanish.

There is no obvious sex in her ethereal elegance. And yet, like the non-smiling things that add up to the smile of the Mona Lisa, she radiates invitation. His jaw sags. Is she real, or merely a projection of his mind? The only reason that he doesn't drop the dinner case is that he is holding it in a paralyzed grip of iron. And that contrasts strongly with his brain, which is a paralyzed glob of jelly.

A reveler approaches her from the side. He sways a bit, and carries a bottle and a half-full glass. He speaks to her. Konteau bursts from his spell, starts forward. But he need not worry. Without seeming to notice the intruder, she says something short and incisive out of the side of her mouth. The seeker gasps, spills his drink, backs away, disappears.

And now he begins to notice a most remarkable audio hallucination. One by one the sounds vanish, as though they had merely been lent out for the occasion, and the true owners have come to pack them up and take them away. The din of voices ceases. Then the shuffling of feet. Then the clink of wineglasses. The swish of clothing. And finally the clickety-click clickety-click of little Tom Thumb, on his tiny eternal rails in the model set-up in that far corner.

No, not finally. That's not the last sound.

In the dead silence he hears the throb of giant dragonfly wings.

Helen smiles and begins walking toward him.